9338

SO VERY ENGLISH

A Serpent's Tail Compilation

Edited by Marsha Rowe

SERPENT'S
TAIL

English Tea by Margo Glantz was published in Spanish in
Universidad de Mexico Review, April 1990; *Wherever I Hang* by
Grace Nichols first appeared in *Lazy Thoughts of a Lazy Woman*
(Virago, 1989); *Dynasty Reruns* by Lynne Tillman first appeared in
Art in America in June 1986 in a somewhat different version;
Leicester Square by Adam Zameenzad is a chapter in his latest
novel, *Cyrus Cyrus* (Fourth Estate).

Library of Congress Catalog Card No: 90-60287

British Library Cataloguing in Publication Data
So very English.
  1.Fiction in English. 1945- -- Anthologies
  I.Rowe, Marsha
  823.91408
  ISBN 1-85242-179-7

First published 1991 by
Serpent's Tail, 4 Blackstock Mews, London N4

Cover design by Roy Trevelion
Cover illustration of 'Ride a Cock Horse' from the 'Nursery
Rhymes' suite by Paula Rego. Hand coloured etching.
Copyright © 1989 Paula Rego. Photography courtesy
Marlborough Graphics Ltd

Typeset in 10/12pt Century Schoolbook by
AKM Associates (UK) Ltd, London
Printed in Finland by
Werner Söderström Oy

CONTENTS

SO VERY ENGLISH

The English – so suspicious of cleverness, fearing it to be superficial, so conclusive about 'taste' as if it was something spiritual, so accepting of eccentricity that it almost appears conventional – are shown here at their most chameleon. Stories by foreigners who live or have lived in England, by one or two English who've observed their country like visitors in a strange land, as well as by those who've lived here so long they may perhaps be described as Guyanese-English or Canadian-English, instead of that concealing catch-all, British. Stories to re-tell the stories that have told the story so far, stories and poems about Englishness.

The English are terribly proud about being no good at things. Like having fun. Just as Victoria Wood said, 'I get overexcited if there's a pattern on my kitchen roll.' Or about being at a loss for words. The English call it understatement. Or about their lack of artistry. David Bailey called it 'the dandruff syndrome'. It's what happens when the English 'mistake sincerity for talent. You've got to have dandruff, wear tweed and sound sincere.'

The English, being superior, know better. It's much better to stick by their tactful silence, as told by Peter Ustinov, 'a friendly foreigner', having been born in

London after his mother fled Russia, eight months
pregnant (thinking incidentally that all stations in
England must be called Bovril). It was a special
occasion. His mother was waiting to meet Queen Mary
who approached slowly 'like a ship in full sail', finally
arriving in front of her while his mother stared rigidly
ahead. The Queen gave a few facial contortions,
stretched her mouth – and said nothing. Beside her,
Ninette de Valois murmured, 'What a pity about the
revolution.'

The English are utterly confident about who they are.
If nothing else, they know what it means to be English.
We, the non-English who live here, notice how often
they tell us that something or someone is so English.
They might possibly speak with irony or a modest
smile, but there's no doubt whatsoever. It's a shock
when, after a time, visiting family or friends tell us we
too are now So Very English.

What? 'Do stay for another drink,' meaning it's time
for you to go – that sort of thing – excessively prude and
polite and privately opinionated to boot, and immune to
pleasure – is that what we, the foreigners, have suddenly
become? And what about politics? And the long, long
continuity of this thing called Englishness? And what
about the way the English talk about other cultures, say
the Irish or West Indian? Often they don't, quite, do
they, for fear of sounding racist, since Englishness
itself is so predicated on creating the otherness of
cultures it has made subject and subordinate. But isn't
it so peculiarly English of the English to go on about
their own ethnic habits, their manners and morals, to
wave them in the public eye like the flag, without quite
saying this is what they're up to, yet making an
industry out of the national heritage, like the Laura
Ashley chain, that 'upholder of quintessential Englishness'.

And it's been like this a long time. The making of
Englishness. An assault course. Centuries of entangled

relations between England and Scotland, Ireland, Wales - and the empire which once meant power, liberty, the creation of wealth, and slavery. Combinations of citizens, denizens, refugees. Englishness has made itself in opposition, crushing, using, annihilating, enslaving. Just as it has also made itself by the rule of law, by justice, tolerance, democracy, by the force of popular citizenship and by art as much as by commerce, by innovation, invention and the ideal of equality - by its ability, as George Orwell wrote, 'to change out of recognition and yet remain the same'.

Marsha Rowe

Colm Tóibín

I grew up in the town of Enniscorthy, in the southeast of Ireland. Every year in the summer we held a Strawberry Fair, and every year, too, the elders of the town would meet to select a Strawberry Queen. One year, they asked a contestant what she would do with the prize-money if she won. 'I'd feck off to England,' she said.

I was a youth then and the words stuck in my mind when I heard them, confirming everything I'd suspected. England appeared before me as a haven of freedom and pleasure. I longed for England.

I was more than thirty years old, however, before I found myself sitting in a private house in England in a room full of English people. They seemed pleasant, the food was good, and there was a lot of drink. I was not intimidated. I watched them carefully.

When an experimental novelist told how his car had been broken into, a sudden silence descended and the room became all ears. 'And what was taken?' they asked him intensely. And thus I learned my first thing about the English: they are very interested in law and order. 'My snow chains,' the novelist said. *His snow chains?* I looked out of the window; it was still a beautiful summer's evening in London. And when I looked back I learned one more thing about the English:

they are very polite. No one asked him what in the name of God he was doing with snow chains in his car at this time of the year.

And when I asked him this, they grew even more polite, and looked at me as though I had said something extremely interesting.

The talk then turned from vandalism to art. During that summer Gilbert & George were all the rage in London, they had a show running on the South Bank. I had a conversation with the woman beside me about Gilbert & George. In passing, I happened to say categorically: 'As far as I'm concerned Gilbert & George should be shot.' 'Don't you think that's rather strong?' she retorted. This I thought was an example of the po-faced English sense of humour I had read about. So I said: 'Okay, maybe they should be beaten to death with his snow chains.' I pointed at the experimental novelist and laughed. It was only when she turned away that I realized that English people often take things literally.

Later, she told the hostess that the party was a great success, especially the Irishman. English people, it turned out, often like Irish people, mostly in retrospect.

Then I went on my holidays to Egypt, where I fell in with a most pleasant English couple, wandered up and down the Valley of the Kings with them on bicycles. We got on well together, we laughed at one another's jokes. On my way through London, I went to stay with them. They hadn't told me that they had an Irish maid, but they introduced me to her as soon as I arrived.

'Where are you from?' she asked.

'Enniscorthy,' I said.

'Where are you from?' I asked.

'Clonmel,' she said. We then went through all the people we knew in one another's towns; the news from Ireland; how long she'd been in England; how she was getting on; when was I going back, among other topics.

I noticed that my hosts were staring at us in wonder and astonishment.

Later, after a bottle or so of wine, they broached the subject. Did I know that my accent had changed completely when I met my compatriot? Did I know that I had spoken one way to her and another way to them? They were amused and curious. Of course I knew, I said. Did they, too, not change their accent and tone, depending on whom they were speaking to? No, they looked horrified at the idea, no, never. And then, in this nice house in a posh part of London, it occurred to me that English people are mono. I had never imagined.

'I'M SO HAPPY FOR YOU, I REALLY AM'

Kathy Lette

LOCATION: *a Soho Literary Club, frequented by the usual assortment of unpublished poets, failed film producers, Instant Celebrities and Chardonnay Socialists.* INTERIOR. DAY. A MIDDLE-AGED WOMAN *sits alone at a table for two. She is one of London's high-powered television executives. Often photographed for* Tatler *and quoted on the* Guardian *Women's Page, she sports shoulder pads, a man's watch, silk lingerie and a Tory Party politician husband.*
A YOUNG WOMAN *approaches* ...

My dear! I *knew* it was you, the *minute* you walked in. I just looked up and thought *yes*. That's *her*. That's just *got* to be Jerome's new friend. He told me on the phone that you looked, well, un*usual*. How *colourful*. You are *brave* to wear that in London, you *really* are ... Besides, you can't see yourself from the *back*, so what does it matter, anyhow? I do so admire you younger girls. It's just so lovely the way you don't feel the need to keep up with fashion. Tea? ... Oh, a drink? By all means. It's just that *I* try not to, you know, unless it's a *special* occasion ... it does so age the skin.

  – Waiter? One gin and tonic...? Yes and top up my tea will you?

So, you're in *love*. I'm so happy for you, I *really* am.
Well – let me take a good look at you ... When I heard
that Jerome had delivered you from the wilds of
the North ... what? Oh Birmingham was it? Well,
wherever ... I just *had* to meet you. That's why I rang
and arranged this little tête à tête. London can be
so daunting. I always imagine that, to an *outsider*
our little customs must seem as mysterious as, I don't
know ... a Japanese tea ceremony. So, I just want you to
know that you can always come to *me* for advice. All of
Jerome's other little friends have in the past. Oh God.
Look who's heading our way ...

ENTER *Another well-known television executive from
a rival channel. She nods in their direction.*

Lucinda, dah-ling, hel-lo ... Rupert? Oh yes. He's fine.
Love the suit. Chanel? I had one just like it ... *last*
year ... Tonight? Yes. I do hope Domingo's on form. See
you at the reception ... Oh, you *weren't?* You won't miss
much. It'll be terribly tedious as usual. All bullying
papparazzi oh, and the *Royals* of course ...

For starters, stay right away from *her*. So *dull*. Don't
you think that should be the only commandment?
Thou shalt not bore? I loathe this place, I *really* do. But
it is *the* literary club of London ... You *are* interested in
books aren't you dah-ling? Jerome always says that the
only reading the working class can manage is the back
of the cornflakes packet. He calls them 'Cornflake
Conversationalists'. But he's very naughty. I mean,
so far, you haven't even *mentioned* riboflavin or niacin,
no, not *once* ... *Anyhow*. I know it's a tiresomely
trendy place and there's absolutely *no* privacy, but I
thought you might like a glimpse of the cream of
London society ... What? No. By 'cream,' I do *not* mean
rich and thick ... Gosh, how refreshing to know that
Jerome's finally *maturing* – usually he goes for the
pretty rather than the *witty* ones.

Oh dear ... you haven't caught a London cough

already have you? Here's some water. That's right.
Take a big long drink. Château *Thames* I'm afraid.
They say each glass has been through at least ten
people already. Ghastly ...

ENTER *Another Chanel-suited English woman.
Having gone to Los Angeles, ostensibly to shore-up
some West Coast business contacts; she has returned
with the permanently startled expression of someone
who has undergone plastic surgery.*

Dah-ling. Hel-lo ... Rupert? Oh yes. He's fine. How's the
little libel action going, you poor angel? Yes, gutter
press. Oh and that frightful boy. Imagine selling his
story ... and to *News of the World.* Absolutely ghastly ...
But you know that your friends believe you and that's
what counts ... Byee.

Can't bear that woman. You must have seen her in
the papers. She's splashed all *over* the tabloids with her
toy-boy. She used to be a very good agent, but *now* look
at her? Did you see her face? I mean, that skin defied
gravity. It's just so embarrassing when a woman can't
act her ... Oh God, now she's *waving* ... Have they left
yet? Good. Still it is *so* nice to see them *together again* ...
Oh yes, I *know* that wasn't her husband. I was talking
about *her legs.*

Well ... I'm so happy for you. I *really* am. I suppose
Jerome has told you that I'm his oldest and closest
friend. That's why I'm so keen to hear *all about you.*
Now start at the very start. *I* first met him through my
editor .... I was only a lowly hack way back then ...
what? No. No, he *didn't* tell me. What section of the
paper are you working on, the Women's Page ... ? The
Fin*ancial* Pages — oh well, how *int*eresting.

Any-how, 'Dah-ling,' my editor said to me, 'you and
Jerome Forsyth were *meant* for each other.' Well, as you
can imagine, I was *intrigued.* I arranged to interview
him on some silly little story or other ... a pictorial on
dogs. That's right ... 'up and coming young artists and

their dogs.' Of course, Jerome doesn't have a dog,
though, by God, he's slept with a few over the years. Has
he introduced you to the dreaded Tiffany? She was last
year's little number. It took me absolutely *months* to
convince him what a disaster *she* was. So, *any*-how,
Jerry and I met for lunch and well, the next thing I
knew, it was back to his squat in Maida Vale . . . Oh, that
squat! It was all smelly socks and women with mous-
taches and stale milk . . . Of course, *then* it was his idea
of *luxury*. Oh, he knew nothing about *anything* in those
days. Honestly, I had to start from scratch. Lots of
potential, but still quite a barbarian . . . At first I
thought it was just sex . . . By the way, does he still have
that little fetish for clingfilm, whipped cream and rolled
up copies of the *Guardian* . . . ? Yes, by all means . . . My,
you *are* thirsty.

Waiter . . .

But, then, silly boy, he went and fell in *love* with me
didn't he? *Too* in love. And, well, I'm *married*. It was
devastating for me actually. I hated to see what I was
doing to him . . . I *begged* him to go out with other
women. Really *begged*. I didn't want him wasting his
whole life pining over me. I've never told anyone this,
but I know I can tell you . . . He used to cry, truly weep,
like a baby in my arms about how he could never, ever
find someone to replace me. But, what could I do? . . .

What? . . . Leave Rupert? I *couldn't*. Impossible. You
see, this has been the tragedy of my life. I'm married to
the most remarkable man *in the world*. Can you
imagine? Most women can't find *one* wonderful man and
I ended up with *two*. And, of course a scandal of that
kind would have ruined the chance of Rupert ever getting
on in the Party . . . Family life is so important to Maggie.
And to me too, of course. And well, let's face it, Jerome is
not exactly the 'settling-down' type, now is he? . . .

You're *what? Moving in?* With *Jerome*? To our, *his*
little flat? Oh . . . well . . . how wonderful. That's . . . I'm so
happy for you, I *really* am.

Waiter? This tea is cold. Another pot.

As I said. I'm just so happy for you. I *really* am. God, you are certainly much more tolerant than I. You obviously don't mind the filthy plates all over the place and all that strange hair in the bathtub and oh! Those cockroaches! I never could break him of the habit of leaving food out. Oh and then there's the toilet seat. *Always* up. And never any loo paper . . . Ghastly. Oh, not to mention the other women . . .

What? *Monogamous? Jerome?* . . . Oh, excuse me laughing. Sorry? . . . A 'Male Feminist' . . . is that what he told you he is? My dear girl, Jerome treats women as *sequels* . . . not equals. Honestly, I don't mean to laugh . . . but, look, it's just not in his *nature*. Jerome and I are old, *old* friends. How long have you known him? . . . Exactly. We always have been and always will be, the best and most intimate of friends. He still has my photos. I mean, the dah-ling man. I saw them the last time I was over at our, *his* flat, at Christmas. Beside his bed, in the drawer. As you know, we do still occasionally go to bed together, just for old time's sake . . . He did *tell* you about that didn't he? No? Oh well . . . I'm sure he *meant* to . . . God. There's that Booker Prize winner. I can never remember his name. Most boring book too . . .

ENTER *A young man. He clearly tries to avoid their table.*

Dah-ling . . . Rupert? Oh yes. He's fine . . . Congratulations. Fab-ulous book. Dazzling . . . The Pinters? Yes, on Sunday. We're being lectured to by some mar-vellous little green man from the Brazilian rain forest, I believe. See you there then. Byee.

I *hate* this place. I *really* do. Did you *hear* him? Dropping his *own name* . . . God, I *hate* being recognized. That's why I loved it so much when Jerome took me abroad on that little artist-exchange programme. The *anonymity*. So refreshing. It was like being an ordinary person again . . . *Any*-how, where was I? . . . Oh yes, I

was trying to tell you why I didn't leave my husband for
Jerome. The point is, that Jerry, dear as he is, is just not
the type to really *commit* ... never will, I'm afraid, that's
the ...

What? *Married*? To *Jerome*? Really ... well ... well ...
that is, well, it's mar-vellous news. I'm so happy for you,
I *really* am. Marriage ... well, well, well. What are you
doing *here* then? You should be at *home*, enjoying the
romance before it fades. To be frank, that's another
reason I chose not to leave Rupert and marry Jerry. It
kept our affair so *vital*, so *alive*. Marriage does, well,
spoil a man. You'll find that once married, his chief
erogenous zone will be the second shelf of the pantry
where he keeps the Mars bars. Yes, I'm afraid the only
stiff thing about a *married* Englishman is his upper
lip.

Waiter ... Whisky.

God, marriage eh. But you know, meeting you today
has reminded me just what a remarkable man Jerome
is. In fact, that is truly one of his best qualities – the way
he doesn't give a hoot about what other people think.
Courageous. That's what he is. Because of course, his
bohemian days are behind him. He's a very successful
artist now. Really, one of the Establishment. And, of
course, everyone expects him to be involved with a
woman, well, with a woman of a *certain type* ... I mean,
it wasn't so long ago that Northerners were considered
to be the dog turds on the sole of civilization. I've seen so
many working-class types scraped off party invitation
lists ... Mind you, not *now*, so much. You don't see *me*
checking the bottom of my shoes now do you? And you
are lucky. You do seem to have lost your accent ...
mostly, don't you think? What? ... Jerome said that did
he? ... Honestly ... well ... well ... Yes. Yes, as a matter
of fact I was born in Liverpool ... but it was terribly
fashionable in the sixties, you know.

But still, lovey, you're really going to need me to guide
you through London's social minefield. What ... ? Well,

of course you can look after yourself. Nobody said you can't . . . No, no, I don't doubt that you know what to *wear* where . . . by the way, it really is a lovely dress . . . Did you make it yourself . . . ? No, no. I'm talking about what to *say* where. Jerome's friends can be terribly daunting. It can be difficult to know what to say to the Harolds and the Antonias of this world. You see, they don't speak *English* in this part of England. No. They speak *euphemism*. Oh, yes, it's a completely different language. For example . . . let's see . . . 'Do stay for *another* drink . . . won't you?' is a *definite* sign that you've outstayed your welcome. There! You didn't know *that* did you? The way we talk must sound positively Russian to an *outsider*, I've always thought. It's sad, but not everyone you meet will be so *broad-minded*. No matter how much you try, they'll never take you seriously. You'll always be Jerome's 'little bit of fluff'. I'm af . . .

New York . . . You're going to live in *New York*? Dah-ling, living in New York is a contradiction in terms. Jerome is an *Englishman*. He needs to be *here*, in the hub of things. Doing his bit for civilization. We *are* still renowned for our tolerance. Someone has to maintain all those values – intellectual debate, the family . . .

But wait! Wait! Speaking of families, yes, well . . . I feel, as a new *friend*, I should warn you that Jerome will *never* consider them. *Children* that is. That was a tiny problem between us. Men just don't understand a woman's *instincts*. There's nothing sadder than the woman who's left it too late because her husband didn't want children, don't you think? I know it's hard to contemplate now, when you're so young . . . -*ish* . . . but there will come a time when you'll get a little wake-up call on the old biological alarm clock and . . .

Pregnant? Really? How far gone are . . . Well . . . that's, well, that's . . . I'm so happy for you, I *really* am. I mean, I'm so happy that you found out so *early*. It makes the little operation so much easier. I know a wonderful little man in Harley Street. *Everybody* goes there . . .

Oh, you both *want* it? . . . You both *planned* it. Really? Before you've established yourself in London, career-wise? Well, excuse me laughing . . . but I thought you were a genuine Feminist?

What? . . . But you can't *keep* the baby. You don't seem to understand . . .

CLOSE UP: – *The middle-aged woman places her teacup crisply in it's saucer and leans forward to scrutinize her young companion. For a fleeting moment she finds herself contemplating a trip to L.A. to shore up some West Coast business contacts.*

It is time, my dear, to *face facts*. What do you mean . . . *I* should? . . . I didn't intend to be quite this frank, but well, dah-ling, I just can't sit by and watch you ruin your life. That's why I always make a point of meeting Jerome's little friends. It's up to me to warn you that, well, it won't last. He's only *pretending* to love you, to spite *me*. The truth of the matter is, you are nothing more than a little inter-city souvenir. Jerome and *I* are *soul mates*. . . No. We *are*. Jerome has *always* been there for me. He *will* always be there for me. He *adores* me. *Forever*. *Nobody* and *nothing* can ever come between us . . .

Do calm down dear. That's a very cruel thing to say. Of course he's always loved me. Just as I've always loved him. Dah-ling, ten years is a very long time . . . No. It is *not* a matter of having left my 'run too late'. My dear girl, you don't understand. Of course, I've had *other* lovers, but Jerome is my Grand Passion. We are made for each other. He'd be *nowhere* without me. If anything ever happened to Rupert, I have always intended to *marry* Jerome . . . Some people, *cruel* people say that I've been stringing him along for all these years . . . but Jerry knows my true situation. He knows that I only stayed with Rupert out of a blasted sense of duty. Not because of the money . . . or the status . . . or the

Party . . . as I know some unkind people have . . .

Sorry? . . .

Who told you? . . .

Who?

Jerome? . . . He *knows* that Rupert's left me? . . . But who told . . . ? How did . . .?

It doesn't matter who he's run off with . . . Well, yes, as a matter of fact it *is* his secretary . . . Ha, ha, ha . . . after all these years, can you imagine? I mean, you'd think that he could come up with something more original. A librarian, or a bloody Lithuanian for God's . . . I mean the Eastern bloc is so sensationally fashionable at the . . . Don't be so ridiculous. It's just the lemon in the tea. It makes my eyes water . . .

Waiter . . .

Do stay for *another* drink dear . . . won't you? . . .

Listen lovey. Save your sympathy. You'll need it for yourself, when Jerome dumps you. Because, of course, he'll come back to me . . . He will . . . He always does you know . . .

The middle-aged woman is now speaking to a retreating back. The waiter approaches.

Yes, you may clear away . . . My daughter? No. . . . *No.* She was *not* my daught . . . Could I have the bill . . . She's just a silly little girl who thinks she's in love. And well – if so, that's grand . . . I'm happy for her, I *really* am.

THE BACK LOTS OF ENGLAND

Shirley Geok-lin Lim

The back lots of England form uniform
rectangles, unevenly plotted with cabbage
rows, a lean-to shack, in the thick loam

those frowsy pink English summer roses:
each Council house brick-solid of late
nineteenth-century empire, empire's losses.

Twenty years ago at Elly's parents',
dark gleaming with polish and faded carpets,
her father walked me through his garden, a gent

forever England. Although daughter
and son-in-law were making do in Asia,
teaching the tropical child. Sallow,

brooding, I had come unexpectedly
for tea with the genial, respectable
working middle-class. Seeing firstly

the ferociously weeded lot
with damson plum and harrowed field,
I wanted to be just so plotted,

sixty feet by forty feet, a land
for leaning mums, resplendent dahlias
every August regular as life, grand

blossoms housed in nation and history,
to live in a brick-brown Council house.
Now the Gatwick Express ricochets

above miles of steady Council yards.
For the migrant no garden will ever
be enough. A different poverty discards

grinding middle classdom, although tea
is always only five minutes away.
Tea is five minutes away only,

and everything else beyond one's lot.
The glory of every summer's roses
left behind, it is the bricks that rot.

Judith Grossman

Wednesday was the group's evening out at the pub, and Brian was nice enough to invite her to join for the duration. Shirley didn't fit in anywhere else; girlfriends and family took up the weekends, and there was no question of introducing her to the dear old mother with the Sacred Heart in her kitchen. Jim, the older brother, was in the States getting a divorce on her account, but he'd only told his Mum there was a separation 'for the time being'. So here she was, with a temporary job in the university library, knowing barely three people in town, waiting till Jim could bring her over.

The way he had introduced her to Brian, asking him to look out for her, was meant to set her up as one of the boys: 'Oh, Shirl can drink all right, can't you love? Head like an iron pot. And she'll buy her rounds, don't worry.'

The truth of that recommendation was tested the first night out: they purposely decided to go to Yates's, where the routine was a small white (a glass of sweet wine) with a Bass chaser.

'Like it?' Brian asked, deadpan.

Shirley had begun feeling premature hangover twinges after the first couple of swallows, but she was going to stick it out.

'The beer's fine,' she said. 'This other stuff is deadly, admit it.'

'White Tornado, that's called – cheapest way out of Liverpool, bar the bus. And faster.'

She puked horribly later, in private. Then it turned out that their regular pub was a nicer place downtown, with Victorian frosted glasswork and special brews on tap, and for the next few weeks they met there. Nobody especially noticed, during that time, the way Brian brought up once in a while this cheap passage to Australia deal he'd read about, until the moment he said in a typical throwaway line that he was going. Five rounds had gone down that evening, but they knew right away that he meant it.

'And what about Maureen?' Terry asked. Terry was the serious one, married already, and Maureen was a cousin of his. She'd been going out with Brian for the past year. Brian had said Maureen was the most attractive girl he knew, but she'd had a kid at sixteen, who lived with her Mum now while she was at her aunt's.

'Told her last Sunday. She wouldn't want to go anyway – obvious reasons.'

'Did you ask her, though? Didya?'

'No. Look, what's the point?' Brian said.

Terry had a drink, and looked up at Shirley. 'She was an absolute golden girl, at fifteen. Then she met some older bloke at work – we never got the name out of her – and the bastard knocks her up, and scarpers. Bloody shame.'

Terry didn't share any of Maureen's good looks – just a blocky-built chap with greasy dark hair – but he had a nice face, if a bit depressed. Always the first one to arrive at the pub, ready with new complaints about his management-trainee job at Jacobs'.

'Hey well! And did you tell our friends at the Cap. Con. yet?' Frank worked in the same insurance firm as Brian: they called it the Capitalist Conspiracy.

'Gave 'em a month's notice a week ago last Friday. Leaving October the twenty-ninth – sailing November the second.'

That stopped them cold. Shirley thought they looked as if Brian had raised the lid to their collective existence and pissed inside. Today was the thirteenth already.

'Well, bugger all!' Scotty said after a moment. 'You're a real prick, Bri. Doing it like that, keeping us in the dark.' It was his place to say that – unlike the rest, he hadn't been to college, which made him the social conscience of the group. Scotty thought about taking courses in commercial art at the Poly, but was stuck in clerical for the present.

'Well.' That would be the closest Brian would come to an apology. 'You have to think it out by yourself. I mean, first. Not to mention breaking it to me Mum.'

'Well I can't deny you're probably right. Got to be more opportunities out there.' Frank ground a cigarette-end forcefully into the ashtray. 'And better 'n being stuck in a groove for forty years, eh?'

It was Shirley's round, and she bought them all double Scotches so they could cheer up and drink to Brian in style.

'Ooh, she's a nice girl,' Frank said. 'Can I marry you tomorrow, love? No? Day after, then?'

A bit later, she was telling them Jim was the one to blame, setting the bad example, going off to the States for a load more money. 'Who knows?' she said. 'We might all be back home in three, four years – flush or broke, who knows?'

'I doubt it. I really doubt that.' Scotty took a drink with deliberation, settling the point.

Shirley looked round the table and thought if she were to pick one of them to go to bed with that night, it would be Scotty, acne scars regardless. They'd all survived a tough neighbourhood together, and the rigours of Jesuit high school too, but only he gave off a sense of having taken the full punishment of that, through some determination not to evade or escape anything. The last fifteen minutes till closing time, she took covert looks at him, at his face with the straight lines everywhere – forehead, eyebrows, short nose, closed lips. He wore a dark shirt, unlike the others who conformed to standard business uniform. She liked that; she herself wore shabby black and purple in the artschool style, maintaining outsider status.

But it was Brian who decided for once to walk her to the bus-stop.

'Scotty's taken, did you know?' he said when they were out of earshot.

'Quick, aren't you? Yes I know, and so am I, don't be *thick* Brian. I'm just drunk. After you leave, I shan't be seeing any of them anyhow.'

'O.K., O.K.'

A harsh wind was blowing up from the river, so they stood back in a shop doorway.

'Anyway,' he said, 'thanks for backing me up. They do feel I'm deserting the side.'

'Well, so we are, to be honest.'

'Right bastards, are we then?'

He moved round, put his hands either side of her shoulders, against the plate-glass window, and started kissing her. To her surprise she felt a spark of response, and put her hands inside his raincoat, pulling him tighter to enjoy the warmth and feel. A bus pulled up to the stop, paused, dinged twice and went on.

'It isn't real, is it?' she said. 'Just the routine.' She relied on what Jim had said about Brian's extensive record with girls. He had kept a deceptively untouched blond sheen to him: the ice prince of Preston Road.

'It's always real,' he said. After an evening of drinking, the Liverpool accent came back to his Rs. 'Not always so good, though. Lucky old Jim.'

At that, she started listening for the next bus, and when she heard it, pushed him away. 'There it is – I've got to go.'

He stood back coolly. 'Well, goodnight, Shirl.'

The following Wednesday, after hours, he took her up to a shebeen on Edge Lane. From the outside it was nothing but a large brick villa with blacked-out windows. To get in, he slipped a ten-shilling note through a letter-box held open from inside; then a heavy man with a squashed nose opened the door. They went through to a large, cheerless back room where there was an improvised plywood bar, and he bought two Irish whiskies. They sat down at a small metal table. Over by the corner juke-box three women stood talking and tapping their feet, and a couple more, in pastel sheath dresses, danced together in a tired way. The only other people in the place were some black men in a group on the far side, drinking out of bottles.

Soon, because of the beer-drinking earlier, Shirley had to piss. The man at the bar told her upstairs, and she climbed an unexpectedly plush staircase, carpeted in purple, with crimson flock paper on the walls. The bathroom at the top was decorated with red hearts on the walls, and a bouquet of plastic flowers.

'It's quite opulent up there,' she commented to Brian when she came back. 'A brothel, d'you think?'

'Well of course,' he said. 'Why else would they be there' – he nodded towards the women – 'and the Americans?'

'It seems quite a nice one. D'you go there ever?' She looked down at herself. It was a new idea, to be compared with prostitutes, and in her dark V-neck and skirt, striped stockings and green shoes, she saw she could only be taken for an amateur.

'Come on, we'll dance.'

Brian's style was close dancing; he had the basic quickstep moves down pat, and he took leading seriously. Possibly he might not be so out of place in insurance as he imagined. They began in a tight pattern, then wheeled out towards the middle, and saw two more women taking the floor together. At the end of the record, one of those dragged-out misery hits started, and they turned back to the table. But a tall American cut in and asked her to dance, so she stayed, and followed him in a kind of slow-motion jive which he could evidently do with his eyes shut just as well as open.

How does he know where I am? she thought, when he let go for a moment and picked up contact on the next beat, with a stroking, upward touch on the palm. Darker than Harry Belafonte, but not as black as the Nigerians at university. He walked her back to the table, but didn't sit down.

'Well, thanks,' she said.

'Thank *you*,' he corrected her.

After he moved away, Brian said, 'I've seen fights in here, over girls. Knives out.'

'Really?' She was sure he flushed slightly. 'Look, I've got to go home. You can come if you want to – I'm going to look out for a taxi, on the road.'

They walked a mile towards town before picking up a ride, and she got annoyed with his silence. Rude questions kept coming to mind: why are none of you over five foot six – who stunted the growth around here? Will you go on wearing such boring clothes Down Under? Why don't you talk about the ethics of making love to your brother's woman?

In the back of the taxi she said softly in his ear: 'D'you go to bed with Maureen?'

He looked surprised. 'Well, no. Not as a general rule. A couple of times on holiday. She lives with her aunt.'

'Jesus.' Weren't there ways?

'It isn't so bad from the inside – for her, I mean. Eventually she'll get married.'

'Will she? People like you and your mates, you always want virgins.'

'Not invariably. Look at you and Jim.'

Shirley was about to say Jim was different, then she caught it that he'd talked to his brother about her, reviewed her history no doubt, this fallen creature he was going to redeem.

'Well,' she said, 'Jim's damaged goods himself, if it comes to that. A bad marriage, and all.'

Then they shut up and began kissing, which seemed to make everything better. Back in her room, with the gas fire turned up and roaring, she poured two more glasses of whisky and got out the packet of chocolate wholemeal biscuits.

'Here, take off that boring tie and have a bikky.'

Soon he tasted deliciously of chocolate and crumbs and firewater, and they undressed and went to bed with the fire still going. Now she could see the family resemblance between the brothers, in the nice proportions of the torso, smooth, rosy, unmarked. And even after a day's work and a night's drinking, he had that ready vitality that she loved in Jim; and they weren't grim in bed, these ex-Catholics – it was so delightful, how they liked to play.

'Sweetie-pie,' she said, feeling his slim prick erect for the second time. 'My sweetie-pie.'

'Not yours, darlin'.'

'Who cares? Just sweetie-pie, then.'

At the eight o'clock alarm they woke up, cheerful and only mildly hung-over. Shirley plugged in the kettle, fluffed her hair in the mirror and went to get dressed, pulling fresh underwear from the drawer. As she put on her bra, she saw four bluish fingerprints on her breast, and felt sore nipples; she was reminded of the streak of cruelty in his love-making which had made her think, before she slept, *enough* – and perhaps too much. Was he intent on out-performing his brother, making so to speak his own impression on her? Too likely, and punishing her at the same time. She looked at him: he was holding his shirt up by the window, examining the state of the collar.

Then he put it on with a small frown. She'd bet his mother did his laundry every day of her life.

Over breakfast, toast and instant coffee in the kitchenette corner of the room, he made a point of telling her how many evenings were booked up in the next week until he sailed: the do with the boys at work, the family gatherings, Maureen.

'It's O.K., Brian,' she said. 'I've got this friend in Manchester, been promising to phone up. Go over, see the Free Trade Hall.'

'Well, suit yourself.' He lit a cigarette, checked his watch and got up to give her a warm, smokey kiss. 'I've to run now.'

But he phoned her at work mid-morning. 'How are you feeling, then?'

'Fairly screwed.'

'Look, Liverpool are playing at home this Saturday. Want to go?'

'O.K.'

'Meet you in the Chester Arms for lunch, then, about twelve-fifteen.'

Lunch was Guinness, brown bread and butter, and plates of tiny cold shrimp tasting as if they had been cooked in sea-water. Afterwards they took the bus out along Scotland Road. It had been raining, and the air was still foggy with wet under an overcast sky; the slate roofs of the houses had a deep-blue sheen to them. Shirley watched the women on the street, loaded with bags in either hand, or with one hand on a pushchair and the other holding the bags. They wore headscarves and drab coats, and she remembered that she was also wearing a headscarf, which would flatten her hair, and a dirty tan raincoat – only three months, and she was starting to resemble them. Already!

On most corners there was a pub; Brian had told her that among the older generation the women often went to one pub to booze on port and lemon, while the men went to another, for mild-and-bitter, or Scotch with a beer chaser when they were flush. The bus went on through areas of brick row-houses with washed doorsteps, and then all of a sudden there were more people on the pavements, men in cloth caps walking in the same direction as the bus. The double stream of them on each side of the road increased at every corner, gathering until it began to spill into the roadway, and the bus changed down gears and ground them spasmodically as it slowed to a walking-pace itself.

'We'll get off, the next stop,' Brian said. 'Might as well walk from here.'

They stepped down into the moving flood of people, all muted and uniform in their greyish or dark raincoats, drab jackets, drab tweed caps. Often the men had a cigarette drooping from one side of their mouths, and made cryptic remarks out of the other side. Brian pulled her over into a pub doorway while he lit up himself; two men beside them were arranging a bet.

'You know,' he said as they walked on, 'our Dad used to send me to the shop for a couple of Woodbines. Just a couple at a time. And Jim'd give me hell, when he was here, because he wasn't supposed to have 'em, with his asthma, and bronchitis. But I didn't have the heart to deny him. I couldn't ever see it.'

At the football ground there were boys milling about with red rosettes to sell, and men with slips of paper and hands busy with money.

'We'll do it right,' Brian said, 'if you don't mind standing room only.'

It wasn't a question. He paid at the gate, and they were pulled along in the current up some steps, and out into a steeply pitched enclosure overlooking one end of the field. To either side beyond the barriers were the higher-priced seats, but here there was just the tilted concrete floor, down to the wall at the bottom.

'This is for the real fans.' Brian waved towards the crowd which had already filled the lower third of the area. 'This is Spion Kop, this here, called after a hill in the Boer War where some local chaps got mangled. So it's only for our side. Visitors, other end please.'

More and more people came in from the stairway, until there were no open areas on the slope; lower down it was packed tight, and farther up they were shifting about, jockeying for a better view. Brian settled for a spot by the side barrier.

'Not the best, perhaps, but we'll get a great view of any corner kicks. There won't be a huge crowd: the boys are in a bit of a slump at the moment.'

A group of taller than average caps edged slantwise in front of them, and he pushed Shirley forward to head them off, but it didn't work. Now she could only see the corner, and narrow segments of the further half of the field.

'These blokes must've cadged extra school milk,' she murmured. One of them turned and spat a gob of phlegm to land a calculated eighteen inches from the toe of her shoe, then flashed her a bleak look which said, unmistakably, *bloody foreigner*. Yet she wasn't the only girlfriend here; there were four or five headscarves among the rows ahead, and two little dollies with chiffon over their rollers had been cavorting in the back earlier.

An orchestrated roar, beginning down at the front and rising through the ranks of the crowd, told them the teams were running onto the field.

'We're the sound machine – that's the Kop,' he said.

'Right. Give us a cig, Brian, would you?' Her feet, in thin socks and light shoes, were already freezing on this damp concrete, and it wasn't going to get any better. 'Your last game for a while, I suppose?'

He lit it for her. 'Well, there's always cricket, and tennis. Not the same, though.'

Moments into the game, cued by a subtle inflection in the roar which she didn't pick up, he came alert and craned high to the left.

'Damn it! Get 'im, you buggers! Oh, Christ –'

No need to ask: the wrong side had scored, rousing a deep and prolonged jeer, and shouts of protest.

'Now,' he said, 'the next ten minutes'll be the crucial ones. Either they've got to score or at least get in a couple of good strikes, at *least* that – or the guts'll go out of them the rest of the half.'

A little way along in the row in front of them was a tiny man wrapped in a muffler over a frayed jacket, who had set up a running tirade: *put the fucking boot into 'em, get it in, yer lazy buggers, put yer arses into it, yer buggers, get a sodding move on, yer bloody sods –*

'What's up with him?' she asked. 'He can't see a bloody thing, surely.'

Brian looked along the row. 'He's pissed. See that bulge in his pocket? That's his half-pint. Still, he knows what's happening all right.'

At the end of ten minutes, she checked again; Liverpool hadn't scored or had a convincing shot on goal, and the little man was quiet, tipping back his bottle. Around him the roar sank to a growling undertone.

'He thinks the same as you do – he's given up for the duration.'

'We know 'em too well.'

At half-time the crowd re-sorted itself, after which they could see a little more of the field. But soon a drizzling rain came on, and the struggle out in the mud bogged down; neither side scored, although the crowd in the home stands kept up a steady level of alternating support and abuse, as the ball zig-zagged up and down the field.

Even before the end a stream of defectors was making for the stairway exit, and Brian nodded to her to move. 'They're saving themselves for next week – there's a big one coming up – as if it'll do any good with this lot. They need some fresh blood: import some Aussies.'

'A trade, then. And the Aussies get you – to do what, by the way? I never asked.'

'I honestly don't know. They give you the names of some firms. Money's what I have in mind. The loot.'

Just inside the turnstile there was a flurry of movement over to their left: two men got a third pinned against the wall and were holding and punching him with short jabs, while their victim jerked to and fro and tried to hack them with his knees and boots. Brian pushed her quickly on through, and the sound of muffled gasping and swearing followed them outside.

She looked back, but caught only the backs of the quickly assembling audience.

'Can't do owt about that,' he said. 'Now you've seen life as she's lived in this place. No action in the game, so they've got to make up for it, see? It's just a dull scene – dull and boring, bloody bloody boring. So what do you do? Get the other bloke in the balls.'

They took the bus back to the end of her road, and ran up in the pouring rain. Inside, he borrowed a towel to dry off his hair, then took out a comb to part it and set the quiff in order.

'Why d'you make it so neat? For all you know I might mess it up,' she said.

'I'll take a chance.'

'And what's it to be – tea or whisky?'

'Ooh – let's have tea with a splash of the good stuff, shall we? Queen Victoria's favourite.'

She put on the kettle. When she came back, he was smiling at the way drops from the leaky ceiling over the window fell in a musical sequence into the array of milk-bottles she'd set underneath. The carpeting there was stained and rotted, and the paint blistered on the wall above. *I should get a reduction in rent*, she thought again, and then remembered her conversation last week with Mrs Skipton, the owner, who lived in the basement flat. Mrs S. had talked about the seemingly nice girl who'd been renting the top-floor, and had left to get married six weeks before. And when Mrs S. went to the service, at St Philip Neri along the street, the bride came down the aisle in white, but sticking out to here.

'Seven months at least – she could have had it there at the altar – and I had no idea, *no idea* such things could have gone on in my house. I didn't even notice.'

This trade-off was better; a few leaks for the right to discreet fornication.

She made the tea, and sat down in the only armchair while he stood and looked out of the window, drinking.

'Tonight it'll be me Mum's cake,' he said, 'and to-morrow me auntie's Sunday dinner. The pair of them are too good for this world: it's a heavy cross. Auntie's Yorkshire pudding alone ought to be worth a few years off Purgatory.'

Then he drained his cup, set it down and came over beside her, reaching down to her breast.

'A farewell fuck, is it?' she said, covering his hand with her own.

'If you don't mind.'

'Well, just this once.'

'Sooner me than another: keeps it in the family.'

Afterwards, getting dressed, he said: 'So – would you have considered Australia, if the subject had come up?'

Shirley was prepared for that one. 'Oh – I expect I would have. If things'd been different. Just, the past two years, going through so much trouble with Jim, it has to have been worth it. You know.'

He looked satisfied. 'Well, needless to say, this episode shall go unmentioned.'

She laughed at that. 'Don't make rash promises. I know you'll tell him. Eventually if not before.'

'Look – if I say I won't, I won't.' But he was blushing, reaching for his cigarettes again.

'I shan't tell him myself, but I really don't care.'

She knew as a certainty that he'd tell. It was his pride in himself: if Jim was to have the more brilliant career, he could at least be the seducer of women, and he'd always be wanting to prove it. She cared, but what was the use? Besides, Jim would be consoling himself for her absence in some comparable way, no doubt of that, and they had both agreed that nothing that happened in this lost time of waiting would mean anything.

'Here – I'm going to drink to you. Success, and a happy trip,' she said.

When he had gone she took the cups round into the kitchenette and washed them out. There was a chop for her dinner, keeping cool on the windowsill; unwrapped, it stank a little but not enough to throw away; she could wash it. And there were potatoes and onions to fry up.

First, though, a bath. She ran the narrow, stained tub half-full, threw in a Jasmine bath-cube from a birthday assortment, and undressed. Yet if she smelled of anyone, it would be herself: Brian never seemed to have a smell, and although she'd told him she had a diaphragm he preferred to use his own supply of condoms – the implication was that he never trusted a woman's word. Lying in the water, she noticed how the marks on her breast had faded to greenish. Then she thought of Maureen, and of Jim's wife, the ones who had been officially deserted, left. Oh, but their friends and relatives rallied round like mad in cases like that – Maureen in the bosom of her auntie and the rest, Valerie and all of Jim's and her former colleagues and friends. Centres of solicitude, the two of them. Valerie might have lost a husband, but she'd kept everything else, as far as Shirley could see. She hadn't been driven out of the fucking *country* over this.

And now, which of the people she'd been friendly with in that damn place could she phone up and talk to? Anita, that was all, and only because Anita was an insatiable gossip.

And seriously, who wanted to be a bloody American, with no Labour Party, and everyone wearing horrible Dacron and white socks, and talking too loudly and making fools of themselves all over the world? Hell – even if Jim were Marx and Freud rolled into one, he could hardly make up for all she was going to lose – herself, even, to be remade in some totally strange place. In seven years there would be complete cell turnover: so much for the corner of a foreign field that is forever England.

But crying into the bath wouldn't help: it was cool enough already. She mopped herself with the towel and went back to her room to dress and put on fresh make-up. Yesterday John Lewis's had had a special offer, so she'd bought grey and plum-coloured eye shadow to try out. After supper, she could go down to the Crack for a drink. There was a good chance someone from the library would be around, and you never knew when the occasional unhappily married man might show up. The best kind, those, absolutely the best, and besides, they deserved anything that happened.

Kevin Coyne

The sky's a sort of salmon pink and Irmgard's just left. It's a bit lonely out here. I'm not sure whether I should be around. Can you imagine how it feels? I'm British, never liked foreigners much.

There are four doors in this room. One of them has a cat flap. A cat's just arrived. It looks hard at me, trembles, then walks past. I give it my special smile, but it doesn't seem to work. It isn't impressed.

Now the sky's changed colour; dark muddy brown with glowing red streaks. The yellow curtains reflect the red; red on yellow, blood. Am I supposed to stay here till Irmgard returns? Mysterious Irmgard, where does she go to in that purple BMW of hers? A glimpse of her underwear used to excite me; not anymore. One of her friends told her I was sexless ('You should read his stories,' she said). I didn't deny it. I'm past trying to prove something.

I came here for love. For some years I'd had fantasies about holding a strong Bavarian woman to my chest under the shade of a large tree in the English Garden in Munich. I was astonished when it all came true. It was exotic, my blubbery grey Englishness was bathed in a new found earthy perfume. No one in Stoke-on-Trent or Hastings (or anywhere in England) smelt like this!

I loved her fingers; long and extremely bony, they excited me when she pressed them into my oversized gut. Were English fingers ever like this? We were a contrast. She was brown with a faint tinge of purple. I was perfectly white. She was tall. We caused quite a stir on Leopoldstrasse.

We set up home together, shared the household chores, talked of forming a rock'n'roll combo. I decided that I was too old for excess. 'You're so so bloody English,' she would say, poking at me with a sharp naked foot. I had to own up; her insistence on walking around naked embarrassed me! Did that make me typical? I immediately thought of my father, how he always bathed behind firmly locked doors. I thought of the little brown kitchen in Stoke-on-Trent, pink corsets draped across the rickety wooden clothes dryer.

'You're amazingly beautiful,' I used to tell her. 'But you won't let me do what I like,' she always replied. England, the fifties, the war, the deprivations of a working-class childhood were all against me. I couldn't relax.

It's good to tell you about her. Is it all in the past? I should draw the curtains but the sky continues to interest me. It's yellow now, totally yellow. Something that looks like an eagle appears to be perched on the garden fence. It's very German, alarmingly symbolic. Is my insecurity subjecting me to delusions again? Am I becoming a victim of my darkest darkest fears? I can hear gunfire in the forest. The petals of the solitary rose (placed so lovingly in a blue and white china vase just before she left) are opening slowly, painfully. A sudden thought passes predictably through my head. Did we really win the war? A failed love affair can draw out the most base and trite observations. I'm embittered, bitchy.

'You're always talking about Hitler!' she snarled before she left (a habit of mine when losing an argument, the proverbial 'low blow'). I know how to draw blood.

Has she gone forever?

She's a mystery.

Could it be her limited (but amusing) knowledge of English? Still, I wish I could hear the purr of her luxurious purple motor. I miss her. I need her. Who's going to talk to the plumber tomorrow when he comes to mend the faulty boiler? My German is terrible.

THE OTHER OSCAR

Mario Vargas Llosa

We were having breakfast in the small kitchen of our flat in Earls Court, when we saw what was unmistakably the head of a mouse peep out from under the sideboard. I rushed to complain to the landlady. Mrs Spence's eyes lit up: 'Ah! It's Oscar!' she said and insisted that we leave out some of that cheese with holes in it for our morning visitor; that's what her children used to do. It was difficult to get her to understand that we did not find the presence of Oscar exciting at all; that for us the very idea of a mouse was horrifying. Mrs Spence just sent me away saying that Oscar, feeling so rebuffed, would most probably leave for another more hospitable abode.

A few days later, after returning from the cinema and turning on the kitchen light, we saw Oscar, Oscar's father, his mother and one of his little brothers all jump out of a basket of fruit on the floor. Come dawn the following morning I was on guard outside Mrs Spence's door. This time our landlady gave in and issued instructions. I had to make a complaint about the pests to an office in the borough of Kensington and Chelsea, appropriately called *The Rodent Department*. I rang and explained my problem. An unsympathetic voice asked for my address and told me I should wait.

The gentleman who called on us the next day looked like an eccentric straight out of an English short story. Tall and bony, he wore a black jacket, pinstripe trousers and a bowler hat, and carried a case that looked like a coffin. He came in, took off his hat and then his jacket, revealing a pair of false cuffs like a cashier's strapped to his wrists. He then subjected me to interrogation: Where had they appeared? How many were there? What size? What colour? He wrote down my answers in a ghostly notebook with a pencil hidden between his fingers.

Once he had all the information he needed he set about the task at hand. His open suitcase was a work of art, a real spectacle. Inside there was a stock of cardboard dishes and countless jars filled with different coloured powders, all packed with fanatical care. Moving around the kitchen like a duck, the man from the rodent department went about his task meticulously. He poured the powders into the dishes, flattened the piles down with a tiny spade and placed them in strategic locations which he had marked on a map in his notebook. He insisted that absolutely no one move the dishes or play with the powder, some of which, he said, was poisonous. The rest was just sand. This, of course, only heightened our curiosity. Before he left he murmured that it would be best to close down the kitchen.

He returned a week later and, from then on, with cosmic punctuality, once a week for a year. We didn't become friends because he was not given to such weaknesses, nor did we say much to each other. As soon as he arrived I would interrupt my work to watch the phlegmatic way he went about his own, and it was not long before I understood the function of the harmless white sand. It wasn't there to choke or to bewilder the mice, but rather to gather their droppings. The gentleman would use metal pincers to pick up the small round black deposits which Oscar and his fellow mice left behind, put them in little jars, and later take them away in his funeral bag. As for the poison, every week he would examine the revealing signs, passing his circumspect gaze over and over the lines, grooves, and footsteps left by the intruders. I soon understood that the range of colours had to do with the different, deathly, composition of the powders; that, since mice rapidly generate antibodies, the gentleman intended to stay one jump of Oscar and his family's metabolism by changing the powder every week.

He never explained what he was up to and when, prompted by curiosity, I asked him, he pretended he didn't understand my English. What were the results of his analysis of the little turds? Yes, yes, of course it would rain. How was the campaign going? Considering the amount of powder the mice consumed, wouldn't the species be degenerating, disappearing? Yes, that's right, Chelsea had won the Cup.

Apart from faeces, he would also take away the fresh corpses. He picked them up with a glove, looked at them clinically for a moment, and buried them deep in his case, wrapped in plastic bags. Many of the mice did die, it's true, but we had the contradictory, fantastic impression that the multi-coloured powders not only exterminated the mice but also reproduced them. Life was becoming somewhat difficult. Although the mice did not venture beyond the kitchen, having it closed meant we had to cook on a toy primus stove, eat in the bedroom, and use the bathroom for our pantry. We hated them for their tenacity, but in the end watching them die made us all feel guilty. They would appear out of nowhere, swollen from their deadly banquet, and drag themselves across the room in slow motion to lie at our feet, where they would breathe spasmodically until they expired, foaming at the mouth. Throwing them into the bin became a thankless task. We felt nauseous and had nightmares. When I wrote, or taught at the University, or read or conversed, the mice and the gentleman were always on my mind.

There were times when the war seemed won: a week, two weeks would pass without a casualty. We'd be excited, and even drink to our victory. The man from the rodent department, however, would carry on just as before, unperturbed, moving the dishes and powders around the corners of the kitchen and taking notes in his notebook. He knew best. For again, the next morning, we would notice those little black granules in the sand and on the dusty tiles. I pestered him: why didn't he just fumigate the house? One day that terrible year he finally explained why. The rules had not been changed since they used to fumigate ships in the nineteenth century, and if we fumigated the house now it would have to be closed down and quarantined for God knows how long. We had no other choice but to wait for him to defeat the mice in his own way.

I couldn't. I looked for work outside London, outside England. I went as far away as possible, putting countries, oceans, continents between us and the mice. But I liked London so much – its surprises – that two years later I returned. Miraculously, we found the same little flat in Earls Court unoccupied and again rented it. The night we arrived we joked with friends from the neighbourhood: nothing had changed, only they were missing. Our friends left, and we had just started to unpack when a hunch made us all turn towards the bedroom door. As in *Myriam*, that story by Truman Capote, there he was, on the red carpet, his head poked round the corner, small, rubicund, welcoming, and promising renewed torture. Oscar.

translated by John Kraniauskas

Emma Tennant

Love. 'The ferocious comedy of England, with its peculiar mark of violence.' Thus Thomas Stearns Eliot; and Thomas Hardy, with his predisposition for women and the gallows, preceded him as a transcriber of the old ballad. Love, betrayal, revenge: raped Philomel to Lucretia Borgia: Hardy hears the strains as he walks the lanes and streets of Dorset; and as they come stronger and clearer in childhood, he revisits Bockhampton, where he grew up, and finds his Tess.

In 1888 Thomas Hardy is nearing fifty. His marriage to Emma Gifford is one of constant illness (on Emma's part) and heavy colds (on Hardy's). He dreams of the village beauties of his youth; in London, in an omnibus, he sees a girl with 'one of those faces of marvellous beauty which are seen casually in the streets but never among one's friends . . . Where do these women come from? Who marries them? Who knows them?' And in Bockhampton, where his mother still lives, he sees the beauty of Augusta Way.

Nothing in Thomas Hardy's life at this point holds any beauty. Three years have passed since he and Emma moved into a house remarkable for its ugliness, Max Gate, at Dorchester, where, due to its elevated position, it is exposed to the full rigour of winds from every direction. True, to the south and south-west it has magnificent views across to Came Wood and the monument to Admiral Hardy; and the downs which overlook Weymouth and the sea. And from the upper windows of Max Gate it is possible to look northwards over the Frome valley to Stinsford church, Kingston Maurward House, and the heath and woodlands surrounding his mother's Bockhampton cottage itself. But the landscape is empty and hollow, to the eyes of a man without love. Obsessively, he studies the murder trials of the time and of earlier in the century; he sees, under the quiet, peace and domesticity which is the smiling face of England, its recurring theme of cruelty, murder, reprisal and revenge. In the seedy, new-genteel suburbs, which Hardy, with his great desire to find himself in company as elevated as the position of his new house, Max Gate, would never dream of inhabiting, are the protagonists of the old ballad come back again: Adelaide Barrett, the 'Platonic Wife' who slowly administers chloroform to her voyeur-husband who has encouraged her to make love to the young, soulful Reverend, George Dyson. Madeleine Smith in Edinburgh, of a refined and strait-laced family who force her to announce her engagement to a man she does not love, Mr Minnoch, and her measured administering of arsenic to the lover who couldn't marry and support her, l'Angelier.

Love. Thomas Hardy goes to Bockhampton, where as a child he went up to the barn at Kingston Maurward House to hear the old carols sung at Christmas; and from there he walks across to the manor of Kingston Maurward. He sees a milkmaid, a beauty who in 1888 is eighteen and who works in the dairy of her father, sharing in the milking and other chores. Her name is Augusta Way; and she will be his Tess, just as her father, Thomas Way, will be Dairyman Crick in the great novel that is forming in his mind. (Note: no shabby-genteel rendering of the old ballad will come from this. *Tess* is a rural drama in a landscape as old as myth, and, to Hardy's great sorrow and sense of loss, turning before his eyes to the new world and away from the old calendar of the countryside: the first cuckoo, the last swallow, harvest, Easter and Christmas, christening, marriage and burial coming round as they always had done and until now had shown no sign of changing.)

No, *Tess* will have none of the sordidness of these contemporary murders. *Tess* will be pure incandescence, the picture of woman wronged, the murderess as saint. Her landscape, metaphorically, could be recognized by the wife of King Tereus, sister of poor Philomel. (Who was raped by the king. The revenge was terrible. But that is another story.)

Love and melodrama. If a seedy note does creep in, it's at the lodgings in Sandbourne (Bournemouth, as we all know) where Tess and Alec spend their second, unloving honeymoon. In these cut-price plush surroundings - as fake as the imposter Alec himself - Tess will be driven to the ultimate act of violence. And by killing him, she inevitably sentences herself.

By killing him, she doubly kills - for it is the terrible betrayal of Angel Clare, clergyman's son, pig and hypocrite husband of an unconsummated marriage - the refusal to accept her when she confesses her lovemaking with Alec, her baby - that she avenges while immolating herself as well.

Tess hangs.

And Angel Clare, after standing under that prison wall with Tess's young sister Liza-Lu, takes the girl's hand and they go off into the future together.

It's no way, really, for a young girl to start out in life. In the shadow of the gallows of her sister. What can have become of them? - as the Victorians used to say.

For now, remember this: Hardy has found Augusta Way. They stand talking in the meadow. (How lovely she is. What a mouth! Hardy is driven insane by mouths.) They go indoors (for in those days there was no marked distinction, in old rural communities, between gentry and dairyman farmer: Thomas Way and his family live in part of Kingston Maurward Manor, a delicate and grand eighteenth-century house that is used just as any house would be by a large family busy with a farm).

Do they kiss?

Kissing is very much on the poet's mind. At Evershot station on the way here, he has discovered some mistletoe that had been there 'ever since last Christmas (given by a lass?) of a yellow, saffron parchment colour'. This mistletoe will come to him again, when he writes of Tess's disastrous honeymoon with Angel Clare and her return to Wool Manor, where they had sworn to be so happy – before she told him of her past – to find it, mocking, discoloured, still hanging as a meaningless symbol above the bed.

Thomas Hardy kisses the beautiful milkmaid, Augusta Way.

It's unbearably dull at Max Gate, the cold, ugly house where Thomas Hardy brought such unhappiness – and after her death, in a fever of remorse, fell in love with and wrote all his best poems – to Emma. It's a 'structure at once mean and pretentious, with no grace of design or detail, and with two hideous low-flanking turrets with pointed roofs of blue slate,' according to one observer at the time of building. And, worst of all, the stairs up to Emma's bedroom go past the walls of Hardy's study. In the last months of her illness, he will hear her mount those stairs – often in agony – and he won't go even as far as the landing to offer her assistance.

No wonder, after Emma's death, he feels remorse!

But at the time, nothing matters to Thomas Hardy except himself – and his new love, of course.

For Hardy has fallen in love – with the young Florence Dugdale – she who sent him a posy of flowers

in her ecstasy of admiration; she who, invited to Max
Gate with Hardy's old friend Florence Henniker, stood
at the front door as she was leaving and drew the great
man's attention to the flowers in his own front garden.

'Until then the faint scent/ Of the bordering flowers
swam unheeded away,' penned Hardy lovingly.

But in the autumn of 1888, the meeting with Florence
Dugdale is seventeen years away into the future.

And Thomas Hardy longs for love. He dreams of a
young woman he sees sometimes in London, Agatha
Thornycroft.

He dreams, too, of Augusta Way, whom he sees when
he visits his mother at Bockhampton.

Most of all, he dreams of Augusta Way. And, in his
dreams, he word-paints Tess.

The old ballad begins to be sung through Hardy, in
that grim house where Emma, increasingly absent-
minded, makes the running of the house and the
management of servants an impossible burden to them
all.

Hardy's best companion is his dog Moss, a brindled-
looking animal, half-Labrador. They walk together, in
the Valley of the Little Dairies and the Valley of the
Great Dairies (Blackmoor and Frome) and on Egdon
Heath, where Moss starts up a hare.

And, as the hare dances away, Hardy sees his love
disappearing too: his taste for love, his ability to love,
his own capability of inspiring love in others. After all,
he is nearing fifty.

Hardy stands alone with Moss, on the outcropping of
green hill that was once an Iron Age settlement and
looks down at the sea and Chesil Beach.

He bends to pick up a stone.

With its worn, rough curvature and an indentation at
the centre under two stripes and a knobbly protru-
berance that is like a nose under eyebrows, he could be
holding an early love goddess: a Neolithic Venus: a

totem for the fertility he feels draining away on all sides - from his loveless, childless marriage, from his own powers as a fertilizing male.

Hardy looks at the stone and it seems to look back at him.

Anonymous were the representations of the individual, in antiquity. All-important was the shape below the casual dash of features, of eyes and brows and nose.

The mouth. The vulva. So shrunk were these goddesses of copulation and procreation that the one stood for the other, and the figurine – round, squatting under its outside baby head – was only a receptacle for a receptacle. The bearer of a hole.

Hardy dreams of Tess's love. He sees in her model – for already Tess is more alive than the original, the pretty dairymaid Augusta Way – and, as to this day, remains so – the mouth of his dreams (perhaps Agatha Thornycroft's mouth, seen and conceivably tasted on those metropolitan visits so necessary to an unhappily married genius who lives in the depths of Dorset) but, unquestionably, first and foremost, the mouth of Augusta Way.

And as Hardy walks back – a long walk that will take him through Powerstock and Toller Porcorum – up onto the ridge of the hill that leads down to Beaminster via Evershot – he fills his Tess with love and hope and dreams – and as surely takes them away again, like the sea dragging and pushing on the stones.

Hardy blows life into Tess. Of course, she's a fictional character when all is said and done and he has to give her the kiss of life – that is, artificial respiration.

When he has brought her back to life – when he has blown his own breath into her mouth – he will fill that mouth with stones.

Of Tess's mouth, the erotic symbol which infatuated both Alec d'Urbeville and Angel Clare, Hardy wrote:

'mobile peony mouth'

'the pouted-up deep red mouth'

'the red and ivory of her mouth'

'her flower-like mouth'

'those holmberry lips'

'surely there was never such a maddening mouth since Eve's'

and

'she was yawning, and he saw the red interior of her mouth as if it had been a snake's ... The brim-fulness of her nature breathed from her. It was a moment when a woman's soul is more incarnate than at any other time.'

and Angel

'had never before seen a woman's lips and teeth which forced upon his mind with such persistent iteration the old Elizabethan simile of roses filled with snow'.

Poor Tess. He shaped her ready for the bloody sacrifice that was bound to follow.

Roy Heath

Debendranath Ghose came from West Bengal. His father, flushed with the newly won independence of India, had taken his wife and children as a body into the thriving Communist Party after explaining to them the principles on which the family was to be organized in future. His five daughters would have the same rights as the three sons and, like the sons, would be educated to the best of their abilities. Their mother and he would act as joint trustees for the two children under fifteen; but the others would be treated as adults and take part in a monthly meeting to discuss family affairs. While choosing different professions for each he declared that any one of them could overrule him and study the subject of his or her choice. Debendranath would do Law and be sent to England, if he approved. Law was a suitable profession for his eldest child, who would be in a position to give advice whenever needed. His eldest daughter would pursue her interest in farming and receive one quarter of all his land. And Mr Ghose distributed his wealth and patronage, allowing every child his due and retaining for himself and his wife an equal share in what remained of a not inconsiderable fortune.

Debendranath, even before joining the Communist

Party, had read and studied the Marxist classics, a process facilitated by the discussions he had witnessed between his father and his father's friends, who gathered in the reception room every Friday to drink tea and listen to his mother play ancient ragas on the sitar. *Anti-Dühring, Das Kapital, The Poverty of Philosophy, Origin of the Family* and Caudwell's *Studies in a Dying Culture* were names familiar to him long before he even picked up the last and, with growing excitement, fell under the spell of its unerring analysis of a bourgeois culture in decay.

He brought the book with him to London, bearing it like a talisman in his scanty luggage, certain that what he saw around him, the statues in public parks, billboards advertising films, a young newspaper seller at the underground station entrance who addressed him as 'Sir', provided evidence for the author's thesis of ineluctable decadence.

Debendranath, having taken up residence in a room he found through the Information Officer of the Indian High Commissioner, lost no time in joining the local CP branch, which held its meetings at a flat in a cul-de-sac branching off from the High Street. An unlikely gathering place, he thought, as he stood in front of the building wondering whether to use the knocker or the door bell. He rang twice, immediately regretting that he had not rung once. The line of plane trees bordering the road gave an uncharacteristic charm to the building, whose unrendered façade stretched about fifty yards and left him in no doubt that behind it were lodgings for the rich. He had surely misunderstood the directions.

Just as he was about to ring again, after a long wait, the door opened and a man in his middle thirties stood before him.

'Yes?'

'I'm Debendranath Ghose. I'm . . .'

'Mr Ghose. Of course! Do come in!'

Immensely relieved, Debendranath felt that his

reception had justified what seemed to him to be an overlong wait before an anonymous door.

'This way . . . No, in here. We haven't all arrived yet. But then you're a little early. Admirable . . . Do you take tea or coffee?'

'Tea, please.'

The host pushed another door and led Debendranath into a small room in the corner of which a timid-looking young woman was sitting on the edge of an armchair.

'Sue, this is Mr Ghose. He's from India.'

They shook hands before Debendranath took a seat by a closed window, while thinking that he had not once seen an open window in the few days he had been in the country. Alan, his host, left them to make the tea.

'How many people are attending the meeting?' he asked the young woman.

'Usually there are three, apart from Alan.'

'Three!' he exclaimed involuntarily.

'Is that . . .? Well, this is the only branch I've ever attended,' she said, glancing at the door.

There were men's voices beyond the closed door and both he and the young woman found themselves listening attentively, like candidates for an advertised post locked in a room until their fate had been decided.

The voices approached and the door opened gently to reveal Alan with a tray, on which a pot of tea, four cups and a bowl with biscuits jostled one another dangerously.

'Donald and Leo, this is Mr Ghose. He's from India,' Alan said, introducing two newcomers.

The civilities over, Alan sat down in the armchair and at once proclaimed that the subject for discussion was 'The Indian Question.'

Debendranath pricked up his ears, eager to find out what he might learn. He put his cup down on the table in front of him and waited for the tea to cool.

Alan continued speaking without the benefit of notes. He told them of India's poverty and its economic crises, the shortage of foreign currency which hampered its development and the help it would need from Britain if it was to survive.

Debendranath glanced at Sue, whose rapturous expression suggested an unreserved admiration for Alan's facility with words. One of the men was trying to dust biscuit crumbs from his shirt front while the other took long sips from the boiling hot tea without flinching. Alan deplored the fact that the British government had no policy for India and, with great clarity, outlined the Communist Party's own plan for the sub-continent.

Debendranath waited for the discussion that would follow. The grandfather clock, miraculously silent, betrayed its working order by the languid movement of an inscribed pendulum; and its discretion added to a conspiracy of silence extending to biscuits disappearing one by one from the bowl into the mouths of party devotees.

No one put a question to Alan, who sat with hands clasped and one elbow propped on the shoulder of his armchair.

'May I ask a question?' Debendranath said.

'I'm sorry!' exclaimed Sue, whose cup of tea tipped over before Alan could reply to Debendranath's request.

'Think nothing of it,' Alan said, jumping up.

He left the room and came back with pages from a newspaper, which he applied one by one to the wet carpet, at the same time attempting to mollify the agitated Sue.

The cleaning-up operation over, Alan said, 'See! Not a stain.' Then, clearing his throat, he asked Debendranath to put his question.

'How can there be an Indian question in England?' Debendranath said. 'India is an independent country. Why not an American question? Or a French question?'

Alan did not answer at once, but smiling indulgently, preferred to make certain that the newcomer had no more to add. In all his thirty-eight meetings as leader of this cell he had not once been opposed.

'Yes, India is independent,' he declared eventually, 'I'm not contesting that. I repeat . . . India is an independent country, but we take a special interest in it because of our long association with it.'

Debendranath took up his cup and devoted all his attention to consuming his tea, believing that he had learned a lesson. Something had been left unsaid, something of such importance it dared not be uttered; and he suddenly became aware of the significance of Sue's clumsiness. He was on alien territory. But he regarded Alan's acknowledgement of India's independence as far more telling since, behind his concession lay a stubborn, unstated contempt for the existence of the very thing acknowledged.

Debendranath could not recall the precise moment when the official meeting came to an end, but he found himself answering questions about his welfare, the room he rented and the winter cold which, they assured him, could not be far off. The warm weather was no more than an early autumnal illusion to lure people out of their houses without a pullover.

Above all, he kept telling himself, he must let no word slip out that had not been examined, turned over, measured and weighed. What better training for his future profession as an advocate? At the same time he recalled the carefree discussions in his parents' home, the porcelain cups with spiced tea, a roomful of visitors unhampered by constraints.

'But now I'm ready for anything,' he thought.

He left when dusk had fallen and the street lights were already on. Drawing his jacket more closely around him he hurried up the road, turned into the main thoroughfare and walked past the restaurant where for two shillings and six pence he had taken his first public meal.

About a week later Debendranath found a note on the

floor by the door of his room. It must have been slipped in before he woke up.

Dear Mr Bhose.

You've been transferred to L branch. It is nearer to your address and you should have applied there for membership in the first place. But no harm done!

Alan

P.S.

I have given Mirabelle G your particulars and she expects to hear from you. I believe their meetings are held at a different time from ours and on a different day. A

Debendranath told himself that the decision was for the best since, in spite of Alan's bonhomie and his cosy flat, he could not have tolerated the arrangement for long. Discussion was in his blood and, having cut his teeth on the classics, he was spoiling for something which bore no resemblance to Alan's paternalistic regime.

He made a note of the new address at which he would be attending Party meetings, then took his breakfast before calling on his landlady to ask her what formalities were necessary to join the Public Library. And in the ensuing conversation Debendranath mentioned the address on the communication he had received.

'Who're you going to see there?' his landlady asked.

'A lady.'

'A lady, eh? Well she would be a lady if she's living in that street, wouldn't she? It's just around the corner.'

Accompanying him to the door she pointed out the easiest route to the address in question and stood watching until he rounded the corner.

The house, joined by a gently rising staircase, stood behind an ample driveway and bore a sign with an arrow pointing downwards which read *Tradesmen's entrance*.

No one answered Debendranath's ring and he left, telling himself he would have to get in touch with the new leader by telephone. He smiled at his reluctance to use the coin-box phone, in the same way that he had resolved to put off a trip by bus as long as possible.

In the library he asked for a card and at the same time enquired about Caudwell's *Further Studies in a Dying Culture* which, the librarian assured him, was not kept in stock. No, he had never heard of it or of Christopher Caudwell. Why not try Westminster Library? You can get there by bus. Thank you.

Perhaps he should have put off joining the Communist Party until he had become familiar with the rules of living in this strange land of brick buildings and closed windows, of courtesies drained of their meaning and eloquent reticences.

On the way back to his room he again took to the side street and went past the house with a Tradesman's sign and gravel underfoot, but resisted the temptation to go up the drive again and ring the doorbell.

'Aren't you lonely?' the landlady asked him, before signing his library application card.

'No.'

'You will be when winter comes . . . If you get lonely come up here and have a cup o' cha. You don't use up your coupons so there's more than enough . . .'

Her loquaciousness, irritating at first, now appeared to be one with her lack of guile.

Debendranath wanted to speak to her about the party meeting, his transfer, and his confusion in the use of buses, but had no doubt she would judge his problems inappropriate to her view of his manhood. Besides, after his experience of the previous afternoon he felt disinclined to take any risks.

'Four years away from your family . . . When I was your age I couldn't stay away four years from my family. I would have died . . . all that way from home. Mind you . . .'

He would not accept the unspoken invitation to sit down.

'Sit down,' she offered, expressing in words what her gestures had suggested.

'No . . . Thank you. I have to go and study.'

'Don't forget, if you feel lonely . . .'

Debendranath dressed in a manner appropriate to a visit to the house with the gravel driveway, not only because he had acquainted himself with its outward opulence, but also because the voice at the other end of the telephone had been the embodiment of self-assurance.

He rang the bell just as he had done the afternoon before and saw through the glass door the shadow of an approaching figure.

'Do come in. I'm Mirabelle. You're Mr Ghose, aren't you?' said the same voice he had conversed with on the phone.

'Yes. Am I late?'

'Oh no. But we've begun, in a manner of speaking. We chat a lot.'

Ushered into the room Debendranath saw about a dozen men and women sitting on chairs and two settees in a way that contrasted so sharply with the scene of a week ago that he could have been in another country.

'Everybody, this is Debendranath. Debendranath, everybody.'

The introduction was greeted with general laughter.

Mirabelle showed him to a seat before herself taking the place of a poodle which she began to fondle while whispering endearments into its ear.

Now Debendranath, seduced by the general atmosphere, forgot the resolution to be on his guard. After helping himself to shelled peanuts on the centre table, he struck up a conversation with a lady sitting next to him, who spoke with a pronounced foreign accent that substituted fs for vs. And their exchanges added to the

general hubbub in the brightly lit room where people
kept arriving singly and in pairs until it seemed that the
hostess's hospitality might be in danger of being
strained.

For the first time since his arrival in the country
Debendranath felt free of the vague anxiety that beset
so many of his countrymen, even after they had put
many years of residence behind them; and when the
meeting was finally declared open he could honestly
say he believed he had found his level.

Mirabelle explained that final arrangements had
been made for the fête to be held in Finsbury Park and
wanted to see those who had volunteered to sell the
Daily Worker newspaper at the gates. Dates of future
meetings were discussed before Mirabelle informed
them that party cards for the following year would be
blue, unlike the present red ones. Then came the
warning she had been saving up for the moment when
she believed no one else was coming.

'A number of Local Authorities have sacked em-
ployees, simply because they were Communists; so
make sure you say nothing about your affiliation.'

Then, after a short pause, she invited contributions
from the rank and file.

One young man suggested that the number of
members in the branch was excessive, only to hear his
objection rejected by Mirabelle who, still caressing her
poodle, looked round the room for further contributions.
The formal meeting might have come to an end, but for
an unexpected outburst from the lady sitting next to
Debendranath.

Bounding from her seat and clapping her hands, she
twittered, 'I'm waiting for the re-fo-lution!'

Mirabelle fixed her with a stare and said, 'We're all
waiting for the re-fo-lution.'

And with that invitation to patience the formal
meeting came to an end.

Debendranath, dismayed at what he had witnessed,

just managed to hold back before committing another
indiscretion. Had he been unfortunate in the choice of
area?

Turning to the impatient revolutionary he asked if
there were ever discussions of the classics.

'Vot classics?'

'Don't you discuss Marx's and Engels's works?'

'My grandfather met Karl Marx once,' she declared,
opening her eyes wide. 'And he said to him, "Ziegfried
. . . you haf a noble head." That is what he said to him.
And my grandfather never forgot that, I can tell you.
But Karl Marx must haf been blind. My grandfather
looked like a turkey that had been beaten in a fight . . .
Now *you, you* haf a noble head. Forget about the
classics; you'll nefer understand them anyway. In
Cherman they are impossible to read. In English! My
Got! In English! . . . Don't you think . . .'

And at this point she came close and whispered into
his left ear.

'Don't you think it is unhealthy the vay Mirabelle
pays so much attention to that poodle?'

Debendranath imagined himself screaming in answer
to the futile question, demanding to be heard on a
matter he saw as being of the utmost importance.

'Lady,' Debendrandath said. 'Lady, are you trying to
make fun of me?'

'Why no! I'm always serious. I vonce had a sense of
humour ven I was a small child and lifed in France. In
those days the whole family had a sense of humour. Ven
ve moved to Chermany it fanished . . . The English could
nefer haf produced a Marx or Einstein. They make too
many chokes!'

'God!' Debendranath declared, looking his neighbour
from head to foot.

'Is anything wrong?' she asked.

'No, lady. I'm just wondering what I'm doing here.'

'Don't you *know*?' she asked, drawing away from him
as though he were tainted.

Anxious not to be the cause of another incident – Sue's accident with the tea came to mind – he said he was only joking.

'You're a choker too, I see . . . That comes from lifing here too long.'

Debendranath stood up to go, thinking that he would need all his self-control to cope with his companion. He shook her hand, bade Mirabelle and the others goodbye and allowed himself to be seen to the door.

'I'll have your membership card sent. You should get it by the weekend. Goodbye.'

He descended the concrete stairs, having made up his mind never to return.

Approaching his lodgings, he reflected on the pleasure he experienced in his landlady's company and thought that he might go up and see her. But, on the way to his room, hearing voices from the upper floor, he decided to spend what remained of the evening over a chapter on Constitutional Law, the first subject in his syllabus.

The next day Debendranath wrote his father a letter in which he informed him, dutifully, that he had attended his first two Communist Party meetings in Caudwell's England, but made no mention of his intense disappointment. After all, the old man had settled in the conviction that London was awash with Christopher Caudwells.

Several weeks later while on his way to the bus stop he met Mirabelle who, wrapped in a voluminous fur coat, was walking two poodles on a single leash. They both stopped and exchanged polite enquiries as to each other's health before going on their way, he to his room, and she to the public gardens so that her dogs could relieve themselves among the dead leaves beside a path.

And years later, as a member of the West Bengal Communist government, whenever he called to mind his first weeks in London, the person Debendranath remembered most vividly was, not Alan or Mirabelle, but the lady whose grandfather had a noble head, according to Marx.

Fay Weldon

'It's all a matter of landscape,' Bente's mother Greta wrote to her daughter from her apartment in the outer suburbs of Copenhagen, there where the land tilts gently and gracefully towards a flat Northern sea, and the birch trees in Spring are an almost unbearably brilliant green, and at nights the lights of Sweden glitter across the water, with their promise of sombre wooded crags, and dark ravines, and steeper, more difficult shores altogether. 'The English are dirty because they are so comparatively unobserved. They can hide behind hills from their neighbours. Dirt is normal, Bente, all over the world. It's we in the clean flat lands who are out of step.'

Bente's mother was fanciful. it was one of her many charms: men loved her absurdities. Her folly made men feel strong and sane. Greta had wide grey eyes and flaxen hair and a good strong figure and a frivolous nature. Her daughter had inherited her mother's looks, but not, alas, her nature. Bente's father had been Swedish born. He had passed on to his daughter, Greta feared, his deep Swedish seriousness, his lofty Swedish standards. He had been killed in action towards the end of the war. Whereupon, at least according to the neighbours, the girl Greta had slept with enough German soldiers to man a landing raft. She was lucky, all agreed, including Bente, to be accepted back into the community. Greta, of course, maintained that she had only done these things on the instructions of the Resistance, the better to gain the enemy's secrets. Be that as it may, there was no arguing but that Greta had gained a taste for sex, somewhere along the line; and Bente had not, even by the age of twenty-three, and with her mother's cheerful example before her. Bente was glad to get away from Copenhagen and the tread of male footsteps on her mother's stair, and to come as an au pair in London, to the Beavers' household.

But within a week Bente rang in tears to say that the Beavers' household was dirty, the food was uneatable, she was expected to sleep in a damp dark basement room, that she was overworked and underpaid, and the two children were unruly, unkempt, and objected to taking baths.

'Then clean the house,' said Greta firmly, 'take over the cooking, and the accounts, move a mattress to a better room, and bath the children by force if necessary, or better still, get in the bath with them. The English are too afraid of nakedness.'

Bente sobbed on the other end of the line, and Greta's sailor lover, Mogens, moved an impatient hand up her thigh. Greta had told Mogens she'd had Bente when she was seventeen. 'But I want to come home,' said Bente, and Greta said sharply that surely Bente could put up with a little dirt and discomfort. Adrian Beaver was a Marxist sociologist/journalist with an international reputation and Bente should think herself lucky to be in so interesting a household and not abuse her employers' hospitality by making too many long distance calls on their telephone. Greta put down the phone and turned her attention to Mogens. Lovers come and go: children go on for ever!

There was silence for a month or so, during which time Greta, feeling just a little guilty, sent Bente a

leather mini-skirt and a recipe for steak au poivre using
green pepper and a letter explaining her theories on dirt
and landscape.

Bente's next letter home was cheerful enough: she
asked Greta to send her some root ginger, since this was
unobtainable in the outer London suburbs where she
lived and she had only four hours off a week, and that
on Sundays, and could not easily get into central
London where more exotic ingredients were available.
Mrs Beaver had objected to her wearing the mini-skirt,
so she only put it on in her absence. Mr Beaver worked
at home: life was much easier now that Mrs Beaver had
a full-time job. She, Bente, could take over. The house
was spick and span. When she, Bente, had children,
she, Bente, would never leave them in a stranger's care.
But she, Bente, liked to think the children were fond of
her. She got into the bath with them, these days, and
there was no trouble at all at bath time. Mr Beaver,
Adrian, said she was a better mother to the boys than
his wife was. She was certainly a better cook!

Greta's new lover, Andy, from the Caribbean, posted
off the ginger without a covering letter. Silence seemed,
at the time, golden. Greta knew Bente would just hate
Andy, who was probably not yet twenty, and wonder-
fully black and shiny. Greta told him she'd had Bente
when she was sixteen.

Bente rang in tears to say Mr Beaver kept touching
her breasts in the kitchen and embarrassing her and
she thought he wanted to sleep with her and could she
come home at once?

Greta said what nonsense, sex is a free and wonderful
thing; just sleep with him and get it over. There was
silence the other end of the line. Andy's hot breath
stirred the hairs on Greta's neck. She knew the flax was
beginning to streak with grey. How short life is!

'But what about his wife?' asked Bente, doubtfully,
presently.

'Knowing the English as I do,' said Greta, 'they've

probably worked it out between them just to stop you from handing in your notice.'

'So you don't think she'd mind?'

Andy's sharp white teeth nibbled Greta's ear and his arm lay black and thick across her silky white breasts.

'Of course not,' said Greta. 'What are you getting so worked up about? Sex is just fun. It's not to be taken seriously.'

'I'm not so sure,' said Bente, primly.

'Bente,' said Greta, 'pillow talk is the best way to learn a foreign language, and that's what you're in England for. Do just be practical, even if you don't know how to enjoy yourself.'

Andy's teeth dug sharply into Greta's ear lobe and she uttered the husky little scream which so entranced and interested men. After she had replaced the receiver, it occurred to Greta that her daughter was still a virgin, and she almost picked up the phone for a longer talk, but then the time was past and Andy's red red tongue was importuning her and she forgot all about Bente for at least a week. Out of sight, out of mind! Many mothers feel it: few acknowledge it!

Bente wrote within the month to ask if she should tell Mrs Beaver that she and Mr Beaver were having an affair, since she didn't like to be deceitful. Adrian himself was reluctant to do it, saying it might upset the children and should be kept secret. What did Greta think?

Greta wrote back to say, with feeling, that children should not begrudge their parents a sex life; you had to take sex calmly and openly, not get hysterical. Sex is like a wasp, wrote Greta. You must just sit still and let it take its course. It's when you try and brush it away the trouble comes. Fanciful Greta!

Bente wrote to say that Mrs Beaver had moved out of the house: simply abandoned the children and left! What sort of mother was that? She, Bente, would never do such a thing. Mrs Beaver was hopelessly neurotic.

(Didn't Greta think her, Bente's, English had improved? Greta had been quite right about pillow talk!) Mr Beaver had told his wife she could continue living in the spare room and have her own lovers quite freely, but Mrs Beaver hadn't been at all grateful and had made the most dreadful scenes before finally going and had even tried to knife her, Bente, and Mr Beaver had lost half a stone in weight. Could Greta send her the pickled herring recipe? She enclosed a photograph of herself and Adrian and the boys. She and Adrian were to be married as soon as he was free. Wasn't love wonderful? Wasn't fate an extraordinary thing? Supposing she and Adrian had never met? Supposing this, supposing that!

Greta studied the photograph with a magnifying glass. Adrian Beaver, she was surprised to see, was at least fifty and running to fat, and plain in a peculiarly English, intellectual, chinless way, and the Beaver sons were not little, as she had supposed, but in their late adolescence and ungainly too. Her daughter stood next to Mr Beaver, twice his size, big-busted, bovine, with the sweet inexorable smile of a flaxen doll. Greta did not want to have grandchildren, especially not these grandchildren. Greta, one way and another, was in a fix.

Greta had fallen in love, in a peculiarly high, pure, almost sexless way – who'd have thought it! But life goes this way, now that! – with a doctor from Odense, who wanted to marry her, Greta, save her from herself and build her a house in glass and steel where she could live happily ever after. (Perhaps she was in love with the house, not him, but what could it matter? Love is love, even if it's for glass and steel!) The doctor was thirty-five. Greta, alas, on first meeting him, had given her age as thirty-four. Unless she had given birth to Bente when she was ten, how now could Bente be her daughter?

'You are no daughter of mine,' she wrote back to Bente. 'Sex is one thing, love quite another. Sex may be a wasp, but love is a swarm of bees! You have broken up a marriage, done a dreadful thing! I never wish to hear from you again.'

And nor she did, and both lived happily ever after: the mother in the flat, clean, cheerful land: the daughter in her dirty, hilly, troubled one across the sea, where fate had taken her. How full the world is of bees and wasps! In the autumn the birch trees of Denmark turn russet red and glorious, and the lights which shine across from Sweden seem hard and resolute and the air chilly, and the wasps and the bees move slowly and sleepily amongst the red, red leaves and how lucky you are if you escape a sting!

Andrew Graham-Yooll

On the bus into London's West End with pensioners going window-shopping, Japanese visitors and adolescents in shouted conversations screaming profanities as if in tribal ceremony . . . after a morning at Colindale Newspaper Library, where the nineteenth-century press reports on the intricacies of Anglo-South American relations provided a form of entertainment or at least of distraction from the drabness of my work as a subeditor, thoughts of the British obsession with spooks ran through my mind.

The telephone caller had said 'Mr Green' wanted to meet me for lunch. 'Mr Green' was the cover name on every message, going right back to the early 1970s in Argentina. Whatever the real name of the British diplomat in Buenos Aires, it was always 'Mr Green' who called at the *Buenos Aires Herald* to suggest lunch. Our meal was paid for by the Foreign Office, or by MI6, or by the taxpayer, although how could M16 pay a bill if few knew what MI6? Officially there were no answers to such a question. I once read in *The Guardian* that MI1 and MI14 existed only during the Second World War. What about the others?

This question shouldn't really be asked – or

answered – but basically it seems probable they did
nothing, but drew pay for it. It is believed that MI1
and MI11 were eliminated long ago because of
confusion between Is and 1s in the accounts
department. As to the rest, it is said that out of the
huge sums voted as 'contingencies' modest amounts
are transferred to MI2 and MI3 and allocated to the
Prime Minister and Home Secretary to reward their
alleged responsibilities for the non-existing MI5 and
MI6. Further amounts, charged to MI4 account,
may be offered either to the Chancellor of the
Exchequer or to the Foreign Secretary to
compensate for loss of tied weekend cottages – and
similar. The large balance (charged to MIs 7, 8, 10,
12 and 13, which are 'notional' only) is used as
necessary to bump up 'invisibles' in specially bad
months to keep Balance-of-Payment deficits below
the £2 billion mark, where possible. But please note,
this is off the record. – A.I. Pottinger, Edgbaston,
Birmingham (*The Guardian*, Monday 22 January
1990).

Foreign agents in London conveyed this to their
superiors arguing for its reliability because of its publication in a great newspaper.

In Buenos Aires it had never seemed to be more than a
good lunch – never anything as serious as 'intelligence'
work. This was mainly because my table companions
did not seem very intelligent: most of what they heard
from me could have been read in the newspapers and in
political magazines. I was merely helping them with
their homework. Later, one of their indiscretions – or
perhaps a genuine exchange of 'intelligence' – about an
Argentine personality might appear in the *Buenos
Aires Herald*. The publication option was the one new
rule I introduced into the game.

'Green' was a cover name, but I understood that a 'Mr
Green', a sort of Mr Big, did exist. His name was used for

all communications, just as some newspapers once used the foreign or features editor's name for all incoming traffic. Only guerrillas used false names in the 1970s. The very idea that a British diplomat might use a false name was risible. 'Green' sounded all right: it could be genuine or a cover.

In 1976, soon after my arrival in London, some members of the British government (other than Customs officers) showed a flattering interest in my person and my past. Their calls always came immediately after I had had a particularly long conversation with an Argentine exile in Paris, or a meeting with an exiled Latin American political figure passing through London, or had visited a suspicious foreign embassy, the Cuban mission, for example. The coincidence never struck me as strange. The timing of the calls seemed just that, a coincidence.

Two or three times a year I was taken out to lunch by men who introduced themselves with very English names that sounded like a catalogue of characters from the countryside: Mr Shire, Mr Wood, Mr Lake, Mr Field, Mr Glenn. Each professed an interest in Argentina and in any contacts that had come my way. The names were false, they admitted later, although the switchboard at MI6 traced each of them easily if I rang to check. A false name gave immunity. These 'Mr Greens' had nothing to hide because everything was disguised by the anonymity of a *nom de plume*. Details of their wives' likes and dislikes, their divorces, their homes, their domestic arguments about holidays were freely revealed to me. A young woman in her late twenties, the only one in that season of secret hospitality, wondered aloud to me how she would seduce, or at least attract and encourage, a young man of her liking who was painfully shy. She wanted to consult an older man on how best to approach another member of his sex. She had to know what men thought of women suspected of planning a catch. Were they flattered or fearful? What did an old man (myself) think about another woman who was trying to thwart her own attempts at conquest? Her interrogation was to insure her success at a summer ball where she hoped the man would approach her. She described the dress she planned to wear and the perfume. The man was a scientist and difficult to entice out of the laboratory and into the arts of human proximity.

Another civil servant had to keep a precise record of the extra-marital relations of every diplomat from a particular group of countries. Thus the details of matrimonial infidelities of Cubans, Venezuelans, Peruvians and others came tumbling out with hilarious detail. It was funny and, in a disgraceful sort of way, frightfully interesting.

Why should England, which has a rich and successful sub-market in spy-thriller fiction, take the spooks business so seriously? To the uninitiated it seems contradictory.

I once asked the novelist Jeffrey Archer about the English obsession with spies and spy stories.

'They all seem to be the same,' he said. 'Whenever I read one, and then the next, I don't seem to have learned much more other than a new name. I suppose that the years of the Cambridge University spies, the 1930s, have puzzled the British public: it is not clear why four educated men, privileged by public school and Cambridge, should have devoted their lives to supporting Russia. So, as an explanation was not forthcoming, the spies became part of our great fictional, non-fictional, factional background. Philby, Burgess, Maclean, and finally Blunt, the Queen's personal advisor on art, were selling secrets to the Russians. The Official Secrets Act was based on our being the most important nation on earth. It is a little out of date.'

In truth the English have been obsessed with popular spy fiction for much longer. Erskine Childers, clerk to the House of Commons for fifteen years, published *The Riddle of the Sands*, about a German invasion of

Britain, in 1903, then was court-martialled and shot for
secretly supporting the Irish Republicans. Childers
seems to be at the start of nearly a century of obsession
with secrecy and secret agents.

In London my lunch dates with 'Mr Green' might be
at the Grosvenor Hotel, in Victoria Station, or at
Manzi's restaurant off Leicester Square, which I
recommend to my friends, or at a series of now forgotten
small places with French names somewhere between
Victoria and New Bond Street. Actually I had nothing
of interest to tell them. Only one man realized that, and
he once complained that nothing useful had ever come
from me. But the 'Mr Greens' could not give up. Long
ago they had been misinformed that I might be a
guerrilla courier with probable links between Latin
American guerrilla organizations and the Provisional
IRA in Belfast. At lunch my 'Mr Greens' would talk of
'debriefing' or of borrowing documents in my posses-
sion. It was a futile exercise, but there was a budget for
conspiracy and it had to be spent in whispers.

Their tip-off about me had originated in the British
Embassy in Buenos Aires. One of the senior counsellors
there used to invite me regularly to lunch in pursuit
of any anecdotes or news of guerrilla groups. He
had kept up-to-date by contrasting my conversation
with that of the Argentine naval officers he had
befriended.

In the run-up to the Falkland/Malvinas war the
spooks were keen to find out what the generals in
Buenos Aires were thinking, but turned from me to more
direct reports from the British Embassy, whose sound
advice in the months before the 1982 conflict was
mostly ignored. The spooks had tired of my company,
and I of their conspiracy and of the catering. By then I
would like to think that they also lost interest because I
had begun to be an Englishman and so was no longer
much use as a foreigner.

'Green?' Oh, him. It was all part of the game. There never was a Green. That last lunch, at the end of the bus ride from Colindale, was paid for by a man who said 'Green' was no longer used as a cover name. They had only kept it going for me.

FLOWERS FOR THE BIRTHING

Jean Binta Breeze

at a busy corner
I stop
ask for signs

a young white woman
smiling says
I'm not from round these parts
a black man intervenes
second left
straight through the lights
first right
our directions are becoming
more precise

I bring flowers for the birthing

at one p.m.
in the maternal ward
under Big Ben
a new black baby
breaks its waters

the Irish nurse
with strong hands
cuts the string
for the Indian doctor
it is not the last one of the day

the mother sings
feeds her
when she can
on mangoes memories

she grows
on crunchy bites of apples
running juice of pears
there are no yams
at school lunches
she is no guest here

she welcomes me
in cockney
offers me
a cup of tea
I smell her
lavender perfume

one day, she says
she'll travel
the Caribbean, Africa
visit the pope in Rome
restrictive myths
are absent from her mind
knowing her history
she makes her future plans
thinks Britain is going down the drain
wants to move to the continent

I leave her
my young British black
it's time to go back home
where I'll tell
our shared grandmother
the transplanted root
has sprung

Nicole Ward Jouve

It was magic: the valley that spread out in front of them. Such space, on all sides, barely bounded on the horizon by blue or purple hills. Stone farmhouses, haystacks, clumps of trees, fields, some a thin green from the winter wheat, some of grass, lusher though shorn and dulled by winter. Ings. Thorn hedges, black, also from winter.

They descended. The road spiralled. Turn after turn. Bend after bend, between bare hedges. Roadsides, a raggy green, with a flotsam of dry weeds. Thawing frost a dew on the taller blades of grass. The rattling twigs of *ombelle*: they'd told her in the summer that it was called Queen Anne's lace. The sky so large, so blue for once. Jocelyne kissed the down on the baby's head. The woollen bonnet with the yellow pompom had slid back, pressing one ear forward, then another, as Olivier twisted his head here and there. *Toi aussi tu veux voir, hein? Ah mon chéri c'est comme d'aller au château de la Belle au Bois Dormant.* She kissed the warm little nose. Such a delicious round nose, such a perfect fit for her lips.

And that is how, on a fine December morning, Alan and Jocelyne came to the house-on-a-bend-of-the-river that was to become their home. Alan came, saw, and bought. The lady that was showing them round, portly, tweed suit with brooch on lapel, and what Jocelyne would learn were called sensible shoes, couldn't believe her luck. She didn't need, not in the least, to celebrate the advantages of the place. She did it anyway, she'd rehearsed her piece and didn't want it to go to waste. 'We've done the improvements as if for ourselves. For our daughter in fact. Engaged, was going to get married. That's why the larder's got this nice modern window, it was going to be our son-in-law's office. Broken it off you know. Flighty. Spoiled.' She'd lowered her voice. 'Still. Better find out before than after, I always say. But Lorna said to me, "Mum, I dream of a turquoise-and-lemon bathroom." And that's what she got. That's what you're getting, you lucky people.' She'd dramatically opened the door. A half-wall-height of turquoise tiles travelled squarely behind the lemon sink, the lemon bath, the lemon toilet. In years to come Jocelyne would vainly scan supermarket shelves for a disinfectant that would not turn a dismal shade inside the toilet bowl ('not blue, no; not green . . .'); she would gloomily leaf through the wallpaper books, the colour charts, in search of shades, patterns, that would match, soften, erase, the vile combination. She was landed with it. Two, three, four children would splash and scream nightly in the lemon bath. Who knew what that did to their subconscious. 'That strange affection of Olivier's for pale yellow socks . . .'

'And look at the kitchen,' Mrs Pearcy was saying. 'We've had a Rayburn put in. Cream, to match the sink.'

Jocelyne looked blank.

'My wife is French,' Alan explained.

'French are you? I thought there was something . . . But I would have said, German or maybe Danish. All French girls are brunettes, aren't they? And you don't have a French accent. Zey talk like zat, you know. Well, well done you. What do they call you?'

She held out her head, ear forward. Ready for the

shock, Jocelyne thought. Greying blonde hair, a mass of neat curls. Rows of little curlers, little sausages with a wire core at the hairdresser's. Pink net, pink shells of ear-protectors, magazines.

–Jocelyne.

–Djoslin?

–Jo-ce-ly-ne.

–Djiou . . .

–Jo.ce.ly.ne.

–Ah! Jousline. (She had said, a-ine.)

–Doesn't matter.

–I'll tell you what. I'll call you Joss.

'Never mind,' said Alan, whom the exchange, endlessly repeated, always put on tenterhooks. Why did Jocelyne insist on people pronouncing her name right, when she ought to have known by now that they couldn't, in a million years.

'Oh but I'm enjoying this,' said Mrs Pearcy. 'My husband and I have been on many visits. Nice, and the Dordogne, and of course Paris. I love French cooking,' she said to Jocelyne, suddenly detaching her syllables and raising her voice, as if to announce to a slightly deaf person, 'I love you.'

'If you like French cooking you'll like my maiden name,' Jocelyne said, perversely inviting more massacre. 'I'm called Caillat. Comes from caille, which means quail.'

'Quaila?'

'You've got it.'

Mrs Pearcy smiled good-temperedly and Jocelyne aimed a broad smile at Alan. Lucky I'm not Indian or African, she thought, and she remembered with shame how she had thought herself charming when she had made halting efforts to articulate the name of a Nigerian man she'd met in London who was called Okunjibido. The irritated patience in his eyes . . . And it happened every time he met anybody . . . Mrs Pearcy was stroking the cream lid of a large metal cupboard.

'And how do you like it here?'

'It's very cold,' Jocelyne said, suddenly longing for chocolate. Mrs Pearcy had just explained how her husband bought cocoa on the Stock Exchange for the local chocolate factory. Mr Porter, husband to Olivier's present babysitter, worked in the chocolate factory, in that other village where they were renting, and loathed the very smell of the stuff. Jocelyne could have done with some though. Got mothering properties, her sister used to say. She was blowing on her fingers inside the kitchen. Olivier, in her arms, was so swaddled in blankets only a round little face peered out, black eyes strangely alert.

'Ah now, you just wait and see,' said Mrs Pearcy. 'You won't get cold with a Rayburn. They're absolute wonders. Keep your kitchen ever so nice and warm, you can cook and bake, they heat the towel rail in the bathroom, takes the chill off the air, you know. And the immersion cupboard! Your towels and sheets are kept ever so dry.'

'Immersion cupboard?'

'Oh you poor dear, of course, you're French. Come and see.'

Ha. Of course, thought Joycelyne. Here, *of course*, the damp would get into everything, even the linen inside the cupboard. At home, they spread the sheets and shirts on fragrant bushes on the *aire* outside the gate, and the sun turned them a magnificent white, and they smelt of marjoram. Here, before they made their slow progress to the immersion cupboard, you dried them in front of the Rayburn. A rope that you loosened from its hook on the wall brought the clotheshorse down from the ceiling. All the bacon grease, the steam from the cabbage, would seep into them . . .

The Rayburn was to become Jocelyne's curse. She had lived her adolescence, her student days, with central heating. Now to get any warmth they had to keep the

damn thing lit, lug great bucketfuls of small pitted
rough coals that had the front to call themselves
Sunbrite Doubles – Sunbright! for Pete's sake as
Jocelyne's more polite acquaintances said. The beast
steadily refused to stay on at nights. In the morning, no
hot drink, nothing but chapped and grimy hands till
you had grovelled, raked ashes on all fours with an
antediluvian contraption that looked like a child's rake
but had a solid bar in the place of teeth. You then shoved
soapy-feeling paraffin-stinking white cakes into the
jaw, till they rested on the circular grate that you could
only see through the lower end, by bowing, knees on the
floor-tiles, as if you were praying to an idol. Everything
there, in the bowels of this monstrous thing, the grate,
the clinkers that you took out, the ash, was a dusty,
rusty pink. The clinkers had the consistency of lava
rocks. It was like having a perpetually ailing volcano in
your kitchen, that produced mounds of refuse and very
little fire: some toothless, spent Hephaestos. Some
mornings, the stove was still warm: hope! A red glow
among the embers as you opened the door. Carefully
place some sticks, some pieces of coal, open all the
dampers out. Draught, bellows, blow! Please please.
Grovel grovel. You looked: out. Kicked it. My right arm
for a cup of coffee. Good thing she still breastfed Olivier,
she could just fantasize the screams if the poor little
mite had been waiting for a warm bottle.

Their few French visitors lived with their coats and
woollens on, went to bed, fully gloved and socked, under
a heap of blankets. The house had been furnished with
troves from a weird warehouse of a place whose endless
resources of rubbish delighted Jocelyne. They'd got
bedsteads for less than a pound, horsehair mattresses.
The beds creaked and sagged. Jacques and Sophie kept
their fur hats on in bed. If you took them a cup of coffee
in the mornings, they looked laid out like medieval
knights. Only the eyes emerged, and you could see them
quiver, wondering whether they might not have been

glued shut by ice, whether they could bear to remove the cover of the eyelids to face up to the full frost of the day. 'Never seen the like of it,' Jacques would say. 'You know what? Here the windows frost over inside. I've heard of, I've seen, windowpanes frosted over outside, but this beats it all. *Elles gèlent dedans. Dedans!*' 'At least that way we find out who our true friends are,' Jocelyne would say. They all sat huddled round the Rayburn in their overcoats and scarves, Olivier happily munching a crust in his little chair, with a healthy shiny pink face and blue fingers. They held slices of bread with a long-handled toasting-fork to the stove-door, hoping the tiny square of glowing fire would toast them before they dropped in, or got charred. '*Ah ces anglais,*' Jacques would say, 'you've got to give it to them. Who in such a cold, damp country would ever dream of devising such minuscule fires? Look at the thickness of the walls, my god, what fireplaces they could have built! The whole length of the wall – to roast a whole sheep in. And what do they do? Make them too small to even roast a *gigot* in –even a piece of steak! And as for their stove! A small safe would be bigger. A jewel-cask would be bigger. Fire-binding, that's what it is. The English form of torture to shape the true-Brit character. If you survive their heating methods you'll survive anything. That's why they conquered half the globe. Couldn't wait to get out of their freezing island. Anything preferable. Sharks, boa constrictors, ticks, vampire-bats, canni-bals. Anything. That's why they stood up to Hitler. After their fires, they couldn't have cared less about the bombs. *Ils s'en battaient l'oeil, des bombes. Plus rien ne leur faisait.*'

Had it not been for the imported visitors, the family, the friends, Jocelyne would have gone mad from solitude. The English visitors looked at the glorious view, the purple hills in the distance, the meadows periodically made into a lake by the quietly swelling river, 'what a

beautiful place,' they said. 'Lucky you,' they said,
looking at the great ash trees with their elastic branches
that the wind broke and scattered, 'so convenient to
light a fire.' The ash had given shelter to baby Jesus, the
vicar who serviced ever so many churches and did them
once a month had explained one Christmas in the
chapel-of-ease where Alan now, out of nostalgia, the
duty of some imagined squirearchy, played the organ
(the organ, rheumatic from the damp, heaved and burst
into smothered notes; four old ladies in the back pew
piped up in disarray, all out-of-tune but one). And the
baby Jesus (the vicar said) had blessed the ash trees by
giving it wood that could be burned green. Not much of
a blessing if you look at it from the ash's point of view,
Jocelyne had thought.

There were long evenings in front of the Baxi fire in
the now furnished sitting-room. It hosted the in-laws'
comfortable three-piece suite, which Jocelyne invariably pronounced 'suit'. 'Sweets are sweets,' she'd say,
and as people laughed, 'how is one to know?' Their
salons, she thought, have to be like their men, suitably
dressed (which is the trousers, she thought; which the
waistcoat?). No Louis XVI armchairs from the great-
aunt, no *Regence console* from the grandmother. Settee,
and twin armchairs. House after house, rows of identical
houses. She had drawn laughter at a sale for buying a
commode. What a bargain for a chest of drawers, she'd
thought, too swamped in the crowd to see the object.
Only half-a-crown and nobody bidding? 'So wet,' the
French visitors complained, their leather shoes sinking
into the mud in the grass-fields churned by cows'
hooves. You had to introduce them to wellies, keep some
spare. It was a game, digging into the old trunk she kept
in the larder that was to have been the son-in-law's
office, trying to find a matching pair. So sweet when
you came across kiddies' wellies, red, tiny, personable,
erect: as if to say, here I am and here to stay.

And what a blessing they were there. Without the

children, they would never have got to know anyone.
Jocelyne remembered the first bleak months, pregnant
from baby number two, pushing Olivier's pram along
the empty roads between the bare hedgerows, and not a
soul in sight. 'Jocelyne must be very fond of Alan to live
in such a place,' her niece from Toulon had said, and she
brandished the memory ('bloody bloody bloody place,
aren't I a heroine') (though to be fair Alan wasn't such a
bad fellow), pulling a long tongue at some inquisitive
bullocks safely contained, thank God, by a wire fence.
Doors closed in the neighbouring villages. Suspicious
stares, frozen faces. Foreigner, she felt they were
saying. Interloper. Once she ventured into a farmyard.
The farmer's wife called her children to her, kept them
close as she gave her curt direction. No trespassing.
Distrustful eyes never left sight of her face till she had
turned. She could feel them on her back as she pushed
the jolting pram down the potholed drive. Jocelyne
remembered how, in the village where they had lived
before, old ladies would grab their cats as she walked
past: some French pilots had been stationed at the
neighbouring airfield during the war, and it had been
rumoured that they snatched cats, and ate them. War
shortages and all that, and everyone knew the French
fed on weird things. Years later, Bertrand, her youngest,
would come home crying with fury. 'Mummy, they keep
asking me if we eat frogs and snails.' 'Darling, tell them
we eat nothing else. Fried for breakfast, boiled for
lunch, in a pot-roast at nights. And tell them, we all go
out at night with a lantern and a watering-can, beating
a drum, to make the snails believe there is a storm and
come out.'

Strange stories, Jocelyne later found out, had circulated about them. They had orgies. They used black silk
sheets. Bearded Alan was an IRA man in disguise,
living (the builder who regularly came to deal with their
septic tank was quoted as having said) with 'that nice
French filly'. The only friendly neighbour, despite her

air of brusqueness, was the lady in the tied cottage across the road. Arms crossed on her ample chest, and not a word too many, and wasn't she giving her the eye! Yes, no. 'Will you do some cleaning for me, please Mrs Wright?' 'Yes.' 'Thank you, that's great.' Silence. It was a truly golden silence, though it took time for Jocelyne, who came from a sunny people, a sunny town, Toulon, the old men and the old women on a bench on the waterfront, in the winter sun too sometimes, chatting away, shouting pleasantries to the fishermen quietly ever so quietly swaying in their boats mending their nets, old people with smile-wrinkles round their eyes telling funny stories on the buses, laughter and good temper showering perfect strangers; and the *crêmière*, groaning and moaning about her aches and pains as she lovingly wrapped a *brousse* in waxed paper, plunged the holed ladle into the shining olives, the fishmonger with her red scarf and huge girth who called all her customers 'Coco', even Jocelyne's ever so dignified grandmother (*'Et alors, coco, pourquoi on fait cette tête?' 'Il est beau mon poisson il est beau. Allez ma reine vous allez vous régaler'*), and the smells of the fishmarket, the iodine and dripping sea-weeds and the exquisite mother-of-pearl of the open sea-shells, the heaps of *violets* and the mussels with the concentric circles on their shells that made Jocelyne think of large black fingertips, the urchins, quills quivering, seeking perhaps to spiral their way back to the glistening rocks from which they had been torn – oh yes, it took Joycelyne a long time to realize how these taciturn people loved a good chat, and could be better than their words – Mrs Wright for one. She was (but it took Jocelyne years to find out) the best gossip around. As her daughter said, she knew what had happened to people before *they* knew. And she loved babies. When she saw Olivier under the big ash tree, she said, her face suddenly lit, and it was the first friendly smile Jocelyne had seen in the place, 'it's grand to see a pram again.'

And that was it. The children, one after the other, did it. Mrs Wright became Jocelyne's best friend. She had trouble making ends meet, but she'd lend you a half pound of butter, a bowlful of flour or sugar, if you were stuck. Jocelyne repaid a bit more – only a bit – so as not to offend. Paid a bit more than she said she would. Years later, Mrs Wright would speak approvingly of people who gave you 'that little bit extra'. The previous owner of the big house, a Mr Soames, a widower, had paid her one shilling a week to do all his washing – sheets and all – and died leaving her nothing. But he had bequeathed a house to Mrs Smirthwaite. Mrs Wright darkly hinted that Mrs Smirthwaite had been more than housekeeper to him. 'And why couldn't she have done the washing as well, I ask you?' They were neighbours, but not on speaking terms. Mr Smirthwaite was a thin, white-haired gentle-looking man, serenely toothless. He looked distinguished. Mrs Smirthwaite looked like an old fairy, eyes like forget-me-nots, white bun, hooked nose, and a rather beautiful singing voice that stood out above the cacophony at church. Difficult to imagine her being tumbled in bed (legs kicking in the air) by a septuagenarian, even one who, Mrs Wright explained, had been a hunting-man, and still kept a circular horn to call his Scottish cattle to the gate. Shaggy longhorns trotting obediently in answer to the old man's call. Wind in those lungs – strength left in – but don't let your lewd imagination wander my dear. Jocelyne learnt not to speak with Mrs Smirthwaite either: how could anyone fraternize with any of Mrs Wright's enemies?

Nobody had ever heard of Queen Anne's lace. One of your fancy names. It was called keksi. *Chiendent*, that the town people had called twitch, was wick. It was the plague of a garden. Hidden networks of white tentacles under everything. On Mrs Wright's instructions, Jocelyne became passionate in her pursuit of wick. The days she spent overturning the rocks of the rockery,

voluptuously uncovering yet another network! Mr
Wright, on the other hand, though a beautiful digger,
couldn't tell a flower from a weed. He would every
spring dig up their telephone wires, and throw the
contact box away. *That* rubbish.

In the early days, Mrs Robson had called. She was the
lady of the manor, of the other manor: for their big stone
house must have disputed the squirearchy with the
other, gloomy, brick farmhouse that was swathed in
oak trees where dozens of rooks nestled. You could see
them circling like a nemesis over the low roof that gave
the house an air of cowering. But Mr Robson owned
most of the land around, hundreds of acres, and Mr
Robson it was that employed Mr Wright as his labourer,
owned the cottage in which the Wrights lived. Mrs
Robson's call was gracious, was lady-like. Yet it was
kind also, and shy: she was one of the old ladies who
sang in the back pew in the chapel, she had a white bun
like Mrs Smirthwaite, who worked for her. Olivier was
at his most cooing for her, and she talked about her
grandchildren, Josie's children. Josie sounded like her
favourite, not to be confused with Josh, her husband. So
Jocelyne eventually learned from other quarters, and
also that Josie the girl had been forced to marry, bairn
on the way you know, and the father a labourer, old
Josh had been mad, cast away his own daughter, his
own flesh and blood, had now come round but wouldn't
see her. Allowed, however, the grandchildren to visit.
Better than in that other village where Alan and
Jocelyne had rented a cottage from a Major MacBride.
His daughter, the girl of the manor, had also made
merry with a labourer. He was married, two children.
His wife had died during a night of rowing . . . The
neighbours had heard . . . Major MacBride had des-
patched his daughter to Switzerland. Now she attended
garden fêtes and charity drives tied to her mother's
apron strings, with a washed out and spinsterish
look . . .

The Robson girls evidently had more robust blood in their veins. The only one still at home, a dark and fierce-looking creature with bounding dogs in tow, was having it off all over the ditches with the local Casanova, a garage-owner with three handsome sons whom Jocelyne looked at with some longing. You could see Mr Harrison's grey Mini parked at odd times near a cover, down a solitary lane . . . the entire countryside chuckled knowingly, or looked deep, and Jocelyne with them once Mrs Wright had initiated her to the mystery of the Mini . . . Contagious, yes, all that illicit sex everybody, but *everybody* knew about . . . as people little by little let on, it took years but eventually you were in with the gossip. You knew that all Sutton knew precisely which days and hours Mrs Ward, who would have been plain had it not been for her amazing green eyes, was having assignations in Colonel Grey's barn with her next-door neighbour, a fetching man, yes, but, for shame, his wife was Doris's best friend! Someone ought to tell her . . . All Sutton knew that Mrs Jordan's husband, nice Mrs Jordan, you know the one, yes, that one, who did the school dinners in the village hall and was so popular with the kiddies – she didn't deserve this, poor woman, wasn't it a shame – but her husband, he was notorious. You should never agree to go anywhere with him, not to look at the improvements in Colonel Grey's dairy, no, he wasn't safe to be with. Well, he waited for his wife to have gone off to work on her bicycle, poor thing, she went potato-picking and everything – and then he watched for his niece. The one that wasn't quite right. Something up there. Ran in the family, on the father's side. A shame. Sharon, yes. The one that used to babysit for you. Nice girl, till she started throwing them fits. That's why she was back at home. Well, the uncle waited for her to walk past, and he followed her. She was man-mad, you see. Yes, in the fox-cover, down by the willows, anywhere. Poor lass, she couldn't get any of the young ones. Honestly, it was

embarrassing, she almost rubbed herself against those
old men and of course they loved it. I had to look away.

Nothing quite so fancy at home, Jocelyne thought. Or
perhaps, her childhood had been too sheltered, she'd
gone to a convent school, her parents' voices had
dropped when she'd come in. She'd heard none of the
adult gossip, and then among the young it had been all
passion, all dead serious, and she'd met Alan . . .

But she was bewildered. It took her years to adjust to
the notions of rural England which the books she was
reading were giving her, to the people she gradually got
to know. Now the children were all reaching school age
one after the other, she was doing an Open University
course as well as helping run the second-hand furniture
business she'd started with her friend Stephanie. She
loved sales. She'd always thought of them as too grand
for her in France, vast sums of money, distinguished
auctioneers and valuers who would look down their
noses at her. Here there were festive crowds milling
around in the outbuildings of farmhouses or on the
village green. People looked deep – nothing made people
look so deep as a bargain to be made ('there's Yorkshire
all over for you,' her mother-in-law said). The deeper
they were involved, the more secretive and unfriendly
they looked. An intentness – a sulkiness – as they
opened drawers, turned plates over to inspect the mark.
You could only joke about what had no value, a worm-
ridden Windsor, a chamber-pot – though since people
had started putting plants in them and the prices had
risen a new note of reverence had crept into the voice
that announced the coming of a chamber-pot. The
auctioneers wore caps and tweed jackets with leather
patches on the elbows and they used an ordinary
walking-stick to say, voice drooling invitingly to lure a
last-minute bid 'you lose it . . . at two pounds'. The stick
hit the palm of the hand if it was crockery, or the table or
chair, the voice rolled on a sing-song note as they said
'pounnnd', purring their voices were, rubbing them-

selves against the imaginary money as Jocelyne's cat in the cat-mint. They were jolly and red-faced and they certainly murdered plenty of pints and when you bid they looked at you as if they loved you. Jocelyne bid sometimes just to feel loved, she was in it, part of it, her foreign accent inaudible since she only had to say 'yes' or raise a hand or nod. She'd learnt to nod, the art around here was to do it almost invisibly, only the auctioneer was in the secret. Only when she pronounced her name – had to say 'McCoy' did the trouble start: she never could say it right, and the auctioneer often found something droll – never cutting – to say.

But that was how she got in. With Mrs Wright sometimes and her daughter Audrey, who always met relatives or acquaintances, and talked. They bid for clay plant pots or for linen which the auctioneer's assistant, who wore a woollen cap with a pompom, pulled out in haphazard lots from baskets. Bits and bobs, Mrs Wright called them, radiant when she'd got some. It made Jocelyne glad she didn't have so much money after all: her rich woman's bidding wasn't so far removed from their bargain-hunting.

Sales and junk-shops. The strange semi-gypsy population of the vendors and sellers. You saw all sorts, the men, loners, the women, shy and passionate, building their little empire of Victorian lace, odd china cups and brass pokers. Independent all. Those were the people she felt at ease with. She loved the shiftiness, the banter, the warehouses where the objects changed or moved from week to week, or stayed, heaped in the gloom, without any order or domestic purpose. Armchairs and carpets on the top of beds, wardrobes next to cookers, the smell of dust, of woodworm killer; penury-stricken county ladies who put on rubber deep-diving equipment to strip pine furniture in an old bath-tub filled with caustic soda, little old ladies who painted the Norman church in oils and made three-piece suite covers with the remnants you'd got on the market from large, combative old ladies . . . Rose and Alice those were called, fat and dyed blonde and they told funny stories as they measured yards of velvet from one end held in the teeth to another bit held at arm's length. 'I couldn't say whether he was a man or a woman, honestly I couldn't, he had jeans on and a T-shirt and he seemed to be a man but with long hair and one of those voices, you know? the jeans were front-opening but what does that tell you these days and they were so tight you couldn't see what was there and so as I bent my head to measure my yards I kept peering down the opening of his T-shirt to see whether there was anything there.' She mimed the act, hands together at her mouth then one arm held out, then again, as imaginary yards flowed through her fingers. It made Jocelyne feel at home, how her grandmother couldn't decide whether the young person who opened the door at her hairdresser's was a man or a woman. 'And so you see when I go in I say "bonjour monsieur" and when I leave I say "au revoir mademoiselle". That way, fifty per cent of the time I get it right.'

No, what shifted, what travelled from one place to another, the nomadic market people who went from little town to little town on different days of the week, the scrap merchants, the gypsy in the next village who could never stay at home and kept disappearing to take up jobs all over, London, Germany, Belgium, then suddenly appeared at midnight, out of the blue, in a taxi all the way from the nearest big town – all these, Jocelyne felt at home with. What took some understanding was the sedentary lot, the genuine country people. You read Wordsworth. You read George Eliot, Morris, Hardy, D.H. Lawrence. You believed them. The English countryside, you felt sure, was full of noble, clean-living if passionate and deeply-moral people, imbued with Methodism and an easy toleration of the ways of Nature. They loved plants and beasts, they had an instinctive blood-togetherness that made them at

one with the circling suns, the revolving seasons, the
forces of desire. They had relationships. The word did
not exist in French. In England you had farmers. In
France you had peasants. Balzac and Zola had written
about them. They had lusts, sudden, amoral. They loved
nothing but the soil. Clods of earth. They would kill for
an extra bit of land, scythe you down over who owned a
fence. They cared nothing for trees. Sure, not so far from
Jocelyne's home, there was Giono country. But it was
getting touristy, Parisians and Belgians and hippies
bought the farmhouses now, made the goat's cheese.
The peasants and tenant-farmers in the back country
where she'd gone as a child had been jolly, yes. Of
Italian extraction, a lot of them, like Jocelyne's own
grandmother. They enjoyed a talk, they smiled, they
grew wonderful vegetables which they handled indivi-
dually, with knowing hands. Some of them did have
wisdom, yes. Generosity some of them had, quietness,
wisdom. Like this old man, Monsieur Aimar, who had
spent his childhood alone on the mountain slopes in the
Alps, guarding his father's sheep. Once a month his
father would come, bringing a huge round loaf of bread.
He dug into the loaf with his knife, milked a ewe into the
hole: that was his breakfast and lunch and dinner,
month after month.

Jocelyne was so filled with the ideal rurals of her
Open University course that it took her years to discover that there was more in common between the
Wrights and the Aimars than between any of the local
farmers and any of the country folk in the novels
and the poems. The Wrights had been terribly poor.
Had eaten no meat but brawn and the occasional
rabbits for years on end. Once a year, in one tied
cottage, Mr Wright had to empty the cesspit of the
outside toilet on to the ash-pit. As it was such a vile job
Mrs Wright got a treat for him. Gave him five Woodbines, bought one at a time with pennies saved through
her rigorous housekeeping. 'Don't you talk to me about

the good old days,' Audrey would say.

Mr Wright, Jocelyne's mother-in-law had explained, was one of nature's gentlemen.

But the rest – where were they, the warm Tullivers and the Prossers and Michaels and Tesses and Mellors? The gamekeepers were more uncouth than the poachers. Indeed, one of Alan's friends, a small, bulky man with an arthritic hip, who'd been a sharp-shooter in Malaysia during the war and almost been killed by a swarm of jungle hornets, had been a great poacher: he was another of nature's gentlemen. On the other hand, you should have seen the local Lady Chatterley, plump-faced and buxom and middle-aged with her quilted waistcoats and artificially curly hair, a good sort, everyone agreed, great at pulling her weight, taking charge of all the sandwich-making at charity drives – and her gamekeeper of a lover, short, stout and as rough as rough can be. No weaving of forget-me-nots for them. The lady one autumn had parked her Landrover in a discreet corner in a field, while she was bent on an assignation in the woods. Fire had been set to the stubble: the Landrover had gone up in flames. And the lady couldn't really complain, furious as she was, people chuckled, because she would have had to explain why on earth her Landrover had been there.

Noble and principled, the farmers? They had the highest suicide rate in the kingdom. Stephanie said her neighbour needed an old-fashioned square shopping-basket to take back all the anti-depressants the doctor prescribed for the family. No pots of butter and honey there. Mrs Dawson, the gigantically fat farmer's wife, the only one in the village itself, manically cleaned her dairy each morning, down on all fours with a pin to prize out the smallest particles. No poetic warmth-of-the-great-bodies-of-the-cows, no foetal desire-inducing smell of straw and manure and milk there. Indeed, Mrs Dawson, though well past sixty, still sucked her thumb. She henpecked her broomstick of a husband, baked at one go three pounds of flour for two. ('They each have half a dozen eggs for breakfast,' Audrey would say. 'With her you can see where it goes, but with him? He must have holey legs.') Mrs Dawson got her kicks spying on the neighbours. Each night she went to empty her bucketful of potato peelings over the bridge that faced Alan and Jocelyne's kitchen, so she could watch what they were up to. One night Alan looked out of the bay-window and saw her moon-like face peering out of the thorn hedge.

Full of principle, the farmers? You've got to be joking, Jocelyne found herself saying one day, many, many years on. They grab land, they fight for it, I bet they'd kill for a scrap of land, just as they do in Balzac and in Zola. They had it right, even if on the other side of the Channel.

First there had been Mr Dawson. He owned the field next to their garden, they had fishing rights over the river bank. He couldn't bear for them to enter his field. He kept putting padlocks and chains on their gate, which Alan knocked off. In the night he would creep in and put them back.

Then the Dawsons went, and Alan bought the field. Every farmer around wanted to rent it from him. One after another they explained why the crop they'd grown that year hadn't made any profit, price of potatoes dropped dramatically, wheat mountain, hay too wet. In fact they'd made a loss, they couldn't pay the rent. Alan ought to be grateful to them for keeping the field tidy. They cropped his hedge mercilessly, breaking the trunks of centuries-old hawthorns.

They uprooted the trees he'd planted on his roadside. 'Trees are nothing but a damn nuisance,' Jacko who'd done it explained. 'Everything that's not under cultivation ought to be under concrete.' Jocelyne thought of Stendhal: *l'affreuse idée du rendement*. It had to be profit, or nothing. Not even nothing. If you couldn't profit, you had to make sure nobody else could either.

Mr Robson, the Père Grandet and Père Fouan of Braidsley rolled into one, kept a dog that bit just to show locals passing on bicycles, fishermen that paid 20p to fish on his side of the river on Sundays, and the neighbours' children, who was master. Nobody dared protest, except Alan, who threatened to shoot the damn thing if it touched a hair of his children. Alan then got a dog, and the two dogs fought, each ferociously establishing and guarding a territory. 'You can't afford to let anyone put one foot into what's yours,' he said. And he was right. When gentle neighbours who'd rented one of Mr Robson's cottages and whom he'd regarded as menials finally got a council house in Sutton, and moved, Mr Robson found out that they parked their car in a wedge of asphalted roadside against their fence. By a freak of fortune, it turned out that the wedge was his, a left-over from ancient ownership. One afternoon when the people were out at work he came with a pickaxe and broke up the asphalt. That way they couldn't park. It was his property.

To Jocelyne's delight, Mr Robson broke his leg falling from a rotten ladder one autumn. He'd wanted his apples picked, but hadn't dared send either of his labourers, Mr Brown or Mr Wright, up the ladder. He'd have had to pay if they'd suffered an injury at work. 'Damn these fancy laws,' he said. His meanness was legendary – and – what Jocelyne could not, but could not, understand – he was liked for it. After Mr Wright had been in his employ for a quarter of a century, custom being to make a handsome present, Mr Robson gave him twenty-five shillings. One shilling per year. People quoted this as a piece of genuine wit. And he owned many farms, he was reputedly worth millions! His wife wasn't allowed to have a fire till evenings in winter, though she was riddled with arthritis.

People admired him. They said, 'he's quite a character.'

He wouldn't mechanize. He farmed in the old way.

That was perhaps why people liked him ... contrary, foxy, canny, mean as muck, capricious, sullen ... the only one who'd got any of these people right, Jocelyne decided, was Charlotte Brontë, in her portrait of Mr Yorke. A strange piece, stranded in the middle of *Shirley*, that she must have thought long about, into which she had poured a lot of knowledge of people not unlike the people in Braidsley and Sutton, though grander – and that, in the end, she'd done nothing with. The embryo of a book: the portrait of Mr Yorke.

If you were French, though, it was difficult to forgive Charlotte for her worship of the Duke of Wellington. Jocelyne was forever having fights with the upper-crust neighbours. She had a row with one brigadier over Waterloo. She'd quoted Stendhal and Hugo at him (Hugo was particularly good ammunition: he said it was the heroic Scots who'd done it, and also Fate). The brigadier had replied with Georgette Heyer. He'd patronized her. 'Napoleon,' he'd called her. Actually, she'd rather liked him. At least her foreignness had meant something to him.

But Mr Robson. '*Ce vieu grippe-sous*. I suppose we should have blessed our stars he wouldn't mechanize,' she was to say later, when he'd died, and the new owner, a trainer of racehorses, an entrepreneurial man, had put the land into intensive cultivation. Put drainage pipes in the fields so that the water now reached the river faster and it flooded more, carrying large chunks of the bank with it. Used fertilizers, and there was scum on the river. Wrenched out the old hedges and the great trees. Made a flat plain of what had been quaint fields, where you went mushroom-picking in the autumn.

'Yes,' Jocelyne said to Stephanie. 'I have to change my tune now. There was some good in Mr Robson. But I'll never forgive him for what people called his wit. Do you know what? One market day at the pub someone was boasting of this new machine he'd bought, a manure spreader, called Ferguson and Massey. "I've no need for that," he'd said. "I've got a manure-spreader, that's better than that." "Oh aye, and what's it called?" "A Brown and Wright." Mr Brown and Mr Wright were his labourers. I can still see them with their pitchforks . . .'

Stephanie was smiling. Jocelyne smiled also.

'Yes,' she said with some exasperation. 'Zola's the one. With all that land-grabbing and greed and rough lust in the ditches. Pity he never came over to do research here. That would have been the book.'

'You little imperialist,' Stephanie said. 'You Napoleon.'

Alan was harsher.

'Tourist,' he said.

John Agard

If you want to be a acrobat
Agile like a tiger-cat
You don't need a supple body
All you got to do believe me
Is buy a cup of coffee
From any British train buffet
And you go turn acrobat today.

When you coming back to your seat
You falling off your feet
The train rocking from side to side
And your coffee going for a ride
Spilling up and down spilling left to right
And you trying hard to be polite.

Sorry sir I didn't mean
to spill my coffee on your *Financial Times*
Sorry lady I didn't mean
to spill my coffee on your clean white dress
Can't you see I'm doing my very best
to wipe away your distress.

The people looking dis West Indian up and down
Some of them giving a little frown
But they can't vex more than me
After all I is the one who lose my coffee.

So my friends take a tip from me
Any time you want a cup of coffee
If it's a British train buffet
Remember think twice before you pay
Cause unless you're a acrobat
It's much safer to buy a Kit-Kat.

Jill Neville

Nancy emerged from the filthy winds of the tube only to be hit by a November gale. A man opened his car door too quickly and had it almost blown off its hinges; a dog sniffing another dog's excrement looked up at the white, emerging moon and definitely bayed. It was that uncanny slice of time between Hallowe'en and Guy Fawkes night and branches flew about the mottled sky as if possessed.

Lakewood Avenue was on the left; 134 must be way down the other end towards Ladbroke Grove. She clutched her jacket around her, careless of its fashionable line, and ploughed through the thrilling wind which knocked over a hessian bag stuffed tight with summer leaves. A few withered brown escapees hurtled upwards, looped-the-loop and ascended with the moon. Nancy was more exhilarated even than usual. From the moment she had set foot in London and breathed its immemorial air she had expanded into herself. Back home there had been something weighing on her; it wasn't just her older sister's vulgarity, it was her insistence that everyone else (especially Nancy) interpret life in the same way, with the same snigger in the face of the imponderable. 'You're kidding me to death,' Nancy had once shouted and felt herself dying in that

place. Often she had stood dangerously on the edge of
the harbour swaying toward the swallowing water. Her
sadness was adolescent; inappropriate; after all her
parents were fine, so was her home life really. But there
was always that dirge inside her, that gene that wailed
to go back to Europe from where her forbears had been
driven by Necessity, Adventure or the Law. She had
been homesick for a London she did not know; the great
sponge that would soon soak her up forever. And like so
many others she had found a cosy interstice; even
despite the usual student poverty.

She hurried on past the great houses. Long ago she
had pruned away any fancy of possessing one as she
had pruned away her love of rubies; lusts that could
only lead to a new version of transportation. At present
she was between lovers. It was typical of her to be in no
doubt of the imminence of the next one; though it was
almost certain she would not meet her fate tonight. The
evening would be far too grand to contain the kind of
man she liked. She shivered. Dusk had come in early
and beyond that, underneath it all, winter was clenching up to strike like a fist.

In the communal gardens, some of the bonfires were
already laid for Guy Fawkes Night, the wind clawing
away at the top layers of branches and broken chairs. It
was the celebration she most enjoyed in London, better
than the anxiety and over-eating of Christmas, better
than the sad bell-toll of birthdays; it was the night of the
long shadows and laughter in the squares when you got
a whiff of heaven's sulphur; when the barnacled heart
moved slowly – like a beast you thought may be dead.

Did this invitation mean she would be accepted into
their circle? That was a silly thought. Crass. She had
her friends, her regiments of eccentrics, not all of them
foreign. But, well Harriet and Joshua Bennett were part
of old Bloomsbury. Harriet was a descendent of the
luminaries. She was the last of all that was left of that
elegant ferment.

On either side of No 134 houses curved away painted
a motley of amusing colours then fashionable; but the
Bennett house, as she might have known, was a subtle
combination of pastels. Despite herself she glanced
down towards 188, now painted fuchsia with pretentious
swagged curtains. She had once lived there, at the back,
when the façade was a crumbling slum. She shut out the
memory of the blighted garden; the landlord who tried
to break down her door. But the huge brown cupboard
she had pushed across the room to bar his entrance
swung open in her mind revealing the stained lining
paper, the row of twisted wire coat-hangers.

The Bennetts wouldn't have a wire coathanger in the
house. They would all be padded by ancient retainers
from former times. There were two bells and a knocker.
One didn't actually use the knocker did one? She
pressed both bells, quelling her nerves. Harriet had
enjoyed her company so much at that party where
they met that she had issued this invitation on the
spot.

'Nancy. How lovely!' Harriet stood there in her grey
wool, her smile slightly askew as if frozen into permanent irony. 'Oh, you're *dressed*. I should have
warned you. Just old chums.'

In the drawing-room Joshua wheeled around. 'Ah-
ha . . .' His spectacles were so thick they obviated all
eye-contact. But he blinked exaggeratedly as if dazzled
by her turquoise velvet dress.

'We've met before.' It was Amanda Goodwin the
biographer whom she had grazed from time to time at
social occasions. It was obvious at once that Amanda
was in that sacred condition of being happily in love.
Marcus, the source of it all, rose from his chair. He had a
kind face despite a tough jaw; it was the jaw of a John
Buchan hero. He was the sort of man she had never
aspired to. She did not realize that she always avoided
such splendid types, fluffed her lines whenever she had
a chance with them, crippled by sexual humility.

A premature bang came from the direction of the communal garden; the sound of children being screamed at, dragged indoors. 'It's odd,' said Joshua handing around more drinks, 'celebrating the man who tried to destroy Parliament.'

How the English purr at their eccentricities. Well, she would purr with them.

'Perhaps that's why it's my favourite time of year.'

'The burning of the old year. Fascinating – the archaeological layers of belief. Substituting modern ritual over the pagan.'

Nancy sank into a chair. She should have left off the chandelier earrings. Every time she moved she heard them jingle.

'All day they've been putting out premature fires in the garden. The children can't wait for November the fifth, the darling little pyromaniacs.' The curtains were undrawn because the moon was full and the gardens so unique. 'Carlotta is supposed to be with us. But she's lying down upstairs with a migraine. We're to start without her.'

This would be Carlotta Riddington, wife of the great thirties poet David Riddington. She must be rather old, poor lamb. Probably not quite up to the hurly burly anymore.

The huge room could have done with a coat of paint, how lovely the moulding would be if picked out in a contrasting colour. Everyone was doing that now. But the chandelier was quite thick with dust; the dowdy authority of the elite. Nancy looked askance at the heel of her shoe. 'I think the shoe industry has mastered the art of obsolescence. I bought them only three days ago.'

Marcus reached down a hand towards the offending item.

She took off her shoe, revealing what fine high arches she had, and handed it to him. He gravely examined the plastic heel. 'If someone invented a permanent heel he would be put on a Mafia contract immediately. This is

ingenious rubbish.' She replaced her shoe amid laughter
that had a touch of relief in it.

Amanda said, 'Harriet, only you can persuade Marcus
to give up this play. It's driving him mad. It's not *him*,
you see.'

'Well I am having trouble with Act Two,' Marcus said.
'It has to be subtle, Chekhovian, because Acts One and
Three are simply packed with adultery and anguish.
The more I rewrite it the more it eludes me,' he groaned
beseechingly in Harriet's direction, who chuckled.

'Your misery is a warning bell, my sweet. You are
stroking your creative fur up the wrong way. Fatal.'
Harriet leant back and twirled her cigarette. 'Why try to
be Lorca? You're Marcus. *Our* Marcus.'

'But it's fun – writing something different. After all
four comedies on the trot! You're always experimenting
yourself Harriet, you should talk.'

There was conspiratorial laughter, which excluded
Nancy. She stared into her whisky glass. Could she be
the hostess's latest caprice; the rough Colonial girl?

'What a divine vase. Such a gorgeous red. Positively
Mycenean.' Amanda wandered over and stroked the
table's centre-piece, her rings reflecting in its ruddy
depths.

'Portobello Road still yields surprises my pet,' said
Harriet, then instructed them all to sit at the table,
leaving one chair with its back to the window for
Carlotta, the late arrival.

Nancy had never seen chrysanthemums of such
paleness. They looked as if they had once been russet
and then had all their blood drained by the vase.

Artichokes were waiting for them, sitting upright in
frilly skirts on every plate. An anecdote charged into
Nancy's head: 'When I first came over from Australia
I'd never seen an artichoke. At dinner parties, I'd copy
everybody else and suck the leaves. I failed to notice
what happened after that. So for years I left the heart
uneaten on my plate.'

'Oh, all those wasted hearts,' wailed Harriet, amused.

'It's wonderful to get away from the theatre.' Marcus wriggled his shoulders as if easing tension. 'All those performing monkeys. Their tantrums. Their melo-dramas. Christ!'

'Surely *some* actors are civilized,' admonished Harriet.

'London is teeming with simply marvellous actors isn't it, darling,' said Amanda, plying him with her blaze of fulfilment. 'Therefore it follows that acting must be laughably easy.'

'Not like writing,' sighed Nancy. Her hostess's face popped round approvingly from behind the epicene chrysanthemums. Harriet had the unyielding nose of the Plantagenets. Nancy's old teacher had possessed such a nose, and she associated it with a ruthless scavenging out of punctuation mistakes.

'Well, has Enoch Powell lost his marbles?' asked someone over the roast lamb.

'The man is unspeakable. A national shame. Absurd blatherings about blacks running wild and rivers of blood.'

Amanda was discussing house prices. 'Thank God you didn't break this house up into flats like so many others.'

'It was built for a housemaid, a cook, a kitchen maid, a scullery maid, a tweenie and a parlour maid, but otherwise it's perfect.' Harriet placed her cutlery parallel on her plate, rocked back on her chair and gazed oddly at Nancy. Night winds rattled at the windows like the ghosts of old house servants. Nancy knew her hostess was drawing back before she sprang at her.

'In your opinion Nancy, who is the greatest English writer of this century?'

Nancy assumed this was a kind of post-Bloomsbury party game. 'Thomas Hardy,' she responded, unthrea-tened. A chair scraped overhead. Could that be the absent Carlotta? Presumably her husband was abroad on the celebrity circuit; lecturing or something. That must be why he had not been mentioned.

'Hardy's *post* Victorian. No, after him.'

'Um. Let's think.' Tension mounted. The faces of the others seemed to close, only the vampire vase flaunted any light. She crumbled a stale bread roll. The meat had been overdone. She thought of Waugh, Greene, Woolf.

'D.H. Lawrence.'

There was a drawing-in of four collective breaths. Carlotta's empty chair loomed spectrally. In the great garden the moon lit up the silhouette of a seven-foot Guy atop the pyre.

Harriet's wrists dropped as if she had received tragic news. She gave a flinty laugh. 'You can't be serious.'

Joshua tore off his bifocals. His two-dimensional eyes angled at Nancy. They were such a pale blue they were almost no-colour. 'What, pray, do you like about that awful man?' White eyes. Sympathy could never find a foothold there; charity, certainly; but she didn't qualify for that. She was too pert. She reached forward and splashed more wine into her glass. How square her hand was. The rest of her was finely-made, but she had to admit her hands revealed something coarse. So, she was on the spot, she was getting the third degree; this was the initiation ceremony; if she passed this she was in. She would have arrived. Oh well, here goes. She gave a merry laugh.

'His grandeur. Think of the other writers at that time: Michael Arlen for heaven's sake. Arnold Bennett. *John Buchan!*'

'Wonderful chap, Buchan,' Joshua laughed.

'Lawrence gives Nature its due. And as for emotions.' Nancy banged on about the tidal nature of emotions; the impasse between the sexes, with only a hair's breadth for manoeuvre. 'Lawrence can convey not just the leaves but the sap in the leaves, the light on them, their smell.' It was into Lawrence she had escaped, that day in the library, aged fifteen, that day when her hand had reached out and drawn forth a book and lo it had been the letters of D.H. Lawrence.

'He makes such a fuss about sex,' Harriet said with her mouth full.

'He makes a fuss about – snapdragons. He makes a fuss about LIFE.' Nancy swept her arms as if to encompass the whole of existence. Marcus was looking at her with pity. She was the pet mouse she'd once tried to drown in the lavatory because it had become deformed. The mouse had swum round desperately as she pulled the chain again and again while it struggled, earless, pustuled, against the raging torrent.

Was she drunk? The image was maudlin. Amanda was now staring out to where some children up too late were cavorting about with torches, gloating over the Guy. 'The man was a sham. A fascist and a bore.' Amanda said wearily.

Nancy jumped in, still eager. 'He could be. But taken as a whole he looms over all these quibbles. We can forgive him *The Plumed Serpent, Lady Chat* and so on because we have the short stories, the poems. We have *Women in Love.*'

From above came the loud thump of footfalls. If only Carlotta would decide to come down, murmuring of her migraine, changing the flow.

They all gazed at the ceiling. If anyone had wielded a machete at that moment all their puppet-strings would be cut, they would loll back, heads awry, legs splayed.

Nancy played with some spilt salt. 'Well then you tell me who you all think is the greatest writer after Hardy?'

'Surely it's obvious? Anthony Powell of course.' Harriet laughed acidly.

Marcus was struggling with his fists as if they had been locked together under hypnosis.

'Powell is the supreme English writer,' pronounced Joshua.

Nancy peered about searching their faces for humour,

but the room was badly lit. Grandees they may be, but they practised small economies. She had an urge to check the lamps. She suspected forty watt. 'Powell is *mean*. It's like comparing a marmoset with a lion.'

Up above the footsteps which had paused for a while continued their heavy pacing. Had Carlotta been listening to them by means of an inverted wine glass? Wisely then she had decided to stay upstairs.

'How *can* you like that lying, raving, over-inflated, sexually obsessed charlatan . . . "*My womb turned*." Ugh . . .' Harriet said scathingly. 'He's sickening.'

'Everything has to be hepped up with him,' piped up Joshua. 'He couldn't write about *ordinary* things like *common decency*. Or people getting on with life. He was ridiculous when he tried. When men gathered together in his books they have to go into a naked homosexual wrestling bout on the floor. Now with Powell, the social comedy, the ironies, the process of time . . .'

Nancy pushed all the salt into a pile and thumped it with her spoon. 'Well, if you only want little emotions I suppose Lawrence must seem overblown.'

Harriet rose. The bone in her nose seemed to be straining with innate authority. 'Let's get the pudding.' Harriet and Amanda disappeared, carrying messy plates. From upstairs came the rattle of a window opening. 'Is that Carlotta up there? Is she coming to join us?' Nancy asked brightly, placatingly.

Silence descended, so tight as to be impenetrable. Outside sacks of leaves containing all that was left of a loveless summer waited for refuse trucks. Did they use leaves to stuff the Guy Fawkes dummy? Her throat hurt. She wondered if she was going down with flu. Perhaps she should never utter again. The wind was wrestling with the branches, garrotting the last of the roses and gusting through the open window upstairs where Carlotta nursed her migraine.

By the time Harriet returned bearing a leaden sylla-bub Nancy had finally learned to endure the awkward silence. Oh well, she had endured worse things.

'Syllabub anyone?' Harriet plonked a helping on to Nancy's plate. 'Mediocrities rush about after Lawrence like blowflies to rotten meat. He thinks only sexual passion is significant; that only sex gives moral worth to life. It is as dangerous as it is ludicrous.'

Nancy pushed her plate away. 'Sexual passion, *not* lechery – Lawrence loathed all those 'l' words: lechery, lasciviousness, licentiousness, lust, libertinage – not that. But the fires of passion. It's the best thing in life after all isn't it?'

'Have you seen the new *Magic Flute*?' asked Marcus. 'Papagena descends in a helicopter.'

When Nancy left, even her arms felt embarrassed; her dress a lurid failure. She turned at the bottom of the step to say the usual final goodbye but the door had already closed.

Outside the tube station she bought a hot doughnut from a sorry figure trying to hold steady the canvas flap above his mobile stall. She bit into its poisonous softness, adoring the cheap jam. 'You're too adventurous,' her mother used to say. 'You'll end up in Buenos Aires harbour drowned by a jealous lover.' Well, there were other ways of drowning.

Some years later Nancy spotted Amanda at a party. Her glow had gone and she kept peering over Nancy's shoulder at the literary celebrities who wheeled and tacked in the prevailing breezes of opinion.

'Good Lord, Nancy. Haven't run into you for years.'

'The last time we met we had a row about D.H. Lawrence. Four against one. Remember?'

'Oh. Yes.'

'I had read only one novel by Powell at that time. *Afternoon Men*. Very funny.'

'An early work. Not typical,' Amanda's eyes suddenly unfilmed as she spotted Melvyn Bragg. 'Yes. It was an edgy evening. But you know – Carlotta's husband had died just an hour before we arrived. His body was still upstairs. Of course Harriet didn't want to make a fuss.'

'You mean. All through that dinner. The body. The *corpse* was upstairs?'

'It hadn't arrived. The ambulance. Or the funeral people. Or whoever is supposed to come.'

It was a Buñuel film. The discreet charm of the bourgeoisie sitting comparing the merits of writers, baiting an outsider, while upstairs lay a cadaver. And no one screaming. No one wailing. No ashes in hair. No rending of garments. No mourning. No admission that something dramatic had occurred. That blood had been shed. A life ended. Real tears were in the house. Carlotta upstairs holding vigil. *In extremis*. Something had happened. Something that had had to be acknowledged, loudly, vehemently. Why could Harriet not have told her at once, on her arrival, told her the truth, told her for God's sake to please GO HOME?

'It was too late to put off the dinner party. So she rather gallantly carried on you see,' said Amanda, escaping with wounding speed towards Melvyn Bragg.

'I see,' said Nancy to the empty air.

Bonnie Greer

'The thing to remember about the English, no matter how nice they act,' Winston said, as the pizza arrived, 'is this: They hate our guts.' He then took his knife and plunged it into the thin crust, cutting himself the biggest slice. Lorraine felt quietly assured. After all these years abroad, he remained the same. Out for Number One.

The restaurant, on the first floor of a listed Georgian building tucked into a street off Covent Garden, was called *The Windy City*, and every inch of wall space was covered by posters and memorabilia of Chicago – drinks named after gangsters, the bar-tender dressed out of a Warner Brothers 'B' movie, the waitresses, bumping into one another with their huge trays, could be expecting a shakedown from the Feds any moment. There was a loud, excited air. Frank Sinatra's incessant 'Chicago' blasting from the sound system made Lorraine anticipate a march from the kitchen to the tune of 'Stars and Stripes Forever'. She had certainly never been anywhere like it back home in Chicago.

'See what I mean about these people? This is supposed to be deep dish, but it ain't shit! Got no heart. Just like this whole damn town.' Winston flung out his arms in a gesture of disgust. On cue, the waitress bounced over and asked happily, 'Having a nice day?'

'See,' Winston ignored her, 'they can't even get that right. She still sounds like the Queen.' He stopped and for the first time since they met at Heathrow, Lorraine could see his face – his once beautiful African face, the luminous eyes, the soft mouth with its hint of tenderness. All his streetwise beauty had disappeared into a vacuum, hostile and vacant. He was giving nothing away. Not even to her. Winston, just like the Bible, 'A man of sorrows and acquainted with grief.'

The man at the next table leaned over, and in a thick, Southern drawl, asked to borrow the salt. Back in the States, he, wealthy and white, would have never spoken to her or Winston. But here she was actually relieved to hear his voice. Three thousand miles of ocean created a strange camaraderie. She knew that Winston felt the same way. She always knew how he felt.

Winston pulled out the postcard he had bought at the National Gallery that morning. *Miss Lala*. The burnt oranges, the turquoises, the light and dark of Degas' painting, blended with the wood in the table, blended with the colour of her own dark skin, blended with the memory of him, Winston, her lover four long years ago. Winston always needed to be obsessed by what obsessed her. Up that morning to see Degas' painting, by nightfall he would be an expert. That was Winston's way. That was how he always maintained control.

Miss Lala at the Cirque Fernando, Paris by Hilaire-Germain-Edgar Degas. She studied the postcard. He was right. The old Jew, Nathan, had been right. She did look like the woman in the picture. The acrobat hanging by her teeth. Even down to her skin tone and the way she wore her hair.

Up until this moment, she thought she had only come to see the painting. Now she understood. She had come instead to climb inside herself. And she would stay inside until she could see daylight.

As a waitress began singing 'Sweet Home Chicago'

Winston threw his money on the table. 'That's it. They're messin' with the blues. Let's get the hell out of here.'

'I want to see the painting,' Lorraine said.

'You crazy?' Winston snatched her from her seat, 'The museum's closed. Forget it.'

PRIVATE ENTERPRISE

Gabriel Josipovici

GAVIN WILLIAMS   *A rich businessman*
ANNABEL   *His wife*
MICH BRENT   *An actor*
SELMA   *A dress shop owner*
MILES   *The Williams's manservant*

1. West End. Mid-morning.
A bell clangs as Annabel enters the shop

SELMA: Oh Mrs Williams! How lovely to see you!

ANNABEL: And you Selma. How are you?

SELMA: You know how it is in the spring, Mrs Williams. Very busy. Very busy.

ANNABEL: That dress you have in the window, Selma . . . The white one . . .

SELMA: A beauty, Mrs Williams. A beauty. Would you like to have a look at it?

ANNABEL: Please.

Selma clambers into the window and brings down the dress

SELMA: There.

Annabel whistles under her breath

SELMA: A lovely thing, isn't it, darling? Audrey only brought it in yesterday. I thought of you the moment I saw it.

ANNABEL: But why didn't you ring, Selma? I might not have come up to town for ages.

SELMA: You know how it is, darling. There's so much to do these days.

Her little dog whines

SELMA: There, poppet, there. You be a good little boysy-boys and I'll give you a chocky.

Dog whines excitedly and jumps about

SELMA: Try it on darling. Try it on. You know the way, don't you?

ANNABEL: Of course. (*She goes down the corridor*).

SELMA: Now! What are we going to give the little boysy-woysy? A nice little chocky? Yes? Yes?

She takes chocolate out of box, unwraps it and gives it to the dog, who is whining shrilly throughout. It gulps it down

SELMA: No. That's enough. Now Mumsy's going to have one too.

She unwraps one for herself and eats it as the dog whines
Annabel returns

ANNABEL: What d'you think, Selma?

SELMA: Marvellous, darling. Absolutely marvellous. You set it off to perfection. And, if I may say so, darling, it sets you off too.

ANNABEL: Yes. I rather like it.

SELMA: I knew you would. The moment Audrey brought it in I thought of you.

ANNABEL: (*Distractedly, as she looks at herself in the mirror*). I wish you'd rung, Selma. It was pure luck my coming up to town today.

SELMA: Darling I'm simply flooded with work! If you knew what it's been like these past few days . . .

ANNABEL: Yes. I'll have it.

She walks down the corridor back to the changing-room. She returns with the dress in her arms. She hands it to Selma

SELMA: You know what I always say, darling? The more you do the more there is to do.

ANNABEL: Wrap it up, Selma. I'll take it away with me.

SELMA: Of course, darling. How would you like to pay?

ANNABEL: Oh, put it on the account will you, Selma.

SELMA: I'm sorry darling.

ANNABEL: What do you mean?

SELMA: I'm sorry. Mr Williams was most insistent.

ANNABEL: Mr Williams?

SELMA: I'm sorry darling. You don't have an account here any more, darling.

ANNABEL: I see.

SELMA: You do understand, don't you, darling? If Mr Williams, who pays the account . . .

ANNABEL: Thank you Selma. I quite understand. Goodbye.

SELMA: Goodbye darling. Mind the step as you go.

The doorbell. The street

2. Dinner. Male Laughter.

MICH: And then he said: (*mimics*) I wonder if you would be so very good as to step off my toe sir. Right off sir. That's right. Thank you. That's most kind of you. And Jim said to him, No no, he said, thank *you*, and he said, What are you thanking me for? and Jim said, for being so very understanding!

Laughter

ANNABEL: Coffee, Mich?
MICH: Terrific.

Annabel rings a little bell by her side

ANNABEL: One coffee, Miles, please.
MILES: Very good Madam.
GAVIN: Well if you've had enough Mich we could . . . adjourn.
MICH: Sure.
ANNABEL: In the drawing-room, Miles, please.
MILES: Very good Madam.

3. Drawing-room, later. Brandenburg concerto on the gramophone.

GAVIN: If you take that path there and turn left round the copse, there, do you see –
MICH: Yes. Yes.
GAVIN: – and keep going round the hill for about a mile, then take this path and about four hundred yards on you come to the crest of the hill and the sea's there below you.
MICH: I don't see how . . .
GAVIN: Here. You cut through just above here, at this line here, and –

*Annabel gets up abruptly and switches off the gramo-
phone*

GAVIN: Is anything the matter darling?
ANNABEL: I'm going to bed.
GAVIN: Darling! Already?
ANNABEL: I've got a bit of a headache.
MICH: I think I'll turn in too if you'll forgive me.
ANNABEL: Don't let me break up the party.
MICH: No no. It's beddy byes for me. This sea air
knocks me out.
GAVIN: Miles should have stocked up your fridge. Call
out if you need anything.
MICH: I will. Goodnight.

Gavin and Annabel are standing side by side

G & A: Goodnight.
GAVIN: You run along. I've still got a bit to do.
ANNABEL: Uhuh.
GAVIN: Sleep well darling. (*He kisses her cheek*).

**4. Gavin's study. He pours himself a drink, adds
ice, settles down at his desk. He sorts out a few
papers, then switches on a machine.**

GAVIN: Marcia, get on to Dewey straight away and
find out what's happened to that order. Then phone
Henderson and make sure he knows exactly what the
schedule is for Thursday. I want him there at 2.30
sharp. Now, take down these letters . . .

**5. Bedroom. Annabel brushes her hair, humming.
She goes into the bathroom, takes an aspirin,
mixes it with water, drinks. She returns to the
bedroom, gets into bed, puts out the light, sighs.**

**6. *Morning. Garden. Birds. In the distance, the
surf against the cliffs steps on the gravel.***

MICH: I'm not disturbing?
ANNABEL: Hullo. Sit down.

He sits on the bench beside her

MICH: Ah! Lovely! Fantastic day!
ANNABEL: Isn't it?
MICH: Sir gone already?
ANNABEL: It's ten o'clock.
MICH: Yes. I suppose it is.
ANNABEL: You slept well?
MICH: Like a log.
ANNABEL: You found all you needed for breakfast?
MICH: Absolutely.
ANNABEL: We think it best to leave our guests quite
free. Miles checks the fridge and the larder in the guest
kitchen to make sure it's well stocked, but that's all.
Most people aren't sociable till they've had breakfast
and Miles has all the garden to do as well so we can't
really expect him to wait about till our guests get up.
MICH: Very civilized.
ANNABEL: It's a good idea, isn't it. (*Pause*) I'm such a
hopeless housewife.
MICH: Are you? Really?
ANNABEL: I'm afraid I am.
MICH: I'm sorry about last night.
ANNABEL: Last night?
MICH: Your not feeling well.
ANNABEL: Oh it was nothing.
MICH: I hope we didn't keep you up?
ANNABEL: No no. Not at all.
MICH: You looked tired. (*Pause*) You still do.
ANNABEL: Do I?
MICH: Yes.
ANNABEL: Oh.

MICH: Ah well, I expect it's just . . .

ANNABEL: Just what?

MICH: Well . . . You know. A bit of the old . . . In bed.

ANNABEL: Oh no. You're quite mistaken.

MICH: Oh?

ANNABEL: No. Gavin doesn't really go in much for that sort of thing.

MICH: Really?

ANNABEL: Oh, he enjoys it all right. He just doesn't have all that much time for it.

MICH: You don't say.

ANNABEL: I'm afraid it's business first with him.

MICH: Is that so?

ANNABEL: It's actually not much fun at all. He won't give me any of the things I want. Or even, to be quite frank, all that much in bed.

MICH: (*Whistling*) So?

ANNABEL: I shouldn't really be saying this to you. His oldest friend and all that. But I can't help it. I'm sorry.

MICH: Oh don't apologize. You know, this oldest friend thing can be a bit overdone. Actually we'd rather drifted apart. Until recently.

ANNABEL: Oh?

MICH: Yes. Until he remarried in fact. (*Pause*) You.

ANNABEL: Really?

MICH: Yes, that's more or less the truth of the matter, I'd say.

ANNABEL: Well, fancy that.

A time

ANNABEL: You know what he's done recently?

MICH: No?

ANNABEL: He's asked the woman I buy my dresses from not to give me credit any more.

MICH: He has?

ANNABEL: It's just spite. The money means nothing to him.

MICH: Aha.

ANNABEL: There's one dress I'm particularly keen on.

MICH: Is there?

ANNABEL: Yes. I like it a lot.

MICH: I see.

ANNABEL: I have to have it.

A time

MICH: How much?

ANNABEL: Twenty-five hundred.

MICH: Pounds?

ANNABEL: Uhuh.

MICH: Well well.

ANNABEL: Yes. Twenty-five hundred pounds.

MICH: Ah, well. (*Pause*) it might be possible.

ANNABEL: What might?

MICH: I might be able to find the money for you.

ANNABEL: You think so?

MICH: Perhaps we could come to some arrangement?

ANNABEL: Oh, I'm all for arrangements. (*Pause*) He goes to Hamburg next week. If you felt like coming over. I mean if you found you'd been able to lay hands on that sum. We could have a little . . . celebration, perhaps. Do you know what I mean?

MICH: I know exactly what you mean.

7.

MICH: (*On phone*) Gavin? It's Mich. Mich Brent. Yes, Hullo. I've been trying to get you for hours. You people must be pretty busy. What's that? Ha ha. Yes. listen. I wonder if I could have a little talk with you. Yes. Soon. Oh, not very long. Just a few minutes. Yes, it is rather important. What? One fifteen tomorrow? Stroll with you in the Park? A lovely idea. Lovely. Yes, I'll see you outside the cafeteria at one fifteen then. Bye.

8. St James's Park. Gavin and Mich stroll along by the lake.

MICH: I said I'd need to look at the script. But I couldn't give a fuck. Frankly. I need the money so whatever they want me to do I'll do, if they pay enough. Which they seem willing to do. (*They stroll*). But there's this bloody case coming up. It's driving me crazy. I don't know where I'm going to get the money from to pay the bloody lawyers.

And you can't keep fobbing these bastards off.

They stroll

GAVIN: Can I help at all?
MICH: They suck you dry, these creeps. For doing fuck-all.

They stroll.

MICH: I just need a bit of the ready. Till the film money starts to come in.

They stroll

GAVIN: How much?
MICH: Twenty-five hundred.

They stroll

GAVIN: I think I could manage that.

They stroll

GAVIN: Here. Let me write you out a cheque.

They sit on a bench. Gavin writes out the cheque and hands it over

MICH: I'm grateful.
GAVIN: That's all right.
MICH: It'll get me out of this shit.
GAVIN: Any time. You're an old friend, after all.
MICH: As soon as the film money comes through I'll –
GAVIN: No hurry. Take your time. Six months'll do me fine.
MICH: It'll get me out of this shit with the lawyers. You know what lawyers're like.

9. The Williams's drawing-room. Brandenburg concerto on the gramophone.

MICH: I thought you said you were a hopeless house-wife?
ANNABEL: Oh, Miles prepared everything before he left.
MICH: But you planned the menu?

She laughs

ANNABEL: Brandy?
MICH: Alas, no. Thank you.
ANNABEL: Alas?
MICH: My liver's rotting. Rotten already actually. The doctor's absolutely forbidden it. (*Pause*) It makes one vice less.

She laughs

ANNABEL: I'm going to have one. My liver's in perfect condition.

She pours herself the drink, returns to sofa

ANNABEL: What's this?
MICH: A little present.
ANNABEL: Can I open it?

MICH: It's yours.

She opens the envelope, counts the notes

MICH: I trust I didn't make a mistake.
ANNABEL: No. No mistake at all.
MICH: I always keep my promises.
ANNABEL: Oh so do I.
MICH: You do?
ANNABEL: Of course. Especially when it's a pleasure. Come.

She takes his hand. They get up

10. Some months later. Bedroom. Annabel taking off make-up at mirror. Gavin lying in bed, reading.

GAVIN: You're very naughty, you know.
ANNABEL: Me?
GAVIN: You.
ANNABEL: What have I done now?
GAVIN: You don't tell me things.
ANNABEL: What kinds of things?
GAVIN: All kinds of things. (*Pause*). I lent Mich Brent some money a few months ago. I rang him today to see how he was getting on.
ANNABEL: Oh yes?
GAVIN: He told me he'd paid it back. To you. It was rather embarrassing, as you can imagine. (*Pause*) I wish you'd tell me things like that.
ANNABEL: Like what?
GAVIN: Well, tell me he'd paid me back.
ANNABEL: But he didn't.
GAVIN: He didn't?
ANNABEL: Pay you, I mean.
GAVIN: I beg your pardon?

ANNABEL: It was for me. To buy a dress.

GAVIN: To buy a dress?

ANNABEL: That's right. I told him about a dress I was particularly keen on and he produced the money.

GAVIN: He produced – ? My money?

ANNABEL: He didn't say it was your money. I took it as a kind of repayment. For all our hospitality.

GAVIN: Our hos – ? How much was this dress?

ANNABEL: Twenty-five hundred.

GAVIN: Twenty-five hundred? He produced twenty-five hundred and you thought it – ?

ANNABEL: It seemed typical of his tact. That's how I took it.

GAVIN: Tact? And you bought a dress for twenty-five hundred? My money? –

ANNABEL: (*Getting up, coming to the bed*) Oh, darling! You don't want me to go about in rags, do you? Your wifey? I'll pay you back. Every penny. I promise you. In bed. Isn't that nice? Isn't that what you like? Darling? Isn't it? Isn't it?

Duncan McLean

Stagecoach were doing a special offer, so after Bap'd cashed his giro he nipped straight to the depot and headed off down to London. He'd been down once before and stayed with a mate who lived in a squat in Brixton, but now this guy had moved to a council flat in an area called Pimlico; Bap was hoping he'd be able to doss there for a couple of days anyway. Next to Pimlico up the back of the *A-Z* was Pilton Place: amazing, home sweet fucking home. Ten to one the buggers there had never even heard of the Great Pilton of the North though. Lucky bastards. It's a part of Edinburgh pal. *Edinburgh*, just over from *Glasgow*. A wee bit up from fucking *Newcastle*.

Bap found the block of flats no bother after a bit of walking; it was half way in between the big Victoria Station and Chelsea Barracks. All these familiar names! It was like walking round a fucking monopoly board.

To win through the front door you had to get by an entryphone system, but the buzzer and/or the speaker was buggered. Or maybe there was just nobody in Pompey's place. That's what he was known as this mate, Pompey, because he came from Portsmouth originally before moving up to London. Bap waited till somebody was coming out the front door and then nipped in, making on he was fumbling for his key or something and not sneaking in illegally to do over a few of the flats, honest guv. He went up the central stairs to the third floor, then out along the balcony to the eighth door. He rang and knocked and rang again: no answer. Three o'clock in the afternoon! What the fuck was going on? Maybe Pompey had got a job.

He sat down on the step with his back against the door and his legs stretched out across the passageway. Out of his back pocket he took a magazine he'd found in the bucket at the toilets at Victoria; it had lists of all the gigs and goings on in London. He sat there reading this thing. After a while he checked the cover: aye, fuck, the magazine was listing events that had been going on a fortnight before. He couldn't afford to see fuck-all anyway. He carried on reading.

Pompey showed up around teatime. It turned out he had three jobs: in the afternoons he gave out leaflets at tube stations, information about new clothes shops or films opening; at nights he worked in a theatre, showing folk to their seats, taking tickets and that; and at weekends he worked in a big record store in Oxford Street. The life of fucking riley in a way. But even so he was having difficulties in scraping his rent together every month; London prices were totally out of order these days. In fact he'd been thinking about moving up to Scotland: it seemed to be a lot cheaper up there, a lot easier. Bap just laughed at this.

After Pompey left for his evening job, Bap sat around for a while and then went out and walked along King's Road. It was a load of shite. He dandered back towards the flat down a series of quiet streets lined with expensive motors, at one point stopping to look over a wall into a beer garden at the back of a pub. At one end there was a fire going and a guy was standing there cooking steaks and burgers and bits of chicken on it. The punters were getting in a round then going up and

buying a plateful of barbequed stuff and taking it back
to their table. There was laughter, and the sizzling of fat
falling into the flames, and the smoke smelled real fine
as if drifted past Bap. The man doing the cooking had a
tall white hat on like a chef. Ho! He flipped a piece of
meat up into the air.

Back at the flat, Bap watched the tele till Pompey
came in about eleven. These ads were totally different to
the ones we get, said Bap.

What're you talking about? said Pompey.

Well we don't even fucking get half of these things at
all. Different beer and that. And even the stuff we do
get, well the ads here are different: posher, ken? Pompey
nodded, looked at the screen. You're a load of rich
bastards and that's all there is to it, said Bap.

Not any more, said Pompey.

How come?

I just spent my next week's pay on same hash to
celebrate your arrival, you tightfisted Scotch cunt.

Spoken like a gentleman sir, said Bap. I'll provide the
rizlas.

They smoked and talked and watched a video of a
band Pompey used to play the drums in. Shame you fell
out and that, said Bap, Cause yous lot were pretty
fucking good, I'm telling you.

Pompey shook his head. Yes yes yes, he said, and took
a long drag. The tape finished and Pompey knelt up to
switch the thing off. So what brings you to the big
smoke anyway?

The big smoke! Bap passed the joint to Pompey. They
both laughed.

No, I just mean, is it a long term visit or eh what?

Getting worried now you bastard?

They laughed again

Well I've no fucking idea to be honest, said Bap, But
I'll tell you: I like the sound of this three jobs per person
scam. In fact, I fancy a bit of that action myself.

Pompey looked at him. I wouldn't want you to think

the streets were paved with milk and bleeding honey.

Och I ken I ken, said Bap, I'm not daft. But jesus: there's not three jobs like yours in the whole of north Edinburgh!

They made arrangements. Pompey was pretty sure that the leaflet distribution mob were on the lookout for new staff, so in the morning Bap should go up to their office in Camden and fill out an application form: they'd probably start him the same afternoon. Pompey couldn't remember the address of the office offhand – he'd been taken there by somebody else himself – but finding it was easy: you just came out of the Camden Town tube, took the first on the left, and it was about a hundred yards along the road, above a hairdresser's or a barber's or something. Pompey said he would go with Bap to Victoria on his way to work, and make sure he got on the right line.

So at half eleven the next day Bap was coming up an escalator in Camden Town tube station. As he arrived in the entrance hall, he stepped to one side out of the stream of folk spewing along in front of and behind him, and leant back against a barrier, looking around. There was a problem. His directions had been to take the road on the left after leaving the station, but how exactly was he meant to get out? There were three fucking exits! There was one over on the right side of the hall: okay, to make life easy for a minute that could be forgotten about. But then there was a main door onto a wide pavement with a big road junction beyond it, and there was a smaller door to the left of that, leading somewhere else.

Fuck. Bap'd borrowed a shirt and tie off of Pompey; there was no need of a jacket, it was that fucking hot. But now he was starting to sweat. He looked from one door to the other for a minute, then walked over to the leftmost one and out.

There was a sign by the entrance: Kentish Town Road. Was this part of London in Kent? Or was Kent a

small part of London? But this was Camden, Camden
Town. In the name of shite. Maybe this area was just
like Kent, Kent-ish. Fuck's sake: it didn't matter. This
route would have to do for starters, he could always
come back and try one of the others.

Bap walked slowly down the road for a few minutes
till he came to a junction; a smaller street was leading
away to the left. The first road on the left? He went down
it, watching out for hairdresser's. There weren't any,
there were no shops of any kind; in fact there was fuck-
all on the street, and within a couple of minutes it joined
a main road again . . . Camden High Street! And about
fifty yards away was the tube station he'd just come out
of. He looked around. Across the road and slightly
along there was a hairdresser's, but it seemed to have
flats above it, not offices at all. Anyway, it wasn't to the
left of the station. Well, it was in a way: it was left exit,
then first left, then across and to the left again a bit.
Surely Pompey could just've said turn right out of the
tube? Hih. Time to try the second option: out the main
door of the station and first left from there.

As he walked back towards the station, Bap checked
his watch, nearly noon. The sun was extremely hot. He
loosened the tie, undid the top button of the shirt, which
was small for him anyway. He passed what must have
been the exit from the right side of the station hall, and
then the pavement widened out and he was in front of
the main door. Now, if he stood here, the street on his
left was . . . Camden Road. Well, Kentish Town Road
was actually further to the left, but in fact behind him as
he stood, whereas Camden Road was at a perfect angle
to the left of ninety degrees, more or less. Anyway, he'd
already tried Kent so . . .

Camden Road looked promising: there were a lot of
shops, also some pubs, offices. So far, however, no sign
of a barber's or the like. There was a manicurist's, advertising false fingernails – surely Pompey couldn't've
meant that? Or maybe he could, the dense bastard. This

fuck up was his fault almost entirely. Something would have to be said, even though the fucker was doing him a favour in a way.

The road crossed over a canal; there was a bad smell coming up off the water. At the far side of the bridge Bap stopped and stood against a wall in a bit of shade. This was getting beyond a fucking joke: he was crawling with sweat, his feet were getting weary in their trainers, and he had the beginnings of a sore head. Plus of course there was no sign of the fucking leaflet distribution office, or even a bastarding hairdresser's. He could ask a London bobby. Could he fuck! He looked at his watch: nearly one. Right: decision time. At one o'clock he would jack it in, if he hadn't found the place by then he'd have a pint somewhere, jump on to a train and head back south. Maybe he would get Pompey to draw him a map and come back tomorrow. Or maybe this hassle was god's way of saying, forget it shithead. Maybe he'd get an evening paper and look for something in the classifieds, or ask at a few pubs if they were needing barstaff. What was the time? One minute past. Right, fuck it: the game's a bogey.

Bap scanned the street. There was a wine-bar type place across the way, but that looked a bit dodgy. Hold on though: a sign at the junction up ahead pointing to Caledonian Road . . . fuck's sake, that sounded good, that sounded pretty fucking homely. Caledonian Road! There would have to be a few good pubs along there . . . he'd maybe even be able to get heavy. Bap crossed the roadway at the lights and headed off towards the place.

Half an hour later he was still walking. Occasionally there would be another sign pointing to Caledonian Road, but the street itself was nowhere to be seen. This was desperate. There are many things in a life that folk not living that life would call desperate, if they kent about them, but this was a bad situation from the inside as well; no, not a bad situation, no, but a desperate situation, aye. Desperate measures were called for:

something would have to be said, asked. There was a bus stop ahead. But only a lassie at it by herself, better not to make any approaches there. But now an old guy was joining her.

Eh excuse me pal, do you ken how far it is to eh Caledonian Road?

The old guy shuffled back slightly, and a worried look came over his face. What? he said.

Eh Caledonian Road, how much further is it like? Aye, it is along this road eh no?

The man looked up and down the pavement, seeming to be in a bit of a panic about something. Sorry, he said, sorry, goodbye. He turned away.

Bap sighed, looked up and down the road as well, and sighed again. He looked at his watch.

If you're looking for Caledonian Road tube it's about twenty minutes in that direction. The lassie was speaking.

What? Oh great, thanks, said Bap. Twenty minutes, jesus. He drew his hand across his forehead, wiping off some of the sweat. Eh Caledonian Road tube, would that be on Caledonian Road itself?

I don't know, said the girl, I think so, probably. Anyway, it's that way, a mile or so.

Well that's great, said Bap. Thanks a lot, I'll get going then. The girl didn't say anything, so Bap started walking on in the same direction as before, the direction she had pointed to. But after a few steps he slowed down and then came to a halt. Fuck it, twenty minutes, fuck it. He turned round and started walking back the way he had just come, moving quickly. In a minute he was passing the old buftie and the lassie at the bus stop; he called out as he strode past: Changed my mind actually, saw a likely place about ten minutes ago, do me fine!

The heat was really getting to him, jesus fuck, the heat and the tramping around these godforsaken streets. Was there no end to the place? He could've walked from Pilton to Craigmillar in this time! But back

a wee bit he had passed under an old bridge of some
kind, an old railway bridge or something, and there had
been a bar, a public house in the shade of the arch,
directly underneath it in fact, right out of the sun
completely; the beer would be fine and cold, and the air
would be cool and quiet, and Bap would get his head
together there no bother. And then out to face London
again. But in a few hours, a few nicely numbing hours:
if he drank enough cold beer, then he could walk around
top hole jeeves for the rest of the day: an internal
refrigeration system, that was what he needed.

This was it. The name painted on the glass of the
door: VICTOR BLYTON'S. Bap pushed the door open
and walked in, smiling. He ordered a pint of bitter and a
cheese toastie. That came to two fifty apparently. The
barman looked on in amazement, mouth open, eyebrows raised, as Bap made to hand over three pound
notes.

Where did you get those from? he said.

What? Eh . . . Edinburgh.

Well well well. And when was this?

Yesterday forenoon! God's sake!

Sorry my friend, but I can't take these.

There's nothing wrong with them!

So you say, so you say. But people won't want this
kind of thing in their change. Sorry, but that's the way
it is. Have you not got any proper money, the legal
tender and all that?

Bap loosened his tie completely, took it off, and
stuffed it into his trouser pocket. I don't know, he said,
I'll have a look. He took his wallet out. What had the
post office given him? An assortment, a variety pack:
Clydesdale, Clydesdale, Royal Bank, BANK OF
ENGLAND, thank christ: a tenner.

Here you go pal, ten English pounds. The barman
took the note and went away to the till. Hih! Thought I
was going to die of thirst there!

The barman came back with his change: a pile of

coins. We used to get people in here trying to pass
Scottish money quite a lot, but not any more; these days
we hardly get any jocks in here at all.

I'm not surprised you cunt. Bap scraped up his
change and said, Well cheers anyway pal, as he moved
away from the bar.

The place wasn't exactly crowded, but there seemed to
be at least one person at every table, nobody talking,
everybody just staring into space. But over at a table
near the fruit machine there was some kind of conversation going on and, jesus wept, that sounded like a
fucking Glasgow accent! What a beautiful noise! Bap
walked over towards the Scottish voice. There were two
guys at the table, looking like builder's labourers: glaur
on the boots, cement dust on the breeks, red fucking
weather-burnt faces and arms sticking out of the muckit
teeshirts.

Can I just butt in for a minute here? said Bap, putting
his toastie down on their table and raising his pint to
them in a kind of salute. They looked up. It's just it's like
music to my ears to hear a Scottish accent after getting
nothing but fucking English all day.

The two men looked at each other. One of them was
beginning to frown, but the other one laughed: Fed up
with the bloody sassenachs are you? he said.

What the fuck're you talking about? said the other
one, now frowning at his mate instead of at Bap.
Actually he had more of an Irish accent than a Scottish
one.

Eh, I could've swore I heard a Glasgow accent there...

You did, you did! said the first guy. That was pretty
fucking well heard of you son, a good bit of listening: to
spot a Glasgow accent across a crowded room at thirty
paces, and me never been there in my life!

Yeah, and me neither! Born and bred in Wicklow,
County Cork!

Och, sorry, I'll eh ... Bap went to pick up his toastie,
but the first guy waved at a free chair at the next table.

No no, come on, pull that over, this is interesting: I must say that was fucking well spotted.

Bap sat down. But how if you've never been there . . .

Yes, what are you talking about, Alec?

My father, my poor old fucking mother and father! They were one hundred per cent Glaswegian. You know that Des . . .

Oh, yes, maybe so . . .

No maybe about it! They came down here, oh, in the forties I suppose it was pal. To work in the steel mills. They were building them up at the time you see.

What, in Camden?

What! Naw! Corby, that's where we're from pal, Corby, a great steel town it was and anyway they needed a great heap of men to do the work you see, and who had the expertise? The fucking Clydesiders did, the good old fucking red Clydesiders! So what did they do? They just fucking carted them down here by the busload, set them up in wee terraced houses . . . fucking social engineering, man! My old man and my old dear, they came from Partick; that's just outside Glasgow eh?

Eh, I think it's actually part of Glasgow. These days anyhow . . .

Aye, anyway, there you have it though: born and brought up in England, but a pure Glasgow accent. Well, pure enough for you to spot it straight off.

Cheers jock! said Des, raising his glass to Alec, then finishing the beer. You'll have another?

Alec looked at his watch and said, Aye aye, same again. Here, listen pal: let me get you one too, it'd be a pleasure!

Aye ok, said Bap, I'll have a pint of heavy, bitter, please.

Alec chucked a pound coin onto the table and Des went away up to the bar. That's not a Glasgow voice you have there yourself, is it?

Naw, Edinburgh actually.

Edinburgh! That means you and me should be fighting eh?

Ach, I reckon we're on the same side down here.

I'll drink to that. If Des ever comes back with them. Oi, come on Finn Macool you slow bastard! Working at this speed is fine, but you should go up a gear during drinking hours!

Des shouted something from the bar; Alec gave him the fingers, grinning, then lent over towards Bap. Of course, he's no more Irish than I am Scottish. Born and bred in County Cork my arse! His parents, maybe, but he's a scouser; born there anyway, lived in Corby twenty year at least. I know he has, cause I've worked with him that long. In the steel first, then in this game. But try telling him any of that! He's proud of the Irish thing. And why not, eh, why not?

Des arrived back, slid three pints onto the table, and sat down.

I was just asking our friend here . . . what is your name anyway?

Eh, Bap, I get called Bap.

Des and Alec burst out laughing.

What the fuck kind of name is that when it's at home? said Des.

Well I used to be a baker, you see.

They looked at him. Oh I get it, said Alec after a minute, Bap as in bun, as in roll . . .

Rolling down the glens, said Des.

Aye, said Bap, Bap as in floury bap, bread roll.

So is that a popular name in Scotland is it? said Des, and laughed again.

Popular name for bakers, said Des, or ex-bakers.

Aha, we're getting to the heart of it now, said Alec. You're down here looking for work, eh? I could see that look in your eye, could see it right away. We know all about that look, eh Desmond?

Too fucking right we do, thanks to you and your fucking militant nonsense.

Been agitating the proleteriat have you? said Bap.

If only, if only, said Alec. Nah, I was just looking out for myself, safety you know, and my mates. I mean there's no point in getting yourself killed for the sake of some yuppie block of flats, is there?

Bap shook his head. So did they give you the big E then?

No, not exactly, they just never gave us a start, neither today nor yesterday. You just have to turn up at six, see, and the gaffer takes on as many as he's needing for the day. Except he was short of a few bodies today and yesterday, and he still never took us.

Not since you opened your big fucking mouth about the scaffolding.

Och, come on! You saw the state of it.

Hold on a minute, said Bap. You mean if I turned up there the morn's morn I might get taken on?

Yeah, but you wouldn't want to be, said Alec, the gaffer's a stupid fucking arsehole.

We'll try somewhere else tomorrow, said Des, we'll get something in a day or two, no bother. There's a lot on the go as long as you're not too worried about pension plans and the Safety at Work Act. And as long as you don't go around with a big mouthed bastard like this cunt.

I reserve the right not to get killed, said Alec.

Bap put down his pint in the middle of a swallow. Hold on a minute. Did you not say that you live in Corby? or was it you used to just?

No, still do, said Des, both of us.

And you have to be at the sites for six in the morning?

Aye, said Alec.

Well what time do you leave Corby then? I mean isn't that away up in the fucking Midlands or something? I mean I've just thought about this: what's going on here?

Yeah, it's a bastard, said Alec. Four o'clock, that's when we leave, four of the a.m. And get back at seven or eight at night. The roads are quieter in the morning you see.

Jesus christ!

What can you do? said Des. I mean at least it's motorway all the way down, and Alec's got the car.

On your bike and look for work, eh! said Bap.

But we're luckier than some, said Alec. I mean what about you for example, you've come four hundred fucking miles, we only come a hundred! At least we have that possibility! I mean you couldn't travel down from Edinburgh to work every day, you'd have to rent a place here; and how would you afford that, eh?

Bap shook his head, downed the rest of his bitter. I think I'd rather not have that possibility at all, he said. And that is saying something, that is really fucking saying something. I mean I had certain ideas, you ken, vague ideas about . . .

TIME GENTLEMEN PLEASE. The barman was banging glasses down on the bar. EVERYBODY OUT PLEASE THANK YOU!

What the hell's this, said Bap, looking at his watch, Two thirty?

Two thirty, closing time, said Des.

Well, where's the nearest shop that's an all dayer?

What? said Des.

Everywhere closes at half past two, said Alec. Afternoon closing, you know.

Fuck me! said Bap. I'd forgotten that completely, the uncivilized state of things down here. Right: that settles it.

Gohar Kordi

It was in 1960 that I entered the Blind School in Isfahan, Iran. It was a residential school for blind girls run by the English Missionaries. My education about the English started then. I learned that the English were punctual, godly; when the bell rang for the prayer we had to be down in the hall promptly and if anyone dared to be late for a minute, such as newcomers, we had a long lecture about the importance of being punctual, especially for God, because at that time God was present in the Prayer Room. Then this prompt response extended from God to them, the Missionaries.

I witnessed how they dealt with Death. Elizabeth, while there, lost her father. When the news broke, Elizabeth disappeared. She's gone to the Bishop's house for a few days to be quiet, we were told. We were given strict instructions not to say anything about it to her when she returned. I could see her in my mind in the Bishop's house in the spare room all alone with a few books. At times she had meals on her own in her room too, and went for long walks on her own. That is how the English do it, we were told. We considered this extremely civilized. It was modern to us, totally different from our experience of dealing with death. What must they think of us when they see how we deal with death, we wondered amongst ourselves, feeling ashamed of our ways?

I remembered my mother mourning my father's death, how she howled and wailed in a group of women, hit her head and tore her hair, how she voiced her grief, 'You've made my children fatherless, my home has lost its caretaker, I've been left all alone, how am I going to cope without you, with all the responsibilities, all on my own, how am I going to manage all on my own, what am I going to answer the children when they ask me where is their father, where have you gone, why have you left us, how am I going to bring up our children all on my own, my poor children, my poor children, left father-less?'

With these words she would express her grief as well as her anger at his early death, that he had left her so early. She would express her children's anguish and distress as well as her own to come, at their growing up without their father. She would talk about their future, it would touch the heart of everyone. Those words, with tears, would draw more tears from everyone else's eyes. The people around her, relatives, friends and neigh-bours would understand, would hear her words, sense her anguish, all would be heard, would be felt, would be shared in a group, her grief and loss had become a group grief and loss.

For up to seven days she was surrounded by people day and night, not left alone for a minute. In this period she did not have to worry about day-to-day chores such as shopping, cooking, cleaning and so on, all those jobs were done by the family, she was given time to grieve.

On the seventh day we all went to the cemetery in a big group, everyone had a good cry and Mother repeated her sayings again, then all came home together to a lunch prepared by some of the family members who stayed behind. The rest of that day was spent in calming Mother down, soothing her, comforting her.

'Now, come on now, it is enough crying now, you've

cried enough, no more tears left in you, for your children's sake you must stop, you have to concentrate on your life now, on your future, on your children,' they all would say. They all comforted her, advised her and left wishing us all good health and long life.

After that day the distant relatives, friends and neighbours left but close relatives kept in contact with us, they would pop in to do a bit of shopping and cleaning now and then. Sometimes one of them would come and stay the night so that being left alone would be a gradual process.

On the fortieth day, again a big gathering took place, all went to the cemetery together and on returning the family helped my mother take off her black clothes. From then on we were left more on our own. Mother was ready, more or less, to stand on her own feet now and start picking up the pieces. But a senior member of the family, in this case my mother's brother, kept a close eye on us. He would call around often and any problems Mother would discuss with him or ask his advice, financial matters and such. In this way we had ongoing support. What would have been the work of psycho-therapy in the West for years was done by the family in these forty days.

I learned that the English were forthright and matter of fact. They would say things like, 'This is not your house, when you have your own house do whatever you like!' And yet, we were constantly told that this was our home. The English had their own quarters, their own cook, their own maids, they had two maids between three of them, full-time. We had fantasies about their toilets, their bathroom, 'What is it like?' we would ask the maids. 'Well, it is like a seat, you see, the toilet.' 'Do you mean they sit on it?' 'I presume so.' We thought that was very grand, very civilized. 'You see they are used to *that* kind of life,' we talked among ourselves. 'And the bath, it is a big, big container. To wash you put water in it and get inside it.' 'You mean, you sit in the water?'

'Yes, I suppose so.' To sit in hot water, with foam around you, what a luxury!

They did not eat Iranian food, Iranian food did not suit their stomachs they said. 'What must English food be like?' we kept wondering and asking the maids. 'We don't know, we never see them eating.' They did not like Iranian music, especially Iranian classical singing. 'It sounds as though they've got tummy-ache,' they said. This embarrassed us. The only music they listened to was church music.

We felt ashamed of our way of life compared with theirs. For instance, our toilets were flat. We squatted on them and washed ourselves instead of wiping with paper as they did. And as for the bath, we used the showers. In every detail our way of life was different from theirs and we considered ours inferior.

We were told we were very much a family there. We called the Principal, mama - mother, something between maman in Farsi and mummy in English. And the rest of the staff were Aunties. The Deputy Principal wanted to be called Hallejan - Halle, in Farsi 'aunt' - jan, 'dear', 'Dear Aunt'. At certain times of the day we were not allowed to go to their quarters, they were either eating or it was rest time, or they had visitors for meetings and suchlike. This did not fit in with the family concept for us.

When I arrived in England in 1971 for treatment for my eye, I was met by a clergyman and driven to a Missionary Guest House. He talked all the way non-stop about his parish and neighbouring parishes and what he did there and so on. I learned that with the English you have to 'talk' in company, remaining silent was considered somewhat impolite. I tried to make intelligible responses, I knew I was doing it wrong all the time, I was too nervous.

In the Missionary Guest House I met a couple with a young family who had worked as missionaries in Iran. They often joked about Iranians, how stupid and slow they were. For instance, how a shopkeeper had not prepared an account, 'I'll give you up to Friday if you still haven't got it done I shall be going on holiday, I won't pay you,' one of them said. 'Friday came and he still hadn't done it. I didn't expect it either. So I left.' 'And you spent the money on holiday, hey?' remarked one of them laughing, then all had a good laugh. When they talked amongst themselves about Iran or other countries they had worked in, it was with mockery, they joked about how uncivilized, backward the people were, how difficult it was working with them. They constantly prayed for strength to cope.

People staying there were either missionaries or interested in missionary work. They had meetings at weekends and holidays, when a totally different attitude would surface, positive images of these countries. They would give talks and show slides, tell something about the country and the people: 'Say in Iran, if you ask a passer-by, "Do you know where Sarsabil Street is?" "Not far at all, only a few minutes' walk, walk straight on, you will come to it, on the right," they will say. You might find you have to walk half an hour to get to it. The reason for this is that they don't wish to disappoint you by saying "half-an-hour", so they say "a few minutes",' they would explain.

In the Missionary Guest House people always asked detailed questions about my life and my family, yet they never said anything about themselves to me. This made me feel resentful, I felt they talked about me, I felt I was on show. They would ask things like, 'What do you eat in Iran? Do you know what a taxi is?' Guests came and went there all the time, I did not feel that I got to know anyone and yet they knew all about me. I learned that the English were private.

I had learned that England was a rich country, a just, fair society, where everyone lived in comfort, equal, happy. I assumed it was perfect. When I first arrived I met Cathy in the hospital. She was in her seventies and had worked for over fifty years in a hospital, from the age of twelve, she said, and during the war she worked day and night, during the day as a cleaner, and in the night on the switchboard. Now she lived in a bedsit in London and relied on volunteers to bring her to hospital and do her shopping. I remember one day we had fish for lunch, halibut it was, she looked forward to it eagerly saying she could not remember when she had last tasted halibut, she was longing for it, the way she talked about it, it was as though having halibut on its own was a good enough reason for coming into hospital. Is this how the individual is rewarded, looked after, after having given half a century of their life to this country, I wondered?

I met Dolly later, a small, timid woman, who dragged her feet when she walked and spoke nervously, especially when men were around. She had always been nervous of men, she said. She had worked fifty odd years in a department store, manual jobs such as cleaning. She lived in a bedsit, she was all alone, not married, had no friends, she had one sister and one niece, and at Christmas she went to her niece and that was her major outing for the year. I remember the conversation one day between her and another woman who also lived alone upstairs. They talked about loneliness with pain. 'Sometimes you don't see a soul for days.' The other one agreed. 'Yes, especially at the weekends and holidays, you get fed up with watching "the box" all the time. Sometimes I start talking to myself just to hear my own voice, just to know that I am still alive, otherwise you think you're going crazy, don't you, silence for ever? Sometimes I wait, I wish someone would come and knock on the door and come in. The tea is there, the milk is there, the sugar is there, everything is ready, if only someone would come.' 'Yes,' the other one agreed, 'but nobody does come, do they?'

The depth of poverty and loneliness I experienced in these two women shocked me. I did not expect this in

England from the English.

I had witnessed as a child my mother's sufferings at the hands of the landlord in the peasant society of Iran – poverty, yes – but loneliness, isolation, she did not know.

As for the treatment of children here, Matthew, a father, said to me, 'Avocados are too good to waste on children.' He loved avocados himself.

And here I witnessed how some friends put their baby in the farthest room in the house so as not to hear his cries at night. One girl said once, 'This holiday, I've managed at last to stop my baby crying in the night.' 'How did you do that?' I asked. 'Well this house where we were staying was an old house with thick walls, I put Ben in the farthest room so I did not hear him crying, now he's stopped crying in the night.' How could she, I wondered? In my experience children were regarded almost as sacred, especially babies, they never were left alone day or night. Blessings were said when the babies were handled.

The English, I learned, were rational, practical, pragmatic. They plan everything, predict events, have control over them, prepare themselves for them. How far can this go, I wondered?

A friend sat outside my house for twenty minutes in her car until it was time for our meeting to come in. It had to be half past twelve: not later, not before.

I was shocked when first I experienced a mother telling her child off for crying because he had fallen over. 'Look, you've made a hole in the ground!' she shouted to him. The child stopped for a second, 'Oh!' I went forward, stretching my hand to stroke him, 'Oh no! he doesn't need that.' The mother quickly moved the child away. This contrasted with the words of that West Indian woman I know who once said, 'When a child is in pain, you have to feel their pain, only then will they get comforted.'

One day, my five-year-old son was trying to show a

schoolfriend his imaginary hovercraft over the garden wall. 'Where is this?' The little boy eagerly asked me. 'It's in his mind,' I whispered. 'He wouldn't understand that,' the mother replied, 'I'm a science teacher, my children are practical,' she said.

I met a friend in the hospital, Angela, an occupational therapist. She took me out one day in her lunch-hour, I bought some fruit and we sat out on the grass having our lunch. I offered her some fruit. 'Are you sure you are giving all this to me?' she asked, with disbelief in her voice, 'can you spare it?' I still remember her surprise at my giving and my surprise at her surprise.

In answer to a question the English never say 'Yes, I know this.' Instead they say 'I *think* this is' – 'I think the high tide is at seven o'clock,' although absolutely sure it is at seven o'clock, since it's just been announced on the news. They never directly disagree with you, they say, 'Yes, but . . .' then state their point of view.

If they do a favour they expect one back. A mum said businesslike, 'I feel I have so many points I've looked after my niece for a week.' Lizzie said, 'My brother's moving in to live with us, I know he's going to expect me to do his washing so I said to him if you do baby-sitting for me I'll do your washing, now we know where we are with each other.'

If they say they will do something they have to stick to it, sometimes at any cost. A change of mind is not allowed, not accepted, they have fear of anything foreign, strange, different.

Just before we moved to this house I bumped into a group of women in the road chatting. 'Hello,' I introduced myself, 'I will soon be moving into this road, No 22, I hope you will be able to give me some help and tell me about local facilities for childcare and things like that.' They all went dead silent. I think they panicked – a blind woman with a foreign name and a baby, did they have to look after me? Foreign, blind, with a baby, each was enough to frighten them.

DYNASTY RERUNS: TREASURE HOUSES OF GREAT BRITAIN

Lynne Tillman

The banner for the show stretched across the width of the National Gallery's East Building in Washington. TREASURE HOUSES OF GREAT BRITAIN, FIVE HUNDRED YEARS OF PRIVATE PATRONAGE AND ART COLLECTING. The letters were gold on a royal blue background, edged with a majestic red. Madame Realism hoped the show would have rooms with dioramas like those at the Musuem of Natural History – with stuffed lords and ladies at tea or in conversation or at dinner, all behind glass, all perfectly appointed. Because 'houses' was in the title, she was looking for rooms as they might have been lived in. When she thought about the past she always wanted to know, how did they live and what did they talk about?

Madame Realism entered the slide show that introduced the exhibition. A taped English voice narrated the images of beautiful countryside and enormous houses. Why aren't these called palaces or even mansions, she wondered. The Englishman's voice explained: 'British houses are as much a part of the landscape as the oaks and acorns'; the people in these houses, 'vessels of civilization,' developed a 'civilized outlook, which helped to produce parliamentary democracy, as well as the ideals that helped shaped Western civilization.' The term 'civilized outlook' set Madame Realism's teeth on edge. Houses natural like the scenery? The divine right of houses? She doubted that something could be both natural and civilized at the same time.

Accompanied by the disembodied voice of J. Carter Brown, the director of the National Gallery, on the audioguide, Madame Realism entered the first rooms, which were called 'From the Castle to the Country House.' Carter Brown told her that the country houses began in 1485, with the accession of the first Tudor to the throne. With relative calm in England and Wales, the castle becomes house because it no longer needs defence - high walls and moats. Madame Realism thought there was always some need for defence, and moats and high walls were perfect metaphors for human ones. Listening to Carter Brown's narration, she felt she was back in grade school. His voice, friendly and authoritative, recited dates and facts that jerked classroom memories. Back then she'd absorbed things wholesale, the way kids do, but now she was able to remind herself that there isn't one history, there are at least two. The official version and the unofficial, whose dates were not taught in grade school - the history of those without access to power. There was no doubt which version this would be, inaugurated as it was by Charles and Di, and funded in part by the British government and the Ford Motor Co.

Madame Realism stared hard at the portrait attributed to Rowland Lockey of Elizabeth Hardwick, Countess of Shrewsbury (ca. 1600). Bess of Hardwick had four husbands, outlived them all and inherited everything, making her the richest woman in England, next to Elizabeth the Queen. Bess's almost heartshaped hair frames a resolute face that is cut off from its body by a high white collar. That old devil issue, the mind/body split, popped into her mind but did it apply to Bess? This portrait was not meant to imply personality or psychology, but, like the other portraits in these rooms, to be emblematic of position and power. Everyone was holding sceptres, wearing important jewels, or being represented in allegories that assure their right of succession and that of their dynasties. Even so, Madame Realism wondered if Old Bess was bawdy like the wife of Bath, what with four husbands – more husbands even than Alexis on TV's *Dynasty* – and were she and the Queen friends? In *Elizabeth I: The Rainbow Portrait* (ca. 1600), attributed to Marcus Gheeraerts the younger, the Queen wears a cloak and dress that have eyes and ears embroidered all over them. J. Carter Brown informs Madame Realism, and others standing with her in front of the painting, that this means Elizabeth had many informers in her employ, maintaining power through a spy system in which she also used her servants. Again Madame Realism thought about *Dynasty*, and imagined that Elizabeth I might have been like paranoid Alexis and Bess of Hardwick like trusting Krystle. Guiltily she looked around her and wondered if anyone else was making such plebeian comparisons.

'There are many symbols everywhere,' Madame Realism heard one woman say to another. 'Everything means something else.' They were standing in the Jacobean Long Gallery, modeled after the picture gallery in the background of Daniel Mytens' portrait of the Countess of Arundel, Alatheia Talbot. Madame Realism and others are directed by the audioguide to pretend they are in the Countess's house, to stroll down the hall and gaze at the paintings. On cue she and several others move in unison. Madame Realism halted in front of the painting of *Barbara, Lady Sydney, with Six Children*, again by Gheeraerts the younger (1596). How had Lady Sydney survived six childbirths? Mother and children look identical, as if stamped rather than painted. Clearly dynasty isn't concerned with individuals, only continuity. So it's faceless. Maybe that was what was so funny about *Dynasty*. Sons and daughters disappear, are thought dead, then reappear with entirely different faces that should be unrecognizable but aren't. Of course the series has to continue, even when principal actors leave for other jobs. The series must continue, she thought, looking around her. And then she heard a man say to his companion. 'They don't have beauty. It's the one thing the British don't have.' What about, she wanted to argue, Vivien Leigh, Vanessa Redgrave, Annie Lennox, Bob Hoskins. She suspected that the man, awed by how much these people did have, may have been comforting himself with the idea that no one has it all.

Madame Realism would never have been invited, in that time, to stroll down the Countess's picture gallery. The British don't fool themselves about all being one happy classless family. She appreciated *The Tichborne Dole* by Gillis van Tillborch (1670), one of the few paintings on view that depicts workers or the poor, and which explained to her the origin of the term 'the dole.' The painting shows Sir Henry Tichborne and his family about to distribute bread to the poor of the village. It's a tradition, she reads in the catalogue, that exists in Tichborne to this day, even though the dole itself is under attack from Thatcher. This painting may have been made to demonstrate the worthiness of that wealthy family, but at least the poor are shown to exist, she thought to herself, which is more than can be said for Reagan's picture of America.

J. Carter Brown was talking to her over the audio-guide, his voice reassuring and almost familiar. The reign of the Tudors passed to the Stuarts in 1603, and everyone kept collecting and patronizing. Upheavals in other countries, such as French Huguenot craftsmen getting kicked out of France, added to British treasure troves. The British made a killing on social upheavals, and, Madame Realism learned, they became rich tourists, taking what came to be known as the Grand

Tour, the title of the exhibition's next rooms. 'The Grand Tour' is dated as beginning in 1714, when Richard Boyle, 3rd Earl of Burlington, made his first jaunt abroad, returning to Chiswick and building a villa there after designs by Palladio. What the British brought back – according to Carter Brown, 'the fruits of these tours' – were 'souvenirs'. A villa in Chiswick, paintings by Canaletto, all these Roman sculptures and busts – souvenirs? Two Venetian Lattimo Plates (1741) did look like contemporary tourist views of Venice on dinner plates. Horace Walpole carried back twenty-four of them in his luggage; she wondered whether he and his family had ever eaten off them.

There were paintings of English gents posing among Roman ruins – Narcissistic Neoclassicism. *William Gordon* by Pompeo Batoni (1766) is wearing a kilt, with a view of the Colosseum in the background and a statue of Roma on a pedestal sharing the foreground – the spotlight – with him. Colonel Gordon's kilt was draped like a toga, reminding her of a letter to *The Times* she'd read when she was in London one summer. A man wrote the editor suggesting that, because it was so beastly hot, men wear togas rather than suits, ties and bowlers. To maintain class distinctions, different kinds and colours of stripes could be sewn on the hems of the togas, and, of course, men could still carry umbrellas. Lots of Englishmen walking around the City in togas carrying umbrellas would turn the English summer into a Monty Python skit. Madame Realism laughed out loud, attracting some attention.

A china serving dish shaped like a boar's head made her chortle quietly; porcelain figurines of prominent 18th-century actors were objects any fan could relate to. In gift shops across the U.S. today there'd be something similar – a little figurine of John Forsythe, maybe. Embarrassed to find *Dynasty* so much on her mind – she might explain to scoffers and nonviewers that she watched only the reruns, as if that made her less

adolescent than the rest of the nation who were
watching it on prime time — she heard a man say to his
young daughter, 'That's where we got off our gondola to
go to our hotel.' They were in front of a view of
commerce in the Campo Santa Maria Formosa in
Venice by Canaletto, one of the souvenirs J. Carter
Brown had mentioned earlier. As accurate as any
tourist snapshot.

Madame Realism entered the room called 'Chinoiserie
and Porcelain' and walked immediately to the state bed.
It had elaborately embroidered Chinese silk curtains
and looked pretty narrow for a bed of state, but then
how many heads of state were expected to lie in it at one
time anyway? State bed or sex and politics. Musing
about 18th-century sex lives of the rich and famous, she
wished that Carter Brown would get even more familiar.
But instead he directed her to the tiaras and crowns,
which rested on shelves in a glass cabinet, so gaudy
they looked fake. One woman nudged another and said
conspiratorially, 'That's why the people rebelled.'
Madame Realism wanted to tell this woman and her
friend, if they didn't already know, about Guy Fawkes
Day, when the English celebrate an abortive attempt to
overthrow King James I. Were they the only people in
the world to celebrate a failed revolution?

The exhibition's brochure claimed that the love of
landscape was 'essentially English', but to Madame
Realism the way the English took the piss out of each
other was even more essential. But wait, she said to
herself, what did they mean by essential? Natural? By
now she was in a room called 'The Sporting Life,'
surrounded by paintings of animals, primarily horses,
like those done by George Stubbs. There were gentlemen
in red hunting jackets, men on horseback in black
jackets, and men surrounded by live dogs and dead
game. Britain's contemporary Animal Liberation Front
might have something to say about the English love of
landscape, populated as it is by dead prey hung next to

portraits of dogs who were much loved by their owners.

Sentiment was very definitely in the air, what with these sweet animal portraits and the works in the last, 'Pre-Raphaelite and Romantic' room. *Love Among the Ruins* by Burne-Jones (1894) was just the kind of painting she might have had a print of on her wall, when she was a teenager, as consolation for yet another broken heart. Now Madame Realism wished she could steal the title, just as Burne-Jones had stolen it from Browning. She liked the title much better than the picture; it was tougher than the wistful backward-looking image. But was that really true? she asked herself, wondering why this kind of adolescent sentiment didn't appeal to her anymore and *Dynasty*'s did.

Parody, she told herself, and walked into the last room, called 'Epilogue,' which was devoted to family photo albums of some late 19th- and early 20th-century collectors and patrons. By comparison with the rest of the exhibition, 'Epilogue' was homey and dimly lit, small in scale in both size of room and in what was on display. Madame Realism thought it odd that an exhibition devoted to the display of wealth and power should end on so mundane a note, though it did allow the spectator a moment to reorient, as in a decompression chamber, for reentry into ordinary life.

Spotlights shone on the albums and photographic portraits. The differences between the paintings and these photographs were overwhelming. Family photo albums compared with paintings meant to last forever. Casual pictures in black and white and posed portraits in magnificent colour. The lords and ladies 'captured' at unguarded moments, letting us know that, in the end, we're all 'just folks'. Especially in these dimly lit rooms.

A small plain book caught Madame Realism's eye. It was, the caption read, a scrapbook of photographs of the servants of a particular household, taken by the lady of the house. Madame Realism wanted to see these photographs, but she couldn't because the book was barely open. These were the invisible people, part of unofficial history, who built the country houses and packed up the souvenirs so that they wouldn't get broken on the trip home. Carter Brown directed everyone's attention to the doll's house replica of an English country house, attributed to Thomas Chippendale (ca. 1745). It was behind glass at the end of the room, but this wasn't the diorama she had hoped for. There was a very long line, and Madame Realism stood in it for a while, only to leave the crowd and return to the small, plain book with its glimpse into . . . The repressed, she said to herself. It's like the return of the repressed. She wondered what Carter Brown looked like . . . Vincent Price?

When Madame Realism got outside, it was snowing. The White House was surprisingly and deceptively invisible. The young black taxidriver, wearing a Coptic cross earring, explained that D.C. had been designed by mystics and visionaries, and that through their writings he knew that the end of the world was at hand. 'God makes no accidents,' he warned.

Back home, Madame Realism lay in bed, thinking about the exhibition and reading Virginia Woolf's *Orlando*, to satisfy her desire to know how people lived and what they talked about in the treasure houses of Britain. There's a wonderful scene in which Elizabethan poet Nick Greene has dinner at Orlando's country house, and though the poet mocks his host and his efforts at poetry, still Orlando 'paid the pension quarterly' to Greene. Woolf is taking the piss out of patrons, while the exhibition had pumped them up. Nothing is sacred in *Orlando*. Madame Realism reached the page where Orlando changes from a man into a woman. She put the book on her lap. Was she expected to be grateful to or respectful of the aristocracy for having first created and then preserved Western civilization? The show's banner could have read: WESTERN CIVILIZATION BROUGHT TO YOU BY . . . It was too

tall an order, and besides, respect was something
Madame Realism didn't like to be asked to give. Just too
much to swallow, she said to her cat, who had sat
himself down on the sex-change page. Closing her eyes,
she had a hypnogogic vision. If Steven, the son in
Dynasty who goes from gay to straight to gay, were to
come back as a woman, would he be a gay or a straight
woman? Madame Realism fell asleep smiling.

Grace Nichols

I leave me people, me land, me home
For reasons, I not too sure
I forsake de sun
And de humming-bird splendour
Had big rats in de floorboard
So I pick up me new-world-self
And come, to this place call England
At first I feeling like I in dream –
De misty greyness
I touching de walls to see if they real
They solid to de seam
And de people pouring from de underground system
Like beans
And when I look up to de sky
I see Lord Nelson high – too high to lie

And is so I sending home photos of myself
Among de pigeons and de snow
And is so I warding off de cold
And is so, little by little
I begin to change my calypso ways
Never visiting nobody
Before giving them clear warning
And waiting me turn in queue

Now, after all this time
I get accustom to de English life
But I still miss back-home side
To tell you de truth
I don't know really where I belaang

   Yes, divided to de ocean
   Divided to de bone

Wherever I hang me knickers – that's my home.

WHY ME?

Leena Dhingra

I couldn't possibly do that. And why me anyway? I wouldn't know where to start. Well yes, I suppose I could give it a try but I don't want to promise anything. It's just that . . . well, I need to feel touched by a topic, connected.

I put the phone down with a frown, grabbed my books, bag and coat, raced through the door and down the street and reached the bus stop breathless. I looked at my watch automatically, and then again more carefully. Could it have stopped? The second hand was going round, but . . . I asked someone, who smiled at my look of incredulity. I had arrived at the bus stop two hours early. I carried my bewilderment into the coffee shop and tried to drown it along with the froth of my cappuccino.

Why did I rush out like that? I was still frowning and my throat felt constricted. I had literally run away - from Englishness! Well, I just won't do it. I'll ring up and say that it's not for me. I started to sip my coffee. In any case, I don't have to do it if I don't want to.

Who are you trying to fool! Ha! I asked myself and returned to folding the froth into the coffee. What was it you said on the phone about needing to feel connected, affected, moved? And can you honestly say you are unaffected?

Obviously there is some problem which I shall attempt to diagnose.

Location, Sensation, Modalities, Concomitants I repeated, having decided to walk to my class in town. Location, Sensation, Modalities, Concomitants, That's what one needs for diagnosis! I remembered my homeopathy seminars . . .

Playing as a child on the Paris pavements, my ten-year-old companion asked me, 'Why do you speak in English? You're not English and you've never even been to England.'

'I don't know, but I just do. It's spoken around me.'

'Well I don't like English.'

'But why, you've never been there either.'

'And I never will! They killed Joan of Arc! *Ça me suffit!*'

'But that was ages ago!'

'And so?'

Back at home I asked my mother why we spoke in English. She shook her head, 'I know it's very bad. I am ashamed,' and immediately started to talk in Hindi, in the manner of an elementary language lesson, as though to jog my memory of my long forgotten mother tongue. In any case she didn't answer my question.

Location, Sensation, Modalities, Concominants I muttered looking around me, trying to imprint some image of elusive Englishness. The location of Englishness is clear. It's here. All around. This is it. Of course, what it is, I don't know. But this is where it's supposed to be. So the first point is: Englishness Eludes. Sensation: What does it feel like? To me, it's a constriction in the throat. A closed club. No admittance. You either are or you're not. Englishness Excludes. Modality. The procedure to find out. I could just try and ask people. See then about concomitants.

I met a friend at the college library and we went out for a coffee.

'What is Englishness? What about the "habit of command'."

'Isn't that a bit cliché or at any rate, passé?'

'Well, yes and no, You know the saying: "The fish is gone but the smell remains." The empire too may be long gone, but you'd never think it listening to the cricket commentators. For them the Imperial Sun shines on undiminishe-ed! That's Englishness! You could write about that.'

'What cricket and all that? I wouldn't know what to say.'

My friend laughed. 'And you want to write abut Englishness!'

'No I don't want to write about Englishness. I've been asked to write about it and I said I'd give it a think.' My tone was defensive and I could feel the tenseness returning.

'Well it's nothing to get upset about. Just say that you don't want to do it.'

'Yes, I think I will. And I'm not upset, it's something else . . .'

'Could it be fear?'

'But of what?'

'Fear of exposure, maybe?'

'Exposure!' I stirred my coffee. This time there was no froth to fold into it. 'Yes, maybe. I'm certainly affected by the whole idea in the strangest manner, quite paranoid. In fact I even found myself trying to diagnose it like an illness, analysing it in terms of location, sensation, modalities, concomitants.'

'What?'

'To find the correct homeopathic remedy for any condition, the symptoms are diagnosed in those terms, and the Materia Medica places them under those headings: location, sensation etc.'

My friend laughed. 'Well some people might agree

with you that Englishness was a condition of a kind. A sort of dis-ease.' He stiffened himself to illustrate his point. 'It's highly contagious as well. I think you've caught it. In fact, I think that we all get affected by it through prolonged exposure. It rubs off. You could approach your writing from that angle. No?'

I laughed. 'It's an interesting idea. But how exactly?'

'I don't know. Something about Englishness and its effect on you? Couldn't you distance yourself from it somehow?'

'I could. I could write as if it was someone else . . .'

'Yes that's right, a character from a play or a novel. You might discover something.'

'You never know. I might. But I'll give it a try. Thanks.'

'Let me know how you get along.'

I liked the idea. I got some paper and wrote: *Englishness and its effect on . . .*

I stopped to find her a name. I decided on an anagram, Neela.

Neela is a woman in her 40s, living in London. She left India, the land of her birth when she was a small child. India was partitioned and her home lost. She was brought up between India, Europe, and England. Of course today, England is a part of Europe, but when Neela was growing up, England never saw itself as a part of Europe. If it ever did, it was always as a part which was apart, separate, a 'precious stone set in the silver sea. A sceptered Isle!' Neela was aware of this difference.

But what did this difference mean to Neela? Or rather how did it feel? Europe appeared to accept her difference and individuality, whereas England demanded that she should somehow conform, assimilate, and yet at the same time, there was no way in which it was possible to really 'assimilate'. In fact it wasn't even allowed. In any case, assimilation never meant any real acceptance or belonging. Basically it grew out of the idea that what the West represented, and the English middle class best of all, was something to emulate, look up to, admire – all the rest was just a bit rude and best if it politely disappeared. This then was the paradox Neela grew up with and had to learn to grow out of.

So, in England a whole part of her personality remained buried. And she had so perfected this technique of politely disappearing, that she had to live almost half her life before she came to realize that she had almost disappeared to her own self! That self now needed to be discovered – but where? And how?

She picked up a pen, and started to write, in English.

'So she became a writer in English, but without Englishness presumably?' asked my friend when we met again.

'I wasn't just trapped in the tower, I also had the key to the door. Do you see?'

'I see that you're a hell of a lot more cheerful.'

'And do you know what I'd like to do?'

'Go out for a coffee.'

'No. Crumpets and tea.'

THE GHOST IN THE WOOD

Judith Kazantzis

She is staying with Harriet. Just one wary night, before she goes to America, at Harriet's weekend cottage in Norfolk. There is a little wood to one side of the lawn, and a large stubble field to the other. Mist is rising, a bat flies round Jen's head and then away over the thatch. An owl hoots.

'Is it always so stunning?'

'In the winter I visit Mummy in Norwich instead. I brought her out here last weekend.'

Her sister Harriet has had the cottage for two years. Harriet knows how to get a cheap mortgage. Such a place is as beyond Jen as Xanadu. Jen's two years older. She has been teaching in North Kensington. Harriet's a property consultant in Mayfair. They don't quarrel.

Suppertime and deep blue dusk. Harriet is barbecuing pork kebabs, which will be as exotic as her long hair swinging blonde white over the glowing charcoal. Jen's hair is coppery/gingery and short. Jeff loves it; he strokes his hand over her head as if she were a child. But when she gets to America she's vowed it will be longer and lighter.

'It's so like Lacings.'

'I'm a country gal at heart. Though I'm off to Singapore on Wednesday. Big deal – big development. Cheers.'

They toast her 'engagement' and Harriet's deal in red wine out of tall crystal goblets. Harriet charmingly apologizes: 'I forgot! Jeff rang before you arrived. He'll ring again. I love the Deep South honey in his voice.'

'Didn't I tell you he's a New Yorker?' she smiles back.

'Sure. What was it like being proposed to by a New York City Planner with a voice to melt molasses by?'

'Lovely.' She's not going to confide immediately. 'Could do without Mommy though. We paid her my first big visit in Brooklyn, she hadn't met me except on the phone. And all she could do,' Harriet, she says silently, what a betrayer you make me, immediately, 'all she could do was ask about the Royals, was Diana as beautiful as in *Newsweek*.'

'Yes, I suppose that would have irritated a Socialist Republican Feminist like you.'

They drink. It's a warm good wine; it hits some little sore spot. Jennifer, she scolds herself, be warm too, more affectionate. Harriet has laid on a midsummer's night farewell, just the two of us, sisters. Didn't we share a bath when we were little, ride ponies together when we were bigger? Just us, fair and dark, peas in a pod, little and large (well, I exaggerate here, she's smaller, more slender; but then Jeff, he's given me new trust in my ass).

'Won't you miss old England?'

'I'll miss the kids. But I'll be teaching again over there.'

Just before the bell on her last day, Sharon and Maria dumped a huge card on her desk: of the Statue of Liberty togged out as Batperson, all welcoming Batcape. 'Good luck and tons of love from 2.3.' X's everywhere. They were all, her included, madly laughing. Michael Morrissey looked at her with his white face. Afterwards she visited the Head. He was short and tended to get jostled crossing the playground. 'Off to the land of opportunity, are you?' he said jovially and reproach-fully. He was more concerned to get her last report on

Michael Morrissey who, now he told her, had a grown brother in the IRA and so, as the Head put it, the family had been made unwelcome in Northern Ireland. 'I'm really sorry to leave,' she said sincerely. 'I hope to teach in public schools in New York, I mean New York public schools.' 'Keep up the good work,' he waved her farewell, 'tell the next child to come in.' On the tube home she felt like crying, not because she had left, but for Sharon and Maria, not to say Michael. For herself she was relieved she didn't have to struggle to harness their zippy, anarchic minds any more to a future of filing and fast food shoppers – till for Christ's sake let's get married and turn on the telly and have some peace. Maybe in another neck of the woods, with Jeff's kind of cheerful, simple yet not stupid, certainty, she would make good . . . For, she thinks, if privileged spoiled people like her can't get off their backsides and put their money where their mouth is . . .

'I love teaching. It's just that the powers that be treat us teachers like dirt. And now with opting out . . .'

'I tend to think,' says Harriet, 'teachers in state schools get paid pretty well. What d'you think of my wine?'

'You know I wouldn't know. But, great.'

'I got given a crate of this, it's Château Margaux, by the small, fat and lecherous owner of one third of Singapore. Chin chin. Actually he was a Jap.'

Jeff, she calls. I'm homesick for you. Just a yearning only, no lust. And call, you snake – Manhattan – Norfolk. Now a tiny red salamander of lust does pierce me. I've seen salamanders in green woods north of New York, with Jeff. Call soon, you snake.

'The kebabs are brilliant.' She'd forgotten Harriet was a great cook. Harriet, fair-plaited, a tea-towel round her middle, another round her front as wide as the nuns still wore their dicky fronts at school. Helping Mummy stir the cake mixture. 'Go 'way. You can't have any. I helped, you were just reading.'

' . . . I'll do it for the Young Farmers sometime.'

'Young Farmers?'

'Not your thing. They're all scientists really, plus businessmen. I'll marry one when I've made my first million, and we'll run an enormous model farm. No hedges, and peas as high as an elephant's eye.'

'Pouring nitrates into the dykes to poison the villagers, sort of thing?'

Harriet sits calmly in her flowery chintz deckchair. She is calm too, of course.

'You really shouldn't believe those funny Green men, love, it's all a scare to queer water privatization. Just because the Government's doing so fabulously well.'

'Harriet . . .'

'You do-gooders are always so serious . . . Listen.'

It's just about dark and Harriet's hair flies out and glimmers as she moves her head. 'I think I heard Maggie just then. She flies around her wood all night. Like the Holy Ghost, ascending and descending on the foreheads of the Apostles, only in Maggie's case it's voles and fieldmice.'

'Maggie is?'

'My barn owl. Isn't England wonderful, Jen . . .'

'But now I want to ask you something, seriously,' Harriet's voice softens. Now they can't see each other's face, just Harriet's hair glimmering. Jen feels sad. Whatever it is, now the moment's here that she came for, that she half foresaw, she won't tell. A long train ride to an owl called Maggie. She drinks up.

'I've been wondering, now it seems, well, you're leaving, why *did* you turn Socialist? Was it the nuns at school? Or Daddy, with all his William Morris-type talk. We turned out so different – I'm curious.'

Curious? Curious way to ask, she thinks. Very funny way, she muses. Daddy dead and Lacings gone. Why ask? Mummy in her Norwich flat now. No more tawny owls in the tall Scotch pines. No more croquet lawn; Daddy, longlegged in shorts and a big blue T shirt, coaching us girls to play. Harriet and I as teenagers bashing each other into the lavender bushes. 'So competitive,' he would mock groan. Of course. Tall man, booming out laughter and orders, watching us, adoring us. Harriet more: the prettier; bumptious, cheeky. But it was she the older, the larger and clumsier, who listened to him over supper. He told them *This Island Story* from Wat Tyler's point of view. He voted Labour even, amazingly; like no one they knew. Down from his stocked shelves he took *Shirley* and *The Ragged Trousered Philanthropists*. 'Jen, try this one. You'll see how . . .' She lay on her bed for hours leading righteous riots of millhands against languid tophatted fops or hardfaced bowlerhatted men of iron and steel.

Harriet, she regrets softly, I've no answer for you.

'Harriet, your cornfield's the spit image of the one at home.' She remembers the way the sun would sink down as the combine sliced out the last ranks of the wheat. Rabbits would dash out of their losing darkness, and the village boys would chase them with sticks and yells, careful not to get in front of the two who had the guns.

That year, she was fourteen? She scrambled over the garden fence and joined them, shy, thrilled. A rabbit dodged between her feet and made it to the hedgerow. A groan from Paul, standing on her right. 'Good old Jen.' He worked at the local riding stable cum farm. She went there for her weekly ecstasy, her Sunday ride. Paul was longlegged, in stained breeches. His yellow hair flopped into his blue eyes as he did up her girths for her. The Sunday before she had asked him to come to tea. 'Would you like to come to tea?' In a mumble downwards. Paul didn't appear to notice.

Also then, they had a cousin, Nigel, to stay. More spots than manly growth. He did have a red MG. Harriet polished the fenders furiously but then she stopped. Nigel had fallen for Jill, the punky purplehaired girl at the garage. Their mother used to click her lips surreptitiously as Jill filled the car up. 'Heard the latest?' said Harriet in the kitchen where they were lounging and doing nothing as usual. 'Paul the Ape Brown is going out with El Tarty Queen of El Garage. Isn't it just too, too, darlings?' Eyeing her and Nigel and speaking to the air. Harriet read film and gossip column mags voraciously. She couldn't summon up a whacky death-dealing reply and went into their mother's beautiful garden to cry. Nigel meanwhile went for the beer. 'So you're a fucking Commie,' he said to her on her return. 'No, I don't think so,' she said, 'I think I'm pretty much in the English Christian Socialist tradition, you know.' Nigel's spots became crimson. 'When Margaret Thatcher gets in you and your bloody unions better watch out.' That was it. She was a Peculiar Young Person locally, a Socialist. She despised them all: dupes, hackettes, lackeys. Harriet played in tennis doubles and her public school boyfriends crowded in to eat her jam tarts. Meanwhile she thought about bosses and masses. She never imagined her little sister, exasperating as she was, would join the bosses.

Harriet. She sees her, the little sister. Earlier memories again. Shelling peas on the sunny lawn with Janey, their help, and Janey getting red with annoyance as she and Harriet ate them up, all but seven. The two of them tickling staid Janey, one on each side until she couldn't help laughing, and the seven peas rolled away. And her saying, 'Harriet, you're so *greedy!*' And Harriet opening her mouth but then both of them giggling wildly. But then, Harriet with her fair-haired plaits and smooth round forehead jiggling off to help Mummy do the shopping. They'd come back chatting merrily. Then they made jam tarts. 'My Princess Harriet,' said Daddy, yes he did, as they paraded in with the silver tea things and the three dead-at-birth jam tarts. She sees: Mummy and Harriet together. Oh well, let them get on with it. It was a long time ago. Later still again, she was doing her A's, there was Daddy talking to them over the shepherd's pie about Keir Hardie, and her saying, 'Oh gosh I see, yes - !' and Mummy laughing, 'Can we all eat and not so much learned talk. Janey's waiting for the washing up and then she's off.' And Daddy, 'Of course, dear. Just one thing, Jennifer...' But those years he would go into his study afterwards with the coffee her mother made, to smoke his pipe and look over a case, and he shut the door.

Then he took them all to Mexico. Mexico! Her balding country solicitor Daddy. It must have cost the earth, package and all. Did he know he would die a few years later? It was hot, hot. They saw the temple of the sun and the temple of the moon, driving out of the huge city past a tangle of ravines and yellow clifftops hung with shacks of corrugated iron and this and that. Fowl, pigs and human kids played among yellow and white plastic rubbish - water containers, Exxon oil bottles. In the heart of the vast city, Daddy again, his brown eyes bright, you could see his sparse hair growing down by the minute into the Hippie pigtail he'd been too young or too old and always too respectable to wear ... Well, he showed them his real find, the Rivera murals, the white-clothed *indigenos* who were being liberated, the obese bosses with their cigars tumbling, the beautiful Mayan prostitute cheeking the bourgeois couple in Almeida Park. 'The Latin races know how to make a revolution,' he said waving his specs in the empty gallery. 'Now this is a truly Socialist country. Even its skeletons dance for joy, for love.'

Poor Daddy. Poor Daddy, she cries. It wasn't the nuns, Harriet, who gave me my guilt, my conscience (do you have a conscience, Harriet?). The day I went up to university I left you all, country gentry all ... country where my father was stifling.

She sees that Harriet is quietly gazing at her in the red firelight. The trouble is, Harriet is beautiful and her sister. She feels soothed in the familiar Norfolk darkness . . . What can she please her with?

'Have I told you about Niall?' she asks.

'No . . . Quick, have some more Oriental plonk.'

'Niall was Mr First. At Oxford. I met him at the Labour Club. I was totally petrified – so I went with another girl, my first feminist incidentally.'

'I was your first feminist!'

'No, you were a crypto-Post-feminist; now you're a fully fledged Post-feminist.' Fair enough. Harriet had gone straight into property after her A's and left home, funnily enough, before she did. It had bemused her, hearing. It was the time of the Miners Strike; just afterwards. She had instructed herself to forget Harriet.

Harriet lights a cigarette. 'So Niall? Was he incredibly handsome?'

'King of the Irish, greeny eyes, Irish eyebrows, Irish lashes. He spoke brilliantly on secondary picketing and the police. Afterwards in the pub someone told me he would probably be sent down. He'd been beaten up once and arrested once.'

'Oh God, the dreaded Scargill.'

'Harriet . . .'

'No, go on. Did he ask you out?'

'Not till the second meeting. I spent the time before it boning up on things like *Troops Out*. So I jumped in, eloquently I thought, to second Niall's resolution, to be released to the press if agreed: that the Labour Party should make annual contributions to the IRA – Yes I did – I was in a wonderful whirl, you see, the whole ant-heap had suddenly become vivid, and, um, deconstructable; I forgot Wat Tyler and Keir Hardie, and saw rich and poor as it all is today, internationally struggling, the classes – well, you couldn't understand . . .'

'I've always admired your conviction,' Harriet says unexpectedly; but then: 'I'm sorry, he sounds dire. Possibly dangerous. You mean he was your First?'

'He was James Connolly to me, anti-Imperialist,

Socialist. Everything right. You ought to listen and learn, Harriet,' she says earnestly. 'D'you want me to go on?'

'Wouldn't miss it,' Harriet says.

'Look – '

'Look, isn't it possible to tease each other about our politics – '

'Look, I simply don't connect with that,' she answers sincerely, 'We should respect each other, just because. Let's talk about something more sisterly. How're your roses?'

'Fine, thanks.' Harriet sloshes her some more wine. In the trees a little wind dies away. 'And so what happened?'

'Well, someone got up and said I couldn't propose throwing redcoats out of Belfast because there weren't any nowadays. I said I was a historian. And Niall got up and said, music to my ears, that Erin's soil wasn't green either but we all knew what it meant . . . Then he went on, to amplify what he called my brave intervention. After that . . .'

She falls silent. Sometimes still, those greeny eyes. She's glad Jeff's are brown. An impression only of Niall's black hair flying, awkward jumble on her hearthrug of arms and legs. She cried out. It was her nail scissors that she'd been searching for for days, lost under the hearthrug and pressing into her hip; and the cry was also her virginity, small and bewildered and gone.

Afterwards somehow an argument started. Were they both unhappy? Niall sending her up in his lilting Belfast voice for claiming Irish blood. 'I've an uncle farming in the Sou – the twenty-six counties.' 'He a Prod, Jenny?' 'It's not the same thing down there. W.B. Yeats was a Protestant you know.' 'I did know,' he said; then putting on the style, 'Your uncle's grandaddy's granddaddy, came over with that murthering bugger Cromwell, did he, English Jenny?' 'Niall, I'm terribly pro

Troops Out . . .' 'Shame on ye, ye plump English
trollope,' he giggled suddenly and rolled onto her again.
She got the scissors out just in time. Now she thinks, not
his cock but his tongue, I should have cut his tongue out
with them, his slow quicksilver tongue; for he partly
took me backwards out of my joy, into an old timidity
that's there still; and it's made a meal of me sometimes
teaching, when the sharper ones have had me squirming
for my lazy luck. Going back to a big house and long
lawns, Jen? said Michael Morrissey's eyes last week.
No, she answers their stare, it's not true any more. If
Niall turns up in the dock for blowing up redcoats, I'll
feel guilty. And defiant, against Harriet and her lords.
And defiant, against Niall and his. And sad, because I
wanted to join him. I wanted him to approve of me. Oh
Jeff, ring, you soft-drawling American snake.

'Well,' says Harriet in the darkness. 'Aren't you going to
spill the beans? Here, you haven't been drinking.'
   Her voice is flat, not bright like five minutes ago.
They've been sitting during this meditation on her
short useless history as a Socialist, they've been sitting
in the dark and now the moon rises, full and amber
against a bar of cloud and Harriet's face is bowed; a
drink at one hand; and a cigarette droops glowing from
the other.
   'It was a washout actually,' she answers. 'I lay on my
nail scissors by mistake – they were under the rug – and
just at *the* moment, well, to be graphic, an awful pain
from *outside* was all I could feel.'
   Pause. 'Well,' Harriet murmurs, 'you always were
untidy.'
   Has she drunk too much? Jen thinks: I don't think I'm
very tipsy at all. This evening seems to be going up the
spout.
   'Er, how about opening another bottle?'
   Docilely Harriet pads off and comes back and they
gurgle out what she knows is the sweated labour of

Singapore. Harriet lights up and recrosses her legs. How slim and white they seem in the moonlight.

Harriet comments, 'When I come to your wedding in the slums of Brooklyn you can do me the honours.'

'We're only going to the old registry office,' she says. 'I wouldn't get married at all except I need to work over there. Jeff thinks the same way.'

'You really are going? You won't miss us?' In the other voice she hears a softness and immediately, softly then, she hears herself answering 'I'll miss you. And Mummy. Visit me, Harriet, promise?'

Harriet is smoking again. She thinks, I wish she wouldn't. But the smoke is fragrant, it curls up into the perfume of jasmine or climbing roses somewhere behind by the cottage door. Which of the two? Oh Lord, she has forgotten the country.

'I don't think you should go, not yet . . .' Harriet says softly.

'Harriet love.' Her heart melts.

'I'm going to be away increasingly in the next few years. With work getting heavier. And so.'

Go carefully, she warns. I'm listening, she pleads: I know we're chalk and cheese but. We took each other, body and soul, for granted when we were little, Harriet, we don't quarrel, we don't.

'Mummy's arthritis can only get worse. Have you thought about what your emigration means to her? Who, to come to my point, is to shoulder the responsibility?'

'I . . . you brought me all the way up here . . . moonlight and dinner, to tell me this?' She laughs angrily. 'Harriet, you shouldn't have.' Shushing herself: calm down Jennifer . . . It's true, I haven't given much thought to Mummy. She seemed thrilled when I told her. I'm not irresponsible, thirty twelve-year-olds over a year . . .

'Calm down,' Harriet says out of moonlight, coldly.

'You think I'm being selfish. That's weird; coming from you.' Woa, Jennifer. We're sisters, I'm a feminist, all we've got. We work to be friends. We respect each other.

'Ah,' Harriet drinks delicately, the moon blanches her hair even paler, even whiter, 'what d'you mean by that?'

Springing up she feels not more powerful but even clumsier, so she sits down again. 'This perfect life of yours, you really just grab grab grab it from others. This was a farm labourer's cottage obviously –' she recalls Niall, this time with some pleasure: 'Why've *you* got it?' She throws out her right hand. 'You wreck the countryside, you wreck the towns, now not content with England you're off to wreck Singapore.'

'You know fuck-all, Jen,' Harriet bursts out laughing. 'Didn't teach you much at Oxford, did they? Who's "you" for example?'

Cow, she implodes. I've better things to do than make a fool of myself with you. O.K. get what you want. 'Thatcherism, the developers, Murdoch, the City, the multi-nationals, the Pentagon, the international arms industry,' big breath, 'the whole military industrial complex!' she yells. She jumps up. So does Harriet. They're eyeballing each other. The cornfield, the wood, whose side are they on? Goddess, she calls happily, I've wanted to shout these things at her for years. The great naming curses flutter into the bland night. And this about their mother. Anyway she's Harriet's guest. Will Harriet turn her out? Shall she sleep in wood or cornfield? 'Sorry.' She sits.

'Oh do go on,' Harriet hovers above, laughing, 'it's not as if we didn't all know how virtuous you feel.'

To hell with guest, she thinks.

'Come off it,' Harriet carries on with a sudden jerk. 'You're all so smug you repel me. You think if I hadn't bought it and done it up at enormous personal cost this cottage would still be standing?' Her voice changes notes. 'While you've been sitting on your intellectual arses alternately pitying yourselves and the so-called workers, it's my hard work, my money that's been keeping this country –' Stalking off indoors; the door shuts.

'Harriet!' Oh to hell with it. 'I don't want to quarrel. It's your patch. Shall I leave?'

'You're jealous.' Tittering from inside. Blonde hair shining, visible, in the shadow, through the mullioned hall window.

'Jealous? When d'you meet any real people apart from those limousine sharks and cordless telephone freaks who never met an ordinary person, don't *know* any ordinary people: how they live, we live, nor how we die, I mean how they die.' Mexicans in the moonlight, surging towards her over the stubble, old wrinkled women, kids with the bulbous stomachs, things to be honest she didn't see because they drove past too quickly on the motorway. But, she defies her, I do know, you stupid woman. How about life in the Westway high rises. The two Bangladeshi boys I had for remedial English all this year. White-shirted beyond belief, incredibly anxious to please, to do the English thing. Of course. They're the lucky ones.

The door unbolts. Harriet comes out with a bottle. 'You are,' she says comfortably. 'You're not the only teacher in state schools I know. Friend of mine's just quit. Awful loutish children, cynical staff. And she went into it out of real idealism, not just as an ego trip to prove oneself to one's dead father –'

'Fuck you. I'm going.'

'Feel free, martyr.' Harriet sits down, begins to hum the Marseillaise. The cork pops up. Jen sits down.

They sit silently. She wants to cry. Why? Then she has some wine. Harriet stretches out her hand and tops her up. 'I'm sorry. Oh Christ. Jen?'

'I'll have to wait for Jeff to phone, that's all.'

After another pause. 'Is it Jeff, Harriet?'

'You're getting out,' Harriet whispers, 'admit you're getting out.' Hardening again: 'Isn't Jeff a way of getting out; as well . . . Why are you so hypocritical?'

It pierces her. My Jeff? 'Damn you. No.' Salamander, I love you. Rescue me. I'm incredibly lazy but I do think I've found the right way or at least a better way than hers to live. No cottage, thanks. 'Harriet, if I got what you get a year, I'd invest it to . . . support the Sandinistas in Nicaragua or something. I wouldn't just use it to grab grab grab with. Or,' she leans forward but only the beautiful hair shines, 'I might just buy a bomb after all –'

Harriet comes out of darkness to pour only herself some more. Jen grabs for the bottle and it drops down on the grass and rolls away, glug, gurgle. They both splutter with anger and burst into silly giggles, wrestling. Harriet makes for her wine cellar. 'Hey, what about my bomb?' she shouts after her.

'Prig, you old prig, even terrorism a virtue. Daddy wouldn't have liked that.'

Two filled crystal goblets later (perhaps she won't go after all), 'Hypocrites, both of you,' Harriet continues. 'You screwing the IRA and Daddy boring Mummy and me over the roast beef with what a socialist champion you were, daughter after his own heart.'

'Cheers.' She waggles her goblet. 'Never knew that, promise. Always felt . . . you were the one, really . . . He didn't much like you being a property shark, I suppose?'

'Property management consultant. Don't try to rile me again, Jennifer, you are my guest.'

'Sorry, no offence meant . . . Just to be clear, what's this "prig", "hypocrite". Not sure if I can stay the night yet. Bitterness not good for our souls, Harriet.'

'Well, prig. You are. You're such a killjoy, misery. I invite you up here and all you think is whether the dyke is full of nitrates poisoning the villagers.'

'Didn't.'

'Did.'

'I said –'

'Guilty. That's what you want to make me. Nuns' stuff. Guilty. Oh I'm not. I'm incredibly proud of what

I've achieved. Of Where I Am Today, just like Maggie, however scornful you get. And wimps like Daddy. Always trying to pass along their failure.' Harriet's voice drops but she's not listening. Harriet's explaining that she gives a service, something about helping people realize their dreams.

'He wasn't a failure.' She's dizzy, she's a long way off.

There's more light, Harriet has switched on the kitchen light. Now leaning forward from out of the flowery deckchair: 'You know he died in debt. No, you didn't, did you, darling. So we lost Lacings. But that's no surprise. The question is, for the last three years, who's been helping to look after Mummy? Who, darling? St. Jennifer, Big Sister, Robin Hood of the workers – Who's been looking after Mummy, d'you imagine?'

'You, she, never told me, never.' The kitchen light skids across the lawn.

'Mummy pleaded with me not. I was beginning to make some money. You were doing your finals. It went on from there.' A flat, furious voice. 'If it wasn't for the drink, I mightn't have told you. Mummy will be upset. You know, Jen, she's rather in awe of you.' The harsh voice. It twists in her guts.

'I'll help of course, now . . .' she mutters.

'It's not the money . . .'

'Oh. Then. You think I'm terrible, unforgivable to go?'

'I don't mind, really, what you are or aren't. It's being here, Jennifer, being here. Someone to be around. Like a daughter? Well, you see, that's how I think.'

Harriet, she begins to talk, feeling the wine in her head, and talking faster, you are telling me how you bought this pretty scenery for Mummy's sake, partly. I understand. Mummy visits from Norwich. Janey can visit too, from where she's retired to. It's all brilliant. I didn't even ask. Janey sends me Christmas cards. I think I will wander in round the lawn, out of the light. I send her cards. Last Christmas she sent me a bluetit and I sent her a robin redbreast, a bloody great Robin Redbreast. I raise my arm, my finger traces a bird on the shape of the moon over the trees in front of me. So, Jennifer, Ms. hypocrite, how d'you feel? Well, nothing. I feel, nothing. To break away, to London, a bedsit, a rather cozy bedsit, laughter and plonk, moaning in the staffroom, and laughter, and exhaustion, and nothing, nothing achieved, not for the kids, not by me. I ... I ... I ... People like Niall, like Michael Morrissey, who do know what it is like to be poor and shat on, the bottom of the whole U.K. heap, they know I'm nothing when they set eyes on me. Nothing. Like my stupid father. What did he ever do? A few cases on legal aid, a sub to the Fabians, maybe a sub to the Nicaragua Solidarity Campaign. It's Harriet who's the something, a good little capitalist something looking after her family plus not to forget the old Babushka. Yes, smiles Harriet, tossing her hair, tearing down hovels and putting up Far Eastern hotels, I'm making the world safer for my family – Bam, punch in the nose for Salim and Sharon and Michael ... I've seen them after all (she's talking still faster) ... for Harriet they're just future factory fodder. All right, less cant ... No, I guess I might not want to spend my life teaching. But, to do something relevant! It'll be better, more straightforward with Jeff and away from home. Bigger country, not one tight little prejudiced clapped out topheavy society, less breathing down one's neck. As for Harriet who supports the family and stays, she doesn't like rough kids, she just plays in a rough ballgame.

Come midnight: the two of us sisters bashing each other into the lavender bushes. Who shall be higher in the eyes of Heaven.

She potters over, 'I'm going for a walk, so if I feel sick I won't puke all over your lawn.'

'Running away again, you hypocrite,' Harriet says drowsily, leaning over to slop some wine into her glass as she meanders past.

Hypocrite, she weeps to herself. Blundering into Harriet's treetrunks. The glimpsed lawn seems all of a sudden to have shrunk, to shine like a tiny stage set, Harriet's slumped figure centre stage and the consoling bulk of the cottage thatch as backdrop. She puts her arms gingerly and tenderly round an inscrutable black trunk. Is it oak, ash or thorn? How do I get to own a tree? she cries up. I want a tree. I want the tall high beechtrees round my bedroom window, I want the night rustle of the wind round the house, in moonlight or the beginning of rain or storms . . . I want the clouds sweeping over the stubble when I creep and stand on the front steps after reading all night, and our owls hoot, and everyone's sleeping upstairs, sleeping sound, in quiet bedrooms.

And all the time I'm taking further steps away. First, here in my own country, a few baby steps, and now, other people, other places, other lands. 'I'll be your home,' said Jeff with loving arrogance when she grew panicky. But one man, one person, can't be home, she has to keep from panicking, trust she's doing right, that's all.

She sees: not Harriet . . . but her mother.

. . . She was crouching over some flower bed, I see her, always, extracting some weed or other. How hunky dory she kept it all. The flowers I loved were hers. She with, it's true, Janey's help, cooked, served, washed up, cleaned, drove us here, there and everywhere, the doctor, school, the dentist, up to London for nerve-racking bouts of clothes shopping, she had the Nigels to stay, and laughed at the Jills at the garage and I'd've died if she'd found out about Paul. She gave us parties and disapproved of me teaching: Jennifer darling, surely you can get a job in a nice private girls' school But when I was 14 and had awful tonsillitis she brought me lemon and honey and sat on the edge of the pillow holding my damp hand. High boned face, blue-eyed, faded permed lock of fair hair flopping over her eyes.

She pushed it back, and wiped the same hand on the Beatrix Potter apron Harriet had made her for her birthday. 'Did I ever tell you about when Daddy and I went to Greece on our honeymoon. I was so pleased,' she looked at me shyly or was it a little slyly, 'I could understand from knowing my Classics what the old peasants were saying. They talked so beautifully to us, they had names like Agamemnon or Thetis. I could understand them but Daddy couldn't. I couldn't help feeling pleased though I was ashamed of myself . . . Go to sleep now, darling.'

Why did she belong to Harriet then? Why? Why does Harriet get everything? Trees, home . . . Her tears are wetting the treetrunk. She pats it apologetically. Perhaps it will tell her why.

Birds of a feather flock together –

Her head is rustling minutely, the back of her skull. She turns round and a white sheet flaps, a white sail sails, a white wraith passes silently in front of her eyes.

Then it's gone into the dark, into the wood further. DTs? No, she's not that far gone. From the insides of the wood comes a piercing screech. Her neck prickles, this must be her hair going up on end. She flounders and leaps towards the kindly light, towards her Princess Harriet asleep on her lawn. Suddenly it's all thorns, she comes to a full stop, caught and blind in a thicket of thorns like Abraham's sacrificial ram.

'Jen? I've got a torch.' Harriet, hiccuping, stands with the beam shining at her feet, waving it unsteadily up into her eyes.

'Stop cursing. You're nearly out.' The edge of the lawn, it seems, is two feet further.

'Now, now, good feminists don't use words like that.' Harriet's doubled up laughing, the beam is shaking on seas of brambles.

'When you lot seize the land back again make sure you know about barn owls first,' she's choking, 'you're so keen on wild life. Ha ha. Teach you to take Maggie's name in vain. Oh. Oh!' Harriet's sobbing and she herself is still cursing and her head's spinning and spinning and they lurch into each other, and Harriet isn't Princess H any more, cool and cocky, she's sad too, mysteriously, unglamorously, and she hugs her and feels how slight she is and it seems she's luckier than Harriet, well, just now.

Inside the cottage the telephone is ringing. 'Come on, Harriet, it's Jeff. Hey, you're gonna have a brother. How about that! C'mon.'

Dancing and swaying and sniffing past jasmine and roses, out of the moonlight, and Jeff says, at last, 'Hi, honey, is that my beautiful English princess?'

And Harriet, clasping the receiver, says nothing and, pale and fragile, hands it over. And she says, 'Come off it, my man, who d'you think you're talking to, a mere jumped up commoner princess.' So Harriet gives a half giggle, half sob. And Jeff says: 'Honey, I've got an urgent message from my mother. She says to tell you she's seen Princess Di's wedding dress in a Coney Island store front and should she check it out for you?'

And she says, 'Piss off, you great hairy Yank, d'you know, actually I love you ever so much.'

Harriet puts her head on Jen's shoulder, her long straight strange hair fanning across Jen's breast as if it were her own hair, and her own short, coppery/gingery hair stops standing on end at the ghost in the wood and begins to flow loose. And Jen thinks: I'll never go back home, never.

A KIND OF DESIRED INVASION

Kate Pullinger

Starting with the Belgian chocolates, desire seemed a potent and dynamic force, like a nuclear engine, high-powered and probably lethal. The chocolates made her melt, sticky, gooey, and desire made her harden, glass blown by fire. She flexed her muscles and felt strong and American, like an airforce base in a foreign country. Strength, however, was not part of the problem.

He, of course, was a married man, a married Englishman, like Trevor Howard or James Mason in an early role. Beneath his pale and archetypally reserved exterior something burned and melted, hardened then softened. She could tell this by looking at his back as he stood at the bar ordering more drinks. His long neck was tinged a bright pink as though reflecting some internal glow. He had just given her the chocolates and she had kissed him. After their lips parted, he sank into the tatty, beer-stained seat, then suddenly stood, knocking his knees on the edge of the table. She felt she had shocked him and his response was to wing slightly out of control.

The colour of his neck faded as he returned to the table with the drinks. They were colleagues at the university. She was not married. She was new to the country and did not have many friends. It was not like her to flirt

with married Englishmen. Her sexual habits had
changed with the times and, besides, in England all the
signifiers seemed different. Here the semiotics of
sexuality were not her own.

Like celibacy, chocolates seemed an old-fashioned
gesture, from another time although perfectly appropriate now. Perhaps romance had snuck back into
vogue, she thought, along with the new sexual caution.
Chocolates, especially European ones, were decadent
and luxurious, like love-letters and long kisses: something one's parents had before they married. Soft-
centred milk chocolates that came as one bit them
seemed almost as exciting as dancing with someone
you knew you were about to sleep with used to be.

His marriage to another woman, an immutable fact,
posed even greater restrictions on their fledgling
nuclear romance. Infidelity had become freshly dangerous, potentially much more lethal to a marriage than
adultery had been previously. Restraint carried with it
nobility, safety, a new kind of self-respect.

'Would you like another chocolate?' she said leaning
against his shoulder. His leather jacket smelt raw, his
jeans felt soft and worn. He was dressed like an
American, it was she who looked English in her patched
tweed jacket and jodhpurs. She looked horsey as well as
strong, like a kind of repellent *Country Living* house-
wife. But her clothes were not literal, as clothes rarely
are; she was as much a bloodsportswoman as he was a
baseball fan. Still, he was married, even if he didn't look
it. What do married people look like?

'Let's go away for the weekend,' he said.

'What about your wife?'

'She can stay home. I'll say it's work.'

'She won't believe you. It's such a cliché.' They
paused and poured alcohol into their systems. 'Anyway,
what would we do? Play chess?'

'No. We'd go for long walks and eat hot meals and
watch the sunset. We'd kiss with the wind in our faces.

I'd hold you close and feel your heartbeat.' He placed a chocolate under his tongue and waited for it to melt down.

She looked at him longingly, Wondering if he really did want to have an affair with her. She had a theory that English men enjoyed sex even less than her male compatriots. She was still allowed to like it, wasn't she? Maybe this new restraint appealed to most people, perhaps everyone felt more comfortable with prudishness.

'I want to look at you without any clothes on,' she said suddenly as she watched him suck his chocolate. His neck began to glow again. He moaned softly. 'I want to see you naked.' The people at the next table moved their chairs forward imperceptibly. He closed his eyes and leaned back. 'I want to run my hands down the length of your legs. Both of them. One at a time.' He moaned more loudly and the people at the next table held their drinks in mid-air. She leaned back against the seat, her hands pressed between her own legs. The lights in the pub flickered like a fluttering heart, a clenching and rumbling nervous gut.

After a while he stopped shaking and bit into another chocolate. Its softness covered his teeth, coating his tongue. In a voice thick with sugar and lust he said, 'You are driving me wild. I don't understand you.'

'What?' she said.

'You are so foreign and yet so familiar. Like sex itself, I guess, a kind of desired invasion.'

They fucked like chickens, their feathers ruffled, pecking and scratching at nothing, everything. She grappled with him as he pressed against her, pushing him away and urging him on. He tried to be controlled, even a bit leisurely, but as he pulled back he could not help but rush forward again. He felt the condom tear inside her. It was all he could do to stop.

'It broke,' he said.

'Shit.'

'Is there another?'

'Over here somewhere.' She crawled away and scrabbled over the junk on the bedside table, returning with the foil-wrapped encumbrance. 'Let's try again.'

They had been fucking like this for a few months, slyly, without letting on to the outside world. They would meet in her flat – the weekend away was still talked about although not realized. He would arrive at her door and they would begin right away, sometimes before he took his coat off. They did not talk much, what was there to say? She saw more than enough in the guilt and pleasure on his face to make questions redundant.

It would not go anywhere; there was nowhere for it to go. She could not take him back to America with her, he could not take her home. They had sex protected from each other, the little slip of rubber a true barrier made of caution and sensibility. Because of it they simply could not plunder on ahead without thinking. They always had to pause and reflect.

'In my country,' she began like a student from abroad, 'the English are often thought of as fey.'

'Hmph. In my country,' he mocked her slightly, 'Americans are often thought of as vulgar.'

'How fey.' He pushed harder today, knowing he would not hurt her. She wrapped herself around him like a clam in formation, her body one big muscle, straining. When he came he had to pull away quickly so as not to spill a drop of his bodily fluids, like the instructions on the box of condoms said.

She reminded him of somebody from a movie, maybe it was Kathleen Turner in *Body Heat*, sometimes Kim Basinger in *9½ Weeks*. Not an old movie star but someone new and less defined, whose character melted into a dozen different actresses. Like her, he relied on clichés for guidance, for cross-cultural understanding. He thought he would like to be more like her; when she

spoke people listened. It was the twang in her vowels
that commanded attention, people thought to themselves 'here's someone from a Woody Allen movie.' And
she capitalized on this, she saw where it could be to her
advantage to be perceived as a celluloid creation.

Some afternoons they talked at cross purposes; it was
not just their vocabulary that differed. He would appear
cold and withdrawn, tormented with guilt over his wife.
She would become overly effusive in response, feeling
hopelessly alone. 'Are you mad?' she would ask,
meaning 'Are you angry?'

'No,' he would reply shortly, thinking she was im-
plying he was mad – insane – with desire for her (which,
in a way, he was). Then they would thrash out their
anxieties in bed, moaning and coming to false under-
standings.

Two cultures rarely understand each other, especially
when one is waxing dominant. The weaker often needs
to copy the stronger – for every one of her foreign
bombing campaigns conducted with supreme arrogance
and ruthless certainty he had his own dirty little war on
distant barren islands, his own vicious murders on the
Rock. Were they playing out these scenarios in sex? Did
he want to be dominated?

One night he put a Belgian chocolate inside her and
as it melted he licked away the cream. 'Do they have
Marmite in America yet?' he asked.

She broke off mid-moan to reply. 'We'll never have
Marmite over there. It's you who will get peanut butter
over here. That's the way Imperialism works.' She was
coated with chocolate as he pushed inside her.

His marriage seemed like the Atlantic Ocean to her,
something vast and unknowable which she could not
attempt to bridge but only fly over at a terrible speed. It
kept them apart, kept them foreign to each other, him
unhaveable, her unhad.

After a year his wife still appeared not to have noticed

the smell of another woman on her husband's face. He was always careful to wash his chiselled visage, of course, but in a year of passion one would think some small scent would have escaped, a tracking odour that would put her senses on alert. It was time for the Other Woman to go back to America. Her academic job had run its course. She had found England a cold place. The rooms where she lived were damp, even while the brief summer had passed. Her career beckoned, the Atlantic Ocean dimmed and became crossable. Still, there was the problem of her married Englishman. Would she simply leave him behind? Would she just move away and forget?

One afternoon in bed in her flat she said, 'I will be leaving soon, you know.'

He sat up, surprised. 'I thought you had the afternoon free.'

'I do. It's the rest of the time I'm talking about. I have to go home.'

'I thought you liked it here, I thought you thought it was fun living in England and sleeping with me.'

'I do. But I can't be a tourist forever.'

They argued about it for the rest of the afternoon, he becoming sullen and sorry, she remaining dispassionate, untouched. She was impressed by his sudden remorse. She had always felt insulated from pain with him, as if the condoms served to forever prevent them from getting unhealthily close. Now he was filling their relationship with a seriousness she had always assumed it could not possibly contain.

'Don't you think,' he began to plead, 'that sleeping together automatically provides us with a kind of contract?'

'A legal document? Fucking gives us certain rights over each other? I fuck you therefore I owe you?'

'You can be so crude sometimes,' he said as though wounded.

'It's in my blood,' she replied.

'I think your blood runs a bit cold,' he said, helping himself to a bit of cruelty.

'You are the one who is married,' she said, 'not me. I know what that means. I know what married people look like.'

'Huh?' he said, like an American. 'What do married people look like?'

She paused and then smiled and said, 'They wear rings around their fingers and have ties around their hearts.'

Moya Roddy

Olive parked badly and swore. Slamming the car door she trotted rather than walked – towards the flat-roofed building dominating the quiet cul-de-sac. As she rounded the gates of the school she saw him sitting on a low wall, his little legs dangling, swinging backwards and forwards.

'Colm!' she yelled.

His head jerked up in her direction then went back to studying the ground. Something was wrong – she sensed it. He kept his face averted while she drew nearer but when she was nearly beside him he turned it to her almost defiantly. She gasped at the sight of the blood beginning to cake under his nose.

'Darling!' Quickly she folded her arms round him then just as quickly pulled back to inspect his swollen nose and mouth.

'What happened? Were ye in a fight?'

Colm didn't answer. He began to swing his legs again, vigorously. He studied them, blocking her out.

'Will ye not tell me what it was ye were fighting over?' Olive stroked his arm gently, coaxing.

He didn't exactly push her away. Instead he stuck his chin in his hand, so removing his arm from her touch.

Olive gave up.

It's all right, you can tell mammy when we get home.
There's a good boy.'

But Colm wouldn't budge. The grim look on his young
face as she washed off the dried blood frightened her.
When she'd finished he sat at the kitchen table,
watching her getting his tea ready, brooding. Thank
God it's Friday, she thought, Steve and her could have a
relaxing evening, open a bottle . . . As she cleared the
table the headline of the *Evening Standard* caught her
eye: ENGLAND MUST WIN! Fuck, she'd forgotten the
World Cup was on. He'd want to watch it. When she put
the fish fingers and oven chips in front of Colm – his
favourites, he almost smiled at her.

'Will ye not tell mammy?' she ran a hand through his
soft hair. Slowly he finished what was in his mouth, his
eyes roaming the plate. Then he raised them and met
hers.

'Mammy am I Irish?'

Olive had been expecting so many horrors that
hearing the question she almost laughed with relief.

'Well of course you're Irish. Haven't we been home
loads to times to where Granny and all your cousins . . .'
A thought suddenly struck her and she stopped.

'Why, has someone been saying you're not?' Olive felt
her temper rise. The school he went to had a fair number
of second and third generation Irish – these days even
first generation – and she was glad of that. She wanted
him to have contact with other Irish kids and families,
as a sort of bulwark against the swamp of English
culture. Was some bastard getting at Colm because his
father was English?

'Is that what ye were fighting over? My poor baby . . .'
She put her arm round him but he pushed her away.

'But I was born in England wasn't I?'

'That doesn't matter. It's not important where you're
born.' She stopped. Even she didn't believe that. How
could she? Quickly she sorted out her thoughts and
began again.

'I mean it's important but it's not the only important thing. I'm Irish and you're my child, so you're Irish. You'd have been born in Ireland if things, history and all had been different.'

She was on firmer ground again. She hurried on.

'It's like a feeling, you know you're Irish even if you're born here.'

She stopped again. Could a seven-year-old understand that?

'But daddy's English and I was born here. That's two things, that makes me English.'

'That's what I'm trying to explain. It doesn't. You mustn't mind what kids say. You're Irish and you're proud of it.'

He shoved the half-empty plate away and jumped up from the table. At the door he turned, his face ashen.

'I'm not, I'm not. That's what they were saying and I fought them.'

His eyes blazed. 'I'm English.'

'Thanks.' Olive took the glass of wine, sniffed at it and downed half in one go. She settled back on the pillow.

'I needed that.'

Steve pulled the duvet over the two of them and began fiddling with the remote control.

'D'you know because so many people switch off their TVs by remote control instead of pulling out the plug, they go on using electricity, the same in one night that would power Leicester for one day. Or is it Hull?'

'Is that what you learned at school today?' Steve teased her. 'Well teacher' – he stopped and upped the volume. 'It's starting. This is the life. Are you sure you want to watch it?'

'Have I any choice?'

'You could wash the dishes.' He put his arm round her. 'Maybe seeing England getting thrashed will cheer you up.' He paused. 'The kick-off isn't for ten minutes. Would you like me to speak to Colm?'

'Not unless he brings it up. D'ye know Steve, I've been thinking. Remember I thought of having him in Ireland – I wish I had. But I suppose I thought it was, like I was trying to tell him today, a gut feeling, being Irish. It's probably a phase he's going through . . .'

'Thanks very much. Some of us are stuck with it.'

Sorry was on the tip of her tongue when a thought struck her with such force she lay back to fathom its meaning. She stared hard at the black curly hairs on the neck of the man she'd married nine years before. She followed the contours of his hairline to the almost kiss curl that hung over one of his eyes, the eye she could see now staring intelligently at a group of men – Englishmen like himself – discussing the prospects of the English team. She heard the various accents and identified them without thinking, Cockney, West Country, and a thick nasal Mancunian. Then she blurted the thought out:

'D'you know I've never thought of you as really English. I know you are but . . .'

'That's probably a compliment.' He looked her straight in the face. 'Colm has a point. He's half and half, in fact a little bit more English if you weigh it up.'

Not quite quickly enough Olive tried to shut out a second thought: that she would never, could never, have married an Englishman. Jesus what did that mean? Whatever it meant she wasn't going to think about it. Not now. Besides it was Colm they were talking about.

'That's not true, I've brought him up Irish.'

'It's all right, I'm only pulling your leg.'

'You can afford to.'

'I have my own problems. You mightn't think it but it would be nice to feel proud of where you come from. That's something you have. Anyway if you're feeling like this maybe we shouldn't watch the match – you might start attacking me.'

But Olive needed to watch the match, needed a diversion from the thoughts spinning round her head.

She punched him playfully.

'We'll watch it, I want to see England beaten by Morocco. I bet they think they can waltz home.'

He squeezed her. 'I didn't know you were a secret football fan. Here, it's starting.

'It would be hard not to be. Tim and Richard talk about nothing else in the staff room. I could give you a blow-by-blow account of how England lost to Portugal the other night. Sorry, how Portugal "stole" the match. England never loses . . .'

Steve held up a hand interrupting her. 'I hope you're not going to talk all the way through it.'

'Fuck off.' But she shut up and lay back forcing her eyes to focus on the two groups of men in their different coloured shirts battling for the ball. She tried joining her mind to the millions of people everywhere glued to screens for this all important match but all she could see was Colm's pudgy little legs swinging backwards and forwards and the grim look on his face as she washed away the crusted blood. It was strange – hard – to think about something she took for granted. Being Irish for her was synonymous with being. Mind you when she went home she noticed her accent was getting worse and worse and she was picking up a sort of English reticence or so they enjoyed telling her. Here she was 'so Irish', a kind of veiled racism or compliment: it depended on her mood or the person saying it how she took it. And now Colm . . . She laughed to herself. Maybe there should be a rule if Irish and English people had children they should be brought up Irish – the way the Catholic Church used to insist on the children of Catholics and Protestants being brought up Catholic. But just as quickly she remembered herself, barely thirteen, standing up in class and saying she didn't think the Catholic Church was fair and the nun, red in the face, asking who did she think she was to question the Pope's teaching. Steve's roar filled the room.

'A goal?'

Steve sighed despondently. 'The English are playing
so they won't lose. No one's taking any chances. Look!'
He glared at the screen scornfully. 'That crossball was
pathetic. They should sack the bloody manager. Y'know
when England had men like Bobby Charlton, they
knew what to do if they got the ball. This shower just do
what they're told.'

Olive loved it when Steve got excited like this,
somehow it always reminded her of her father.

'Look there's Hoddle – he's good when he's playing for
Tottenham but look at him now.'

Names like Danny Blanchflower and Christy Ring,
shouts of 'Up Down' and 'C'mon the Dubs' crowded into
her mind from the dinner tables of her childhood. The
voice of Michael O'Heiher on the radio . . .

'Daddy who's playing?'

'Ssshh – go and play, there's a good girl.'

Steve slumped deflated. 'It's a real example of
Thatcher's Britain. Do what the boss says even if it
means annihilating yourself.'

'I'm glad. I want them to lose. C'mon Morocco!' she
cheered but it was half-hearted. She snuggled closer
into Steve's body searching assurance. 'I thought you
wanted them to lose too.'

'Well at least Morocco are trying to score,' was all he
replied.

'If you've just joined us,' the commentator's voice
droned, 'there's no score in this all important match but
England can be admired for holding their own, down to
ten men and against a Moroccan team that's used to the
sort of heat . . .'

'Did you hear that Steve, they wouldn't say the
opposite if it was raining.' She stuck her tongue out at
the television. As she did one of the English players
danced across the screen and up the sideline, outwitting
several of the Moroccan side who tackled him from all
directions. Olive grabbed Steve's arm.

'That's Hoddle isn't it? C'mon Hoddle, waddle, dawdle, kick it!'

'You're getting very excited.'

'I can't bear them being such idiots . . . eigits,' she corrected herself quickly using the Irish word.

'Cheer Morocco then.'

Olive wasn't going to admit it but she was finding it hard to identify with the Moroccans.

'Oh no,' Steve groaned, 'they're bringing on Steven. They should put Barnes in.'

'Who's he?'

'He's brilliant. Got the best goal ever scored against Brazil. Steven is a bloody midfielder.'

'What does . . .'

'Sshh . . . Hoddle's got it . . . he's going to try.' Steve's voice was at breaking point. 'C'mon. C'MON . . .'

'Score England, score' Olive screamed. She grabbed Steve's sleeve, their eyes in unison watched the ball sail through the air and high over the net. They both sagged. After a moment Steve looked at her.

'You cheered England.'

Olive stared back at him. She felt flushed and drained, angry and ashamed all at the same time.

'I can't bear seeing them throwing it away, that's all. You were cheering them to.'

But Steve had gone back to the match, his face rigid with anticipation.

'There's only a few minutes left, they'll never . . . wait, wait, Steven has it, he's come from nowhere and yes, he's going for a shot! . . .'

Olive closed her eyes. 'I'm not watching. I hope they lose.' It was ridiculous getting so excited over a game. How would she explain that sort of behaviour to Colm? Oh, she knew well enough there were thousands of Irish who followed English clubs but there were thousands who would choke before they'd cheer an English team and she was one of them. She'd got carried away on Steve's excitement, that was all. That's not true, she

told herself. Admit it, you wanted England to win. She
stiffened. C'mon, secretly just between you and me the
voice persisted in her head, it would be hard not to.
They're your team really. You're half English now
anyway, you live in England, you're married to an
Englishman, Colm . . .

The commentator shrieked into her reverie. She
opened her eyes and not trusting her tongue any longer
simply looked at Steve.

'It's over. No score.'

She turned over and buried her head in the pillow. She
felt sick. She wished she hadn't watched the match. She
wished she could turn back the clock. But to when? a
voice asked. To earlier when they'd turned on the TV?
To when she collected Colm from school? Or right back
to the day she married Steve, or took the boat to
England?

Or maybe even further than that: to those warm
sunny days when she sat watching her Daddy and
asking him questions and he told her like he always did
– 'Go and play, there's a good girl.'

THE CROSS IS GONE

Ben Okri

It was a day of fairs
Yellow music on the wind, feathers
Of dead birds whirling beyond
The green trees.

We walked up into the Heath
Passed a man riding a baby's bicycle
And the paths confused us.
It had rained, the earth was soggy
Beneath the deceptive grass.
We strayed past trees that bore
The features of dying men.

All around us the trees were heaving.
Their comrades had fallen
The great spirits trapped in their monstrous
Trunks sang in the cold air
Songs of white mermaids
Corrupted beyond their time.
Their comrades had fallen
They who had witnessed the sordidness
And the miracles of three hundred years
Felled in an instant of nightspace
By the karmic hurricanes
Of an unconfronted history.

Like old elephants, their trunks inscrutable,
Breathing lamentations on the unforgiving
 earth
Into which they will not be reborn,
The trees sang to us of a darkening age
With mysteries dying
And yellow spirits in the wind.

We passed their hulks
On the graveyard of the Heath
We said nothing about them
We talked about a single voice
From oppressed spaces
That could bring down thunder on corrupt
 lands
And about tyranny unleashing wounds on
 itself
That bleeds through us, the innocent
 journeyers
Into forbidden zones of dying gods.

We passed them quickly
Noting the character and psychology
Of each surviving tree –
Then, from the valley, we looked up high
And saw three kites,
One red, another of blue,
The third of gold, invisibly attached
To a black cross,
Bold against the sky.

We climbed Parliament Hill
Our spirits heaving, our breaths
Quickening, the earth slipping beneath our
 feet.
The sky quivered with silent birds.
With our ascent we noticed a gathered crowd,

An old woman with a yellow scarf
A black man with a red beret on his bald
    head
Children playing with strings
A nun with frozen hands
An Irish priest wearing metal-framed glasses
An enormous bible under his arm
A wand in one hand, the string of the red
Kite in the other.

We approached them, holding
Fast to our invisible trail, breathing
Heavily the rarified air:
And when we gained the hill top
The Cross shivered
A strong wind, smelling of incense and
    radiation,
And disease and French perfume and
    hidden wars,
Blew over from the distant Thames.

We saw all the world laid out
Before us in the air
A city perceived in a moment's enchantment
Whose history, weighed down with guilt and
    machines,
Laughed all around us like ghosts
Who do not believe the existence
Of men.

We saw the city and marvelled.
We dream the city better
Than it dreams itself.
The air and distance weave such burning
Miracles from the houses and church spires
The towers and glass offices of
    multinationals.
We dream the housing estates, built on

marshes;
The woods, sad and defiant;
The chaos of buildings, the threaded streets,
Where madmen wander alone,
Where men dream of impossible women,
And women of non-existent men,
With each pursuing instant fulfilment
Orgasm without end
Love without responsibility
Miracle without pain
Transformation without knowledge
Difficult dreams, doomed to abortions
And sick births
Blind births, one-eyed births.
In the phantasm of the city
Glacial vision prevails
While voices from the marshes vainly cried
   out
That they are the victims and hostages
Of the history their parents accepted
In silence.

The world lay before us
And the wind stayed still.
We wandered round the Irish priest
Not daring to approach
How would we be received?
And then a bitter wind blew the kites
And one got stuck, blue on green, against
The branches of a fallen tree –
We wandered round the crowd
And gazed at the cross
Upon which was written, on that wintry day,
Summery with the blessedness of its
   naming –
For it was Easter Sunday –
The words, clear as glass:
Christ is dead

Christ is risen
Christ will come again –

And our spirits soared, mixing with the
 clouds
Of deep colour –
A child's cry of delight
Sent the golden kite upwards.
The priest's cassock lifted and was whipped
By the winds of four directions.
Voices became sweet on the air.
In the distance below, the three lakes
Shimmered – the wind carved its many
 names
On the face of the waters.

We went down and dwelled
In the solitude of swans.
We talked of painting, love, and adventures.
My friend's face was reddened by her red
 coat.
We heard the fair and followed the jangling
 music
Through the wet trails
And came upon cacophony.
We dwelled in the fair, listened to the
 conflicting
Noises, watched the faces of ticket sellers,
And the machines like windmills sending
The children into the air
Of artificial stimulation
And the gadgets and games and bumper cars
That once filled our adolescence with
 longing
But which left us hungry and empty now.

We left the fair followed by the smell
Of mass-cooked sausages, by dogs

Dragging hamburgers between their teeth –
We left the day behind us, with the view
From Parliament Hill
Forever bright in our vision.
We went back to our lives of ordinary
  miracles
With the joy of that day lost in us
Till three days later when she returned
From a long walk –
She didn't look sad, or disappointed:
But in that tone of voice we reserve
For events that should be underlined
Except we don't know why, or how, or with
  what accentuation
To underline them
Make them speak
Make them significant –
And with a disturbed, imperceptible tossing
Of her head
A movement of her shoulders
A hand launching itself into the air
But holding back
She said, simply, without mystery:
'The cross – That cross – is gone.'

Hanan Al-Shaykh

Like a thirsty horse making for water, I lunged. But I wasn't thirsty. I was on fire. I threw the water over the English boy and his friend, and the fire blazed in my head and heart and between my legs.

Images kept on coming at me which, like a crazy horse, I tried to resist, defiantly tossing my head high, but each new picture flashing into my mind enraged me more and more and I shook my head frantically from side to side.

Seeing Saad laid out on the floor, dumb and silent. Saad, whose mighty voice had welled up from his entrails. Now his wife seemed to have snatched his voice to lament for him, joined by her daughters, by his aunts and sisters, all beating their faces and rubbing ash and black soot on to their cheeks.

The English pigeon devouring the remains of the couscous, without a pause, immersing its whole beak and head in the grains while I smiled at it, saying: 'You seem to like couscous from a packet. I suppose it's because you're an English pigeon. You're used to things out of packets.'

Aisha's insistent words in the grain store, as she shook her gold earrings and the bangles on her wrist, urging me to stay at home, but I could only gaze at her shoes and marvel at how exactly they matched her handbag.

Then I am standing in Aisha's house with its Moroccan furniture and Moroccan smell, hardly able to believe that I'm in London, having braved the customs official who turned my passport over and over in his hands.

The letter with my name in English on the envelope, a Moroccan stamp, and a list of requests from my family for a white bridal veil to go with my sister's wedding dress, surgical stockings for my brother and a china dish for my mother.

Offering the blond English boy – the one I was throwing water at now – half my lunch, and sitting there full of gratitude because he smiled, because he liked the taste of the piece of chicken dipped in cumin and saffron and he had smiled at me for the first time. I wanted his approval because he was English. I wanted the approval of everyone from the bus conductor to the Pakistani shopkeeper, because he owned a shop and spoke English. Being lost in the underground, tears running down my cheeks. Learning to decipher the names of the stations. Learning them by heart as if they were magic signs.

I was throwing water at the English boy and his friend and they were yelling, 'She's crazy. Jesus Christ, she's completely crazy!'

I was transformed into a raging bull, and everything turned red. He started up at my scream and I saw the dark blood on him and on me. Then he'd jumped to his feet as if he'd been bitten by a snake, shouting, 'You're a virgin! You're still a virgin! I don't understand you.'

I didn't chew my nails with regret at giving him my virginity, furious at my weakness in lying down for him, and taking this boy in my arms just because he was English, a citizen of that great nation which had once ruled half the globe: nor did I blame myself for clinging on to an idea even though it meant severing my links with my country, and travelling to London alone without any member of my family. Instead of striking my face and grieving aloud because my hymen was no longer intact, I wondered, 'Is it because he's an Englishman that he doesn't feel proud he's taken my virginity, or is he frightened that now I'll try to force him to marry me?'

I tried to tell him that I didn't blame him for deflowering me but he wasn't listening. He just went on saying in a shocked way, as if he had lost his mind, 'You're twenty-five, thirty years old? And you're still a virgin? Jesus Christ, I don't understand you. I just don't understand at all.'

He didn't go to the bathroom to wash, he stayed in the room. Out of the corner of my eye I watched him wipe himself with Kleenex tissues and drop them on the floor, indifferent to the smears of blood on them. He pulled on his trousers and went quickly over to turn up the music, moving his head from side to side in time to the beat. He lay face down beside me, not knowing that I was now painfully aware that the threads which bound me to home and the inevitable marriage had snapped once and for all. I could see myself on the roof of our house, as, for the last time, I spread the couscous out to dry on a sheet in the sun before my journey to London: I could see the village below me: the tops of the trees, the minaret, the ancient wall which ran round my village. I could think of nothing except going to London and finding my way among its tall buildings studded with lights.

I remembered the friend of Aisha's who'd helped me escape from her house in London, carrying one of Aisha's children, while I took my suitcase and dragged the other child along with me. I could see her English neighbour shutting her front door in our faces, and yet all the same we left the two children there, rushing away after I'd pinched their cheeks to make them cry so that she'd have to come out to them.

I walked in the cold of London without tights, without
an overcoat, without a jumper. In Marks and Spencer's
there were hundreds of dresses and jumpers and
beautiful nightdresses. I paid the woman at the cash
desk and smiled at her. She smiled back and said the
coat I'd chosen was really pretty. I was overjoyed. She
approved of my taste and I'd given her the right amount
of money for the red coat which I still haven't worn.

Eagerly I was bending over the vacuum cleaner. It
was a magic broom to transport me to another world,
from poverty to riches. The implements available
here for cleaning were as many and as varied in colour
and smell as the places which I had to clean. Aisha's
gold chain which I'd carried away from her house
hidden among my clothes was in my hands one moment
and the next on the counter in the Oxford Street
goldsmith's.

The red of my anger bubbled up like the rosy orange
juice squeezed by the vendors' machines in the main
street in our village. It ran down between my eyes and
made me see everything blood-red, even though seconds
before my mind had conjured up a pleasing vision: the
English boy's sister. She was polite, she gave me a
small box of chocolates with a thank-you card and
kissed me and shook my hand when she came for a meal
on Sunday. She had been different from her brother and
from his friends who used to visit, make themselves at
home in my clean room, on the clean bed, delighted to
find a video and a cassette recorder and cassettes, who
ate my nice food and listened to loud music and
swallowed the drink they brought with them. They all
said they wanted to visit my country and I nodded my
head, promising it wouldn't cost them a penny, thinking
how the people in the village would crowd around them,
look at their coloured hair, some of it short and some
long. I smiled at them, heaped more food on to their
plates, poured more mint tea or coffee into their cups. I
wanted their approval, even if they did smell so terrible,

the reek of their hair in its stiff, bright tufts mixing with
the fumes of alcohol.

I began to alter my standards of hospitality, offering
them my pale, cold face when their music grew louder,
when they began laughing among themselves and
didn't take the trouble to explain their jokes to me as
they had before, or repeat their words until I understood
what they were saying. The English boy showed the
others all the implements and products I had collected
for cleaning and disinfecting, telling them I had a
mania for cleanliness, and I'd once decided to wash all
his clothes and he'd had to stay indoors the whole day.

I felt revolted by them and began to sleep in the hall,
dragging a pillow and a wool blanket off the bed and
leaving the room to them, in the hope that they would
understand my anger, that they would no longer stay
till the early hours of the morning, stepping over me as I
lay asleep, leaving overflowing ashtrays and empty
glasses and cans and bottles strewn about the floor.
Sometimes they were so drunk they fell asleep where
they were and lay without pillows or covers until I
returned from work, and then I would rage at them in
Arabic, telling them that thanks to them my room was
no better than the Italian's pigsty at home; we used to
spit on the ground whenever we went near it, children
and grownups alike, shouting exclamations of disgust,
even though all we could see of it was the outer fence.
Why was I doing this? Pouring water over them while
they yelled back at me? Perhaps this is what happened
in the neighbouring rooms, which were occupied by all
different people. Their noise had stopped me sleeping:
shouting, shattering glass, the word 'police' echoing
here and there.

How glad I'd been in those first nights with him. I'd
believed the English boy would protect me from these
sounds. Now they were happening right inside my own
room. I tried to shout like the two of them, but my cry
came out strangled and distorted; I just couldn't express

my anger in English. So I reverted to the role of crazy
horse, raging bull: wheeling, rearing, plunging, now
attacking, now drawing back. Were they shouting? No,
they were laughing. Actually laughing.

It was the music that had brought me in from the hall
where I had been lying. A single note repeated over and
over again, throbbing in my head, making my chest
tighten. I had to be rid of them, I decided. I had to be
rid of the English boy. I'd give him a choice: he could
either stay on his own or leave. I knew he had no home,
but that wasn't my problem. I had to go in there
immediately. I had to pull the tape out of the machine,
interrupt the music right in the middle of the song. It
had been on loud all evening, and now it was the early
hours of the morning. They had no sensitivity, no
conscience.

I charged in like a bull. When I saw no one in the
middle of the room, which had been full of music and
smoke and pungent with the smell of hashish, I thought
he might have forgotten to turn off the music before he
went to sleep. I found myself thinking affectionately
that I ought to be straightforward with him; the English
liked that. Perhaps he didn't understand why I'd
become so angry and distant. Suddenly I stopped and
stood still, staring in amazement. A man was lying by
his side. They were both naked. They were lying in each
other's arms. I saw their uncircumcised members as
clear as day and shuddered. That was the first time I'd
seen a man's penis so clearly and my mouth and throat
went dry. I went dry between my legs for several
seconds, then I charged again. Shocked, they started
up, but they made no attempt to cover their nakedness.

Then, as if they'd recovered from the surprise, they
began to laugh, snorting and giggling in delight at the
water being thrown at them, like two children playing a
game.

I had to be dreaming. What I was seeing was surely
the opposite of what was actually happening. In reality

they should have been dumbfounded and embarrassed,
wishing the floor would open up and swallow them. Or
hiding themselves from me, resorting to a whole range
of lies and excuses. How could the English boy go on
living now that he'd been found out?

They continued to call on Jesus Christ, trying to dry
themselves off, then laughing again. The English boy
pointed to my face, unable to control his mirth. I must
have looked like the mad ape that wandered the streets
of our village with its gypsy owner.

Their laughter so infuriated me that I began to have
thoughts of revenge. But how, when he had nothing
that I could take by force, steal, hide, break in front of
him, tear up or trample underfoot, to vent my rage and
spite? All he owned were the clothes on his back and a
few cassettes which I'd partly paid for anyway. I looked
wildly about me a hundred times, unable to think what
to do; then I threw my coat on over my nightdress,
pulled woollen socks over the wool trousers I wore to
protect me from the cold, and ran to the door, without
listening to what his friend was trying to say to me. I
went out and slammed the door behind me, turning the
key in the lock as if I wanted to safeguard the proof of
the crime and its only witnesses, repeating the same
English phrase, over and over again, 'Just you wait and
see.' Then I went on in Arabic: 'You'll be sorry. Everybody's going to know. I should have noticed. You've
been with me for a whole week now and you might just
as well have been a girl, or a boy without balls. What
was I doing admiring you for being so well-behaved,
sitting there for hours content to have your arm round
me? I even said to myself, "He's English and yet he
understands." Still I wanted you to go all the way with
me. London's very far ... and I'll never go back home.
I'll always live here now. I should have been on my
guard. How was I to know? If you'd had a big fat bottom
I might have guessed. But you're all scrawny. Your
bum's hardly bigger than a fist. I'm crazy. I let your

white flesh and your skinny body and your blond hair blot out things that would have made me shudder at home.'

I rang his sister from a public phone box. When she heard my voice, she asked drily, 'What do you want?'

'Your brother . . .' I began.

She cut in. 'Are you getting me out of bed at this hour to talk to me about my brother?' she demanded.

'It's urgent,' I replied.

At this she changed her tone, and asked quickly, 'Is he all right?'

Why did I bother to tell her, only to have her shout at me, accuse me of being crazy to wake her up for that and tell me to keep my nose out of her brother's business, especially since it was nothing to do with me. As her parting shot she told me never to phone her at this time of the night again. but then her anger seemed to have woken her and she continued, 'I know you went to a lot of trouble over the meal, but my brother's sexual proclivities aren't any of your business, or mine either.'

'Bitch,' I screamed down the phone at her then, remembering how much they like dogs here, I shouted in English, 'Whore! Whore!' I walked along, trembling with anger and misery, not through the London of beautiful houses and clean streets that I'd dreamed of, where people wore only elegant, expensive clothes, nor between buildings that soared into the clouds, but in the darkness past trees planted at infrequent intervals and council houses with their unlit windows, all alike; I passed people asleep, protected from the cold in cardboard boxes, and rubbish in untidy heaps or neatly tied up in black plastic bags and empty milk bottles with traces of sour milk lingering in them, and I marvelled once again that the dairies were trusting enough to leave them lying about.

A voice rose from a heap of clothes on the pavement, accompanied by the stench of alcohol-laden breath, a voice begging for a drink or money to buy a drink. I used to smile at the people who stopped me in the street, not knowing what they wanted at first, until I discovered that there were actually beggars in London. I gave them money, full of pride that I was richer than at least one English person, even if he was a beggar.

I walked along with something boring a hole between my legs. Now I was conscious of Aisha's words when we stood together in the storeroom and she tried to dissuade me from going to London: 'Go alone to London without an aunt or a husband or your mother and they'll say you've sold your soul. You'll be known as a bad girl even if you're as pure as the Prophet's daughter.'

'What are you talking about?' I'd said to her nervously. 'I'll be staying with you!'

Aisha's annual visits home had sown the seed of travel in my spirit and this seed had grown and opened out and reached my eyes and tongue. On her last visit I'd been unable to take my eyes off her gold earrings and her bangles. I'd dragged her into the storeroom and begged her to take me to London, saying my family wouldn't allow me to go without her. It was not only her matching handbag and high-heeled shoes which fired my enthusiasm. The smell of couscous and other grain which filled the air constantly reminded me of my own situation. All I wanted to smell from now on was the fragrance of England which Aisha exuded. I urged her to listen to me and to feel what I was feeling. Then I took off my little gold earrings and felt in the folds of my dress for all the money I'd saved or stolen from my brother's pockets over the years, and placed both the money and earrings in the palm of her hand, forcing her fingers shut around them. As I gave her an exaggerated account of my clashes with different members of my family, she continued to discourage me, saying that the work in London was hard and that exile was no easy way of life. I thought she must not like the idea of my going on the plane with her, then coming home every year laden with presents. How could she compare the task of dusting and polishing the magnificent English furniture to the drudgery of cleaning our house, where there were only torn rags, a broom and a pail of water, and you had to go down on your knees to scrub the floor and do the endless piles of washing by hand?

The man at the British customs was much sterner than the magistrate who came from the capital to investigate crimes committed in our village. This man would forget the purpose of his visit, at least for a brief spell, and the fact that he was on official business, and drink tea and eat a good meal in the prosecutor's house, crack jokes and make amiable conversation, and sleep through the heat of the day. The British official behind his high desk asked me numerous questions which I didn't understand. When all I could reply were the two forlorn words, 'No English,' he asked me if I knew French. I nodded my head to find I had opened Ali Baba's cave merely by answering all his questions with the one French word, '*oui*'. His features relaxed and he stamped my passport. Without realizing it he had let me know that using French words, however few and halting, has a bewitching effect upon everything in London, animate and inanimate alike.

I'd woken up the next morning at Aisha's place, not convinced that I was really in London: her flat was like any flat at home with the same smell, the same coloured ottomans and rugs, the same pictures on the walls, the brass tray in the middle of the room, and the loud shrieks and wails of her two children puncturing the air. However, this sensation evaporated as soon as I looked out of the window, when I realized how imprisoned I was by my ignorance, which Aisha seized upon, exploiting the fact that I didn't know how to flush the toilet, work the shower, turn on the oven or boil the electric kettle to make tea, and that I couldn't understand what her older child or her next-door neighbour said. I couldn't even answer the phone. Inventing far-fetched excuses, she left me trapped in her flat and made no attempt to help me look for work.

From the window I saw the flats opposite, their even lines making them look like children's drawings. Noisy voices floated through their windows. I let my gaze wander to the open grassy strip at the side of the block, which was almost completely empty of life, and then on to the red buses and cars hurrying along the main road. Fixing my eyes on them, I couldn't help cursing Aisha, wishing she was dead, swearing by the Prophet Muhammad that I would have my revenge because it was she who was stopping me walking those streets and riding in those red buses to find work and a flat or a room of my own. When Aisha returned from work, coming through the door weighed down with plastic carrier bags, her coat smelling of perfume mixed with cigarette smoke, I gave a shiver of anger: I wanted to carry shopping bags like that and wear a coat like hers!

Since everything seemed out of my reach I was reduced to making friends with the pigeons who were everywhere, and whose gentle murmurings I'd grown accustomed to hearing. I put the remains of our dinner on the window ledge to attract them, and when one of them alighted near me I called to it, 'Taste this couscous, steamed and mixed with oil, English pigeon, and tell me if it's nice.'

I'd been amazed that in London you could buy ready-made couscous in packets, and that the English used it in their cooking. I'd imagined that they would eat food fit for kings, and look upon our food with distaste.

I left Aisha's prison in the following way: one day a woman from the same village as Aisha and I came to pick up her sewing machine. She asked me if I was happy here and I sighed. She responded with an even deeper sigh. I found myself lying to her, although my lies seemed to me to represent the truth as soon as I was out of Aisha's house. I told her how Aisha kept a close watch on what I ate and drank and how I had to take care of the house and children to pay for my board and lodging. The woman nodded her head in agreement and remarked, 'Yes. Everybody says Aisha's become like an Englishwoman. She must have saved herself about thirty pounds a week having you there, because she used to pay her neighbour to look after the two children for her while she was out at work.'

Immediately we joined forces against Aisha, criticizing her and insulting her. The visitor told me things about her which I didn't believe, but still I nodded my head as if to confirm what she had said. For my part, I told her that I was sure Aisha had a lover and we began searching for proof. We broke into the single, locked cupboard, and although we only found some new clothes and shoes with jewellery stuffed up inside the toes we assured each other that Aisha received money from her lover and liked leaving me in the house with the children because it made it easier to cheat on her husband.

Only the walls heard this delirious talk, but I was suddenly seized by a guilty fear, and became convinced that the two children were taking it in and that it was ringing in Aisha's ears at work, and I rushed to pack my suitcase before she came back. The visitor left, forgetting to take her sewing machine, and I left with her, knowing full well that I would never see Aisha again and that news of my forcing the lock on her cupboard would reach my family and the whole village well amplified, so that I'd end up accused of stealing all of Aisha's possessions.

I took the woman's advice and looked for work paid by the hour. I discovered that time was money and threw myself into cleaning offices, restaurants and hospitals. Picturing the pounds mounting up in my handbag, I pushed myself harder, indifferent to the veins aching with fatigue and the bits of my body which cried out with exhaustion and craved for sleep. I only stopped working frenziedly hour after hour after I met the English boy I'd just thrown water over moments before.

I left the woman's house as soon as I found work and a room to rent. When I was told that I'd have to share a kitchen and bathroom with strangers I couldn't help thinking how this would astound the people at home, how they would snort with laughter at the idea that this could really happen in England, mother of civilization. The English boy used to work in the hospital for a day at a time, and then be off for several days. At tea breaks and lunchtime I never saw him eat more than a bar of chocolate or a biscuit. I never saw him talk to anybody. He would just put headphones on and close his eyes. He had blond hair, light eyes and a thin face. I suppose I fancied him although I told myself that it was just that I felt sorry for him. I decided to offer him some food. When I approached and held a piece of chicken out to him he opened his eyes in surprise and at first refused to take it. I insisted and he put out his hand, asking me if I was sure. I smiled. I no longer took what the English said seriously. 'Are you sure?' they ask without fail, regardless of whether you are offering help or an invitation to lunch, giving them a cup of tea or paying their bus fare.

After eating the piece of chicken dipped in cumin and saffron which he must have liked, he asked me where I came from. I told him and it was as if I'd opened Heaven's door. His face softened, his pupils grew bigger, and his irises went deep green like olive oil. Enthusiastically he told me that he'd always wanted to visit Morocco, live there even, and that our hashish was the best of all. Was it true, he inquired anxiously, was it really cheap there? I answered him with lies, happy that he was so interested after I'd been certain that he'd never say a word to me: I told him that I grew it myself, my family grew it, and it was everywhere like green grass and empty milk bottles in London; it was really amazing hashish: wherever I threw its seeds it sprang up like flames leaping into the air.

Dreaming of the hashish and the sunshine he said,

'You left all that sun for the sake of these grey clouds
and this miserable country?'

'What can I do with the sun?' I answered. 'Sweep it off
the rooftops?'

In my imagination I could feel the monotony of the
days in my country, the poverty and the nothingness. I
remembered the threatening looks of the men of the
family, the attentive stares from the ones in the street,
my mother's harsh way of talking: and I repeated it to
myself. 'What can I do with the sun? Sweep it off the
rooftops?'

I was happy in London, free, mistress of my self and
my pocket. Here it was impossible not to be happy. At
home I was thought ugly. In one week I listened to the
English boy singing the praises of my dark colouring
and frizzy hair, felt him kiss me on the cheek with
obvious pleasure whenever I cooked a meal and when I
came in from work, or when we sat watching television
together, and found him waiting for me at the end of the
road when I was late back for some reason.

I encouraged the English boy to move in one evening
after he had taken me to a pub, and I felt this urge to
have a hold on all the different sides there were to
London. Even though I didn't say a word in the uproar
and drank only water, I was standing there like them in
the crowds and smoke, proud and glad and sure of
myself.

As soon as he entered my room that night, he declared
provocatively that I must be rich to have such a bed and
quilt, as well as cassettes and a television and a video.
He'd expected it, he added, since he noticed that I had
my own plate and cup at work, and bought tea for
whoever was sitting with me. I smiled, nodding my
head, not unhappy that he'd jumped to the wrong
conclusions, but surprised that he didn't know the
secret of paying by instalments. He flung himself down
on my bed, trying it out in different positions. 'How
clean it is!' he exclaimed. 'How comfortable! I've never

slept in a bed like this before.'

Was I hearing him right or had I missed the point as so often happened? When we talked it was like two people playing with a ball: sometimes it went into the goal, sometimes it grazed the post, but most of the time it went high in the air and missed completely. He hadn't slept in a bed like that before, yet there were all those advertisements for them on television, and they were on display in shop windows and in almost all the big stores in London so that I'd imagined them in all the houses I could see from the bus.

Quite at home in my bed, he fell fast asleep until dawn.

In the little streets and neighbourhoods where I wandered, London did not sleep. And when it did, the hoardings stayed wide awake. Hoardings about films, pop concerts, milk, drugs and AIDS . . . AIDS? My thoughts suddenly became alert: he was going to die of AIDS. I should tell him, extending my finger in a threatening manner: 'You'll die of AIDS.' Then I found myself shouting, inside my head, '*I'll die of AIDS. O, my God!*'

Then partly reassured, I thought, 'He entered me twice, but he came outside me.' Then again I cried out in terror, wordlessly, 'Who knows? Maybe a germ slipped out of his prick and landed on me. 'And with an involuntary movement I raised my eyes to the sky – where God was – beseeching Him, wanting Him to see my fear and my contrition. But I couldn't see the moon or the stars, only the gloomy sky. I lowered my head quickly, as if to acknowledge the truth spoken by the old woman Khadija when she heard of my decision to travel to London. 'Foreigners have no God,' she claimed, as if she wanted to weaken my resolve and then, correcting herself and asking God's pardon, she changed this to 'Our God, the God of Islam, is different from theirs in the West.'

Then, again asking God's forgiveness, she said that

there was no God but God, and the trouble was that
Westerners didn't follow His instructions or live by His
law. At this she rose, washed her mouth ten times to
make amends and performed twenty prostrations for
her scepticism.

I had to go back to the room, as if I needed to tell the
place where I lived of my feeling. As I accelerated my
pace I asked myself what I was doing here, and I didn't
know the answer. Why didn't I go home to my own
country taking with me the sheet which bore the stains
of my virginity. I had purposely left it unwashed,
stuffing it in a suitcase because I might need to spread it
out on my bridegroom's bed in the dark of night.
Bridegroom? I would save some money and then I
would find a man to marry me, especially if I promised
to bring him to London. But why was I here? Was it
because I was out of reach of the prying eyes of the men
in my family and their questions about my comings and
goings, and far from my mother's interrogations about
why I slept on my stomach, or why I took so long in the
bathroom? The God of my far-off country must remember that I used to pray four times a day and still
love me. Now I had to be on my guard against AIDS and
the Devil. I opened the front door and heard the voice of
Warda Al-Jazairiyya flooding through the door of my
room. Pushing the door open, I was confronted by a tall,
blonde, green-eyed version of myself, the Englishman's
friend dressed up in my clothes, with my kohl on his
eyes, wearing a pair of my earrings. He was swaying his
head in time to the Arab song.

I stood before my blonde other self, wondering at my
calmness, contemplating my clothes on the English
boy's friend. After the long conversation with my
brown self out in the street and being confronted now by
a blond self, the haze lifted and all the images became
clear.

I no longer had to push away the picture of Saad laid
out on the floor, or banish from my imagination the

sound of his huge voice, louder than the roaring of the wind, dumb for ever. The women of the family struck their faces and smeared them with soot. Saad had taken his own life the night the news had gone round that he'd been caught sleeping with a travelling shepherd. He could speak no longer: he'd swallowed his voice, choking on the words, while his wife's voice, which had always been weak and incoherent before, rose high into the air, followed by those of his daughters and his sisters. When Saad's note proclaiming his innocence was discovered there was an outcry in the village. Saad's family rushed to try and have their revenge on the witness who had announced the news like someone possessed, and who cared less about Saad's death than about convincing the whole community of what he had seen in the hut that burning noonday. The village was divided between those who wanted Saad's name cleared and those who wanted the accusation against him proven even after his death. His soul would have no repose and would hover over the place, flying through the night.

As I remembered I laughed. My blonde self laughed at the people of my village. I imagined Saad lying down with the English boy and the two of them flirting and giggling together. The boy came over and put his arm round me, as if he could not quite believe my laughter and my lack of agitation. I smiled at both of them and told his friend my clothes suited him. He asked if I had a caftan he could borrow. I shook my head regretfully – I hadn't brought it with me, thinking the English would look down on my caftan with its silver belt – although I saw garments like it selling here at huge prices. I was still laughing. I imagined the beggar from the London streets sitting with the old woman Khadija in my village. I had a mental picture of the conductor on the red London bus talking to Hammouda the village postman, of the English boy's friends playing with Khadija's grandson, especially Margaret, whose hair reminded me of the coloured feather duster Khadija's grandson had pleaded for everytime he saw it in the market, thinking that it was a toy or a bird. I saw Margaret talking to Saniyya, the daughter of the woman who ran the bathhouse. I saw people springing up from the ground and letting down ropes out of the sky, boarding red buses, jabbering in English. Englishmen climbing the ancient village wall with their bowler hats and black umbrellas. Englishwomen, some pushing their pushchairs along the winding muddy roads, other older ones fanning their faces with trembling hands and still wearing their coloured woolly hats.

The television blared, and then I noticed the electricity advertisements: an electric stove, an electric heater, an electric boiler. I'd have to buy an electric boiler to replace the gas one which had been leaking for a week now. The gasman had told us it would blow up and had stuck on a warning sign to remind us.

I turned, intending to ask the English boy why he lived with me, why he liked my company. Once he had said I showed him a concern which he had never met with before, even from his parents, and that he would love to visit my country one day. At the time I didn't believe him because I wasn't used to hearing the truth from people's lips, preferring to believe what I thought rather than what I heard.

Instead I found myself thinking 'AIDS'. I looked at the two of them, 'You ought to go and have yourselves examined.'

I was thinking I would boil the sheets that evening and ask the chemist for a powerful disinfectant and give myself a vinegar douche to get rid of all the germs inside me.

They went into the kitchen and I started to tidy the room, gathering the plates from here and there and scattering the remains of the food on the window ledge. The pigeons flocked around it immediately, though dawn was only just breaking. I knew the neighbours complained that the pigeons grew used to coming close to the windows, but I didn't care. 'Eat up,' I told the nearest bird. 'You're lucky I'm feeding you, not eating you. Where I come from, if we see a pigeon we throw a stone at it. If it falls we accept our good fortune, kill it and eat it. If it carries on flying we shrug our shoulders and say, "it's the angels' turn today". You're not beautiful, you're not white, or even a nice light brown. You're grey and black like a big rat, but I love you because you're English and you wait for me every day.'

Translated by Catherine Cobham

Deborah Levy

On the tragedy and the hilarity of being in an uncomfortable place:
Yasser Arafat jokes that he lives in an aeroplane because being made homeless, he might as well live in the air. In Salman Rushdie's *The Satanic Verses*, two Indian men, Farishta and Chamcha, fall out of an aeroplane and hang suspended in the air before landing on the shore of Britain, where they begin to reconstruct their identities.

I am nine and-a-half years old and sit in front of the television in England with my brother, watching characters like Meg and Sandy argue in the *Crossroads* motel, while fat Benny, the tele West Country moron in woolly hat, eats lots of pies. And somewhere through the hotel muzak lurks the sensation that things used to be different, that we (my brother and I) hadn't always been wrapped in jumpers, silent, staring at the screen, that the days used to be hot and long. That we used to walk home from school at one p.m. in the burning sun and play barefoot in grass that was dry and scratched our calves. That we would wait for our mother to come home from work with 'Lucky Packets' full of sherbet, that most of our childhood had been outdoors and here we were inside, with our dad home again, our dad who we hadn't seen for four years, here we were having crossed the equator with nine suitcases, where flying fish leapt from the sea, to be in this place. Wembley Park, London, no money, no furniture, no nothing, short winter days and starless nights. Here we were on swings in small parks, our hair that had been blonded by the African sun now turning dark, as if another person was emerging, slowly, day by day, and with it our accents changed too, so that we spoke in multiple mangled voices as we moved endlessly, six times, seven times, eight, nine times through different versions of Englishness. Here where class and its rituals, football teams, chips, queues for everything, council estates, three storey houses, pebble dashed suburbia, languages we'd never heard, the tube, children who'd grown up with TV programmes we'd never seen, pubs and warm beer (when we saw COURAGE written on pub hoardings we thought they were left over from the war to give people morale), tea and gasfires and pets, having to make appointments to see people in advance rather than just arriving, suspicious politeness, all of these began to reveal themselves, intricately and ambiguously.

We arrived in England in 1968. Tee shirts had the black power fist, Angela Davis and Che Guevara printed on them.

I was born in Johannesburg, South Africa in 1959. When I was fourteen months old my mother was arrested. There was a knock on the door in the early hours of the morning, she had curlers in her hair, and my father, thinking it was for him, told her not to panic. But they took her away instead and she was in gaol for a day and a night; they released her because the State of Emergency (1960) which allowed the government to detain political prisoners without charge, had not yet been legally declared.

When I was five years old, my father was arrested. Another knock on the door, he packed a small suitcase while the police dug up the garden for 'subversive' literature. The charge was membership of, and working for, the banned African National Congress.

I am six years old and eat pickled herring with my father's mother Miriam Leah, who has changed her name to Mary. She tells me that when she came to South Africa from Lithuania in 1910 and met her husband Abe Moses, she could only speak Yiddish. Together they owned a fish shop called Levy's Provisions and Fisheries. Abe Moses, who was also a poet when he was not gutting fish, died while the children were still young, and Miriam Leah, who stunk of fish, decided to go into something more glamorous. 'Chinese Lingerie,' she says, staring at the silver belly of her herring.

We all wave goodbye to my father on the stoop as he is taken off in a little red car.

I will not see him again until I am nine years old.

I am nineteen years old and at college in rural Devon, away from friends and family and the city where I spent ten years of my life. I really feel a foreigner and walk up the drive cursing the mud that has ruined my gold stilettos. I look like a refugee from a Verdi opera, stranded in the damp gentle valleys of South West England, where no one has yet introduced me to wellington boots or the useful strategy of invisibility. But I make three best friends. One is a Nigerian man, one is an Indian woman and the other a Kurdish man. What I have in common with the Kurd is green eyes, the fact that he came to England at the same time as I did – and that he too looks like a refugee from a Verdi opera. The Nigerian who is six feet four inches tall, tells me about his audition to get into this college. He turned up at the dance studio in a pair of very skimpy tight shorts and observing that everyone else was very white and wore towelling track suits, and seeing that he was very tall and very naked, got nervous so went for a walk and smoked a joint. Then he came back and did the class.

'How did it go?'

"I danced like Nijinsky.'

There is a sort of joy in persuading the English you are the right person for them by dancing like a stoned Russian. The Indian woman was born in Kerala, Southern India, and came to this country when she was six. She tells me how her mum and dad know everything there is to know about fish, and tried to teach her. But as an Indian woman, and the only daughter among seven brothers, she resisted all attempts to teach her how to cook and clean fish and how to prepare spices for sauces. Her brothers could learn for themselves. Now, here in Devon, she suddenly wants to know all about why a fish is oily near the spine and how you cut and salt it. She wants to catch up on everything they can teach her about themselves, because then she can learn about herself. She feels she needs this information to defend herself.

The drama students at this college are discussing theatre very seriously and sociologically when the Nigerian comes in late, long and loose limbed. He has pinned a little square of material onto both his knees so that when he drives, the fabric of his best trousers will not rub against the steering wheel.

'Hello wankers.'

The very blond student from Birmingham we have nicknamed Madam Mosely goes red with the terrible burden of always being right.

'Why are you late?'

'Extra curricular activities.'

Every time one of us dares contribute to the debate, she tells us with thriftiness of spirit and consonants of flint that we have no common sense. And she is absolutely right. We have no sense in common. She feels imperialized, that everything familiar to her is being disturbed, the peace is being disturbed, and that our ways of telling (form) and what we have to tell (content) are simply not something that should be on an agenda of any kind. Which is interesting because here the three of us are, thinking about what it means to belong somewhere, what it might mean to belong to this idea called 'theatre'. And we are discovering that we are not interested in exploring the finer points of alienation with tea cuppery, but that the theatre can be a bridge of bone between sickness and health – that our language will somehow always be on the edge of poetry and that image and metaphor are our natural tools – they best express whole worlds and histories in collision with each other.

'Why don't you just talk straight.' Madam Mosely sucks a mint with vigour.

When the Kurd talks to his mother in Teheran from the telephone in the common room, he can hear bullets being shot just outside her front door, and we hear him tell her to take the phone away from the window. This is happening while students play pool and pinball machines, and right next to him, Madam Mosley knits a scarf and talks about making good sensible entertaining shows. Had she known it, there was no peace to be disturbed. A martyr of tolerance, I think she would like not to just purse her thin prim lips. I think she would like to burn our houses down.

I am thirteen years old and go to a girls' school, predominantly working class, at the Elephant and Castle, London. I don't know any of the Beatles songs and the girls sing them on top of their desks. A lot of their boyfriends are skinheads who go 'paki bashing'. We all wear mutated versions of the school uniform and platform shoes. Everyone supports Millwall. I am at the bus stop and have dropped my busfare. As I search for it on the pavement, one of the girls says, 'Look at the yid licking the gutters for pennies.' And then she says, 'You're from South Africa aren't you? My mum and dad go there every year.'

'The English molest their children and love their dogs.' This is the sort of cheap bitter jibe we love to say to each other when we feel wronged by life and attribute it to the lukewarm stew of Englishness. That they're cold and formal and anal. That the principle of pleasure is sacrificed to the principle of endurance and eroticism and sensuality replaced by sudden repressed explosions of rage and abandon. But who are they?

My English friend Annie was more or less brought up by her nan in a back-to-back in Manchester. Her nan had lost her hearing working in the textile mills. Because she had no garden, she improvised a sandpit for the children to play in. She took an old carpet, filled it with soil and put it in the front room, where Annie and her brother spent the day. When it was time for them to go, she rolled up the carpet full of soil and put it in her bedroom. Later on she taught her grand-daughter how to sew, how to make tripe, and she taught her politics. Annie, now in her thirties, talks about what being working class means in terms of self-image and worth. Of how there are no accurate contemporary represen- tations of her life, only this heritage stuff about happy agricultural labourers with straws in their mouths, or chirpy cockneys eating winkles. She says she needs to gather up, in her post-modern skirt, all the creative, affirmative, intellectual parts of her childhood; she needs to know how her folk survived, and when she looks for them in England, on TV, at the theatre, in art galleries, in advertising, they're invisible.

Whether it's fish in Southern India or tripe in Northern England, the need to *place* ourselves is the same.

That put him in his place.

The phrase has always interested me. It means something has been said or something has happened that has put the subject of the remark into an *uncomfortable* place. Is 'Englishness' a comfortable place? If as Marx said, the working class have no country, what does it mean to have a *place* in a culture anyway? And what language do we use to name that place, or rather whose language? What if your place has been described for you as being a so-called 'minority', or an 'emerging voice'? What are the multiple repertoires of identity buried in this word Englishness? What does it mean to be 'English' when so many people are disenfranchised in this country? Here where the streets are not paved with gold, but with garbage. Garbage and the people who sleep amongst it.

Violet next door to me, who I help sometimes rake over her allotment, is eighty-five years old, and if one was to draw a graph of her life from 0-85, it would be one of unremitting poverty. She tells me that when she was a nippy (of course I say what's a nippy and she tells me it's a waitress) the worst sin the girls could commit, sackable instantly, was to whirl the pencils which were attached by string to their aprons. 'It was the first thing you wanted to do,' she says. Putting sticks into the ground for her beans, she says, 'Oh the kids will take these. Y'know, kids love a stick.' The kids on the estate have nowhere to play. Similarly, when she catches me watering my plants on the balcony we share, she says, 'Shame you haven't got a patch to muck about in.' Violet has mostly dug up her patch and planted vegetables in it, but she has left a little strip of grass, about three foot long, which she mows with a lawn mower she bought at a jumble sale for two pounds. Annie has a little rug in her bedroom the same size, and every day she hoovers it.

I think the real English gardens are not the manicured

lawns of the home counties (usually nurtured by someone 'who comes to do the garden') but precisely these
little pocket handkerchief gardens and allotments;
places of little rugs and doormats and tiny bits of land
for which rain is prayed, cultivated with beans and
tomatoes and cabbages and roses, a respite from the
rest of life, where people are autonomous, in control of
something they are making. Places to think in, mull
things over, escape to. They are full of cats and tools,
improvised sheds and extraordinary devices to keep out
birds. When the temperature rises to 59°F Violet says
there's a heatwave.

The man next door has spent the last year making a
kennel for his dog. This plywood structure has grown
bigger and bigger, and he has even carved gothic spires
on its top. The neighbours complained and when he
asked if I minded, I said I loved the kennel and hated the
dog. He hasn't talked to me since, but Violet tells me she
has explained to him that 'some people are funny about
dogs'. She has also warned me that the little porcelain
giggling buddha I've put in the tomato plant pot outside
my front door 'will probably be nicked by the Arab boy
who delivers the newspapers.' Apparently, the milkman
will not be tempted.

I am sixteen years old. I have lived in this country for
seven years. People ask, 'Are you English?' And I don't
really know what to say. People ask, 'Are you South
African?' And I don't really know what to say. I love it
in the summer when London is full of tourists.

An Englishman with Eton accent and broken NHS
glasses stands unsteadily in a pub in the East End of
London. He begins to read, beautifully, lyrically, with
heartfelt empathy, a poem by Wole Soyinka in which
the poet tried to rent a room in London in the 1950s, and
the landladies on the telephone ask him just precisely
how black he is. For some reason this inspires the

barman to tell me there were a lot of good boxers in the
1930s because they were hungry.

A group of Turkish workers in South London buy
lamb and bread and take it on a coach to the striking
miners in Wales (1984). The roads are full of snow and
the coach is delayed. The Turks are worried that the
meat they so painstakingly prepared will not be as tasty
as it should be. The Welsh miners and their families and
the Turkish workers and their families eat well together,
exchange song, dance and poetry, while around them
hang banners of solidarity with Chile, the African
National Congress, and the women of Greenham
Common. The children secretly throw away the rings of
raw onions in their kebabs.

As peoples shift from one part of the globe to another,
from one self to another, in various states of exile,
dispossession and displacement, the dominant feature
of the late-twentieth century has to be the search for
place. It is these people who are uniquely *placed* to
observe the culture and comment on it. They had been
hurt by it and have had to seriously think about how to
make themselves better.

A pinstriped youth in his early twenties, fingernails
bitten into a raw and livid mess, drinks a cup of fake
cappuccino in a Eurobar. The theatres around the bar
play out all the trifles of TV soap life, larger, its little
pains domesticated, microwaved and packaged into a
popular night out. He stares at the streets near him and
hopes the grief he sees there is something that happens
to other people. He is standing on his own two feet – on
the face of someone else.

In 1989 the tee shirts have ZAP, INSTANT, WOW,
HELLO and PALM BEACH written on them. In the
last months of 1989 the people of Central and Eastern
Europe take it upon themselves to address the future
and make it a different place to be in.

I am thirty years old and have lived in this country for twenty-one years. Rain pours down the window panes of my London flat and I am reading the letters of black political prisoners in the country I was born in. One man describes reading the biographies of Maya Angelou, popstars on the radio, vegetables they have been allowed to plant and harvest. He talks about news of the education cuts in England, and is aghast when there is such a thirst for education all around him. But most of all he is anxious about the children of friends and comrades. He wants photographs of them, information, he wants them to be well. He wants to know where they are living and what they are thinking.

I am eleven-and-a-half years old and have lived in this country for two years. I am on a swing in a small park with my brother. We push ourselves higher and higher into the air and our shoes fall from our feet on to the concrete below us. We watch the train shuffle and rattle across the tracks where we collect blackberries and know, soon, when it gets dark, we will have to come down to collect our shoes.

This is dedicated to Simon Levy

GOODBYE DUNCAN

David Deans

All evening they sat in silence until Catherine brought Duncan his supper.

— Duncan, I want to talk about something, she said.

— Not again, replied Duncan irritably, looking up from the *News*.

— I want to move to London and get a job.

— I've told you you'll hate it down there.

— I want a job Duncan.

— What d'you need a job for anyway?

— You know I want one.

— It's no' as easy as they say to find work these days, even down there.

— But Sheila moved down to London with Bob and she got a job no bother.

Catherine was staring earnestly down at Duncan over her coffee. Duncan buried himself in the paper and with an air of finality he said,

— Well I've got my job here and I'm happy with it.

— But I just hang around the flat all day getting bored.

Duncan put down the paper. There was rancour in his eyes.

— In a month you'll be bored with your job.

— Sheila's not bored. There's things to do in London.

— It's all a big con. Look I'm tellin' you . . .

— Duncan, I want to go.

— What am I meant to do with my job then, eh?

— Duncan, I'm leavin'. I'm going to London.

There was a pause. Then she added,

— Sheila can put me up until I find a place.

Another pause. Duncan looked up and protested.

— But we're just married a couple of months.

— We've been living in this flat over a year Duncan. I wanted a new start.

— You've got to give it a chance.

— How long Duncan?

— It's different now we're married.

— I've always wanted to go to London, I told you before.

— It's crazy. We've just got settled in this place. What the bloody hell did you go an' marry me for if you wanted to go to London? You don't know what the hell you're on about, you've no idea at all.

— I'm sittin' here waitin' for nothing. I'm still young, Duncan, I want the life. Sheila's havin' a good time and she's getting a bit of money too.

— Well bloody go then, but you're mad Catherine, bloody crazy.

Catherine moved to Sheila and Bob's, and Duncan was left alone.

One Saturday night he'd been drinking in front of the telly when he decided to phone Sheila's place.

— Hullo, is that you Sheila? he asked.

— Aye, came the answer.

— It's Duncan here, is Catherine there?

— Um, no, she's no' in at the moment.

— Will she be in later on d'you know?

— Um, she could be, aye.

— Right, I'll probably call back later then. Y'all keepin' well down there?

— Aye.

— I won't keep you then Sheila, cheerio.

Duncan went back to *Hill Street Blues* and the scotch. At a quarter to twelve he phoned back. And after a while it was answered.

— Hi ... It's me again, is Catherine there yet?

— This is Catherine, Duncan, she answered coldly.

— Oh ... em, Catherine, how are you?

— Fine, Duncan.

— Did you have a good time tonight then?

— Yes.

— You got a job yet?

— Yes.

— Oh ...

— Duncan, it's five to twelve.

There was a space of silence.

— Yes ... well, I'd better be off, hadn't I?

— Yes.

— Well, goodbye then.

— Goodbye Duncan.

Adam Zameenzad

I was sure I was not being followed.

I looked behind me just the same.

I was being followed by a crowd.

A crowd of pink white brown and black people; all blue with unnatural cold, grey from lack of oxygen, and yellow with pent-up bile.

All climbing up the stairs in one mad rush trying to get out of the hell-pit of the London Underground tunnels, after having escaped from the claustrophobic strangulating suffocating hold of the London Underground Tubes, marginally cleaner but less picturesque than those of New York.

They couldn't all be following me, of course not. Even I knew that.

But was there *one* among them . . .? I hesitated for a moment on the stairs, turned round and tried to look at some of them, to see if there was a familiar face, a suspicious or suspecting face, a face I could place, a face that could . . . I was nearly knocked down the steps then nearly carried up the steps then nearly trampled upon then nearly asphyxiated then completely ambushed engulfed surrounded then wholly abandoned. All in a flash. Soon all who were following me were leading me so the chances were that they were not following me though they could still be following me by leading me and then waiting around to ambush etcetera etcetera; but of course not. No, there was no one following me.

Another crowd was following me.

Another train had arrived.

Yes, I was not being followed. Any more. The feeling had gone. But a feeling remained. I tried to shudder it away. But it remained.

I was out on Shaftesbury Avenue, facing Eros, the heart of Piccadilly, in the guts of Soho, the cunt of London. Or so I had been told. It was rather a loveless heart, the guts were sagging, and the cunt was the driest coldest and most shrivelled of cunts, if indeed cunt it was and not an asshole in disguise. It certainly made an asshole of visitors. A real let down, especially after all I had heard about it, not to mention all that nudge nudge wink wink from the son of the house in East Ham where I had found a room, and so much eyebrow raising and snorting from the father. I had been quite looking forward to sampling its unsavoury delights. Unsavoury, yes; delights . . . you must be joking, to quote a famous British phrase. All promise and no delivery. It was about as frustrating as trying to masturbate with your hands tied behind your back. Nothing was what it claimed to be. There was none of the so-called obscenity – real sex shops and real sex films or honest free-trading prostitutes of either sex, or any allied pleasurable activities: the scourge of the righteous. Instead there was true obscenity, the obscenity of deceitfulness and come-on lies. And to cap it all, the bland sleazy boredom of it all. Quite a contrast to equivalent places in European cities, even New York.

I rambled aimlessly for about an hour, in and out of dirty narrow streets, their only saving grace being their brevity, in and out of a variety of shops, bought some oranges from the market stalls, the most interesting feature of the wretched place, then went in to see an 'explicit sex' film and was presented with a badly mutilated and heavily censored version of some third-rate continental film which I left within the first fifteen minutes. By that time I was hopelessly lost and hopelessly bored.

Perhaps because this was the first time I was all alone in a big city in a new country. I had always had someone to go round with, while in Europe, or in America; and good company, any company, can make an enormous difference to one's perception of whatever one happens to be perceiving. And London was different. I had got so used to the straight criss-crossing North-South, East-West roads of most American cities that I would have to acquire a taste for the more complex and possibly much more fascinating spread of London lanes.

Perhaps I was in the wrong place, the wrong part of the town. Perhaps I was going about it the wrong way. Going to the wrong places. Had the wrong attitude. I could have gone to one of the libraries or museums, art galleries . . .

Perhaps I had the wrong expectations. Too high. London was, or should have been, the most exciting place in the world. After all, Great-Grandmother swore by the British, or the English, *angrez*, as she called them. And though she would never admit to it, I was sure there were moments, however fleeting and however infrequent, when she wished she'd been with the Church of England, rather than the Roman Church. For Americans she had scant respect and considered them to be nouveau riche upstarts, not good enough to hold a candle to the *real* thing: the true English gentry, the *real* ladies and the *real* gentlemen. Even Father had all but stood to attention at the very mention of the *pucca angrez saab*. Loyalty to crown and 'country' sometimes exceeded in the colonies that in the core of the Empire itself, especially among the poor and the powerless. Glory by association was one explanation

for the phenomenon, gullibility and impressionability
were two more.

And despite my inbuilt irreverence for all sacred
stones of all establishment temples, I too had grown up
with an aura of awe for the British and all things
British, and London was meant to encompass represent
and symbolize the best of the best of it all.

I came back to my earlier proposition. I was in the
wrong place. The wrong part of the town. I picked up the
Evening News from one of the street sellers and looked
through its entertainment pages. In times of disorienta-
tion, intellectual or otherwise, it is sometimes best to
stick to the familiar, cling to the known. I decided to go
and see one of the Bond films which was on in a cinema
at Leicester Square.

I didn't know exactly where Leicester Square was, but
I did know it wasn't far from Piccadilly, I had seen it in
one of those tourist maps I had in my hand a short while
ago, didn't know where it went, probably left it in the
cinema showing the explicit sex film which wasn't.
Even if I might have wandered away from Piccadilly, I
couldn't have gone far, and anyway I didn't mind
walking. Provided no one was following me.

All I had to do was ask for directions.

I saw this good-looking redhead with a bust to
challenge Shakti's – a sight which was getting rarer
and rarer as women were made to get thinner and
thinner for the convenience of the multi-billion dress
designing industry, much easier and hence more eco-
nomical and hence more profitable to clothe a bean pole
than an hour glass – walking my way. Could you please
tell me the way to Leicester Square, I said, speaking
softly, in my best voice and with my toothiest smile.

Perhaps I was showing too many teeth which could
make me appear roguish and untrustworthy. She sort of
froze for a moment, tried to smile and not smile at the
same time, looked uncomprehendingly at me, turned
ever so slightly towards the farther side of the road from

me and walked away with quick nervous steps.

I tried the next time with a very dapper man, all pin-stripes and umbrella. He didn't even stop or turn his head to look at me. I don't think he heard me. Perhaps I spoke too softly.

Perhaps I was not saying the name of the place correctly. I wasn't. I was uttering three distinct syll-ables: Lei-ces-ter Square. Not merely that, I was putting my strongest accent on the syllable that wasn't! I ought to have known. After all I did know through my discussions with Pasha regarding the plausibility of King Lear's plot that the Earl of Gloucester was really the Earl of *Gloster*. But I failed to make the connection. Anyway, since the English language, not unlike its speakers, and the climate in which it was reared, did not necessarily adhere to the principles of predictability, even had the thought of the good Earl occurred to me, I may still not have surmised that it gave proof positive one way or the other re the acceptable pronunciation of the Square's Christian name. What's more, were I sure I was mispronouncing, I might not have worried that much. After all, in Paris and Rome, Copenhagen and Amsterdam, I had frequently made a complete mess of whole sentences, much less place names, and had generally been set in the right direction, after a little bit of repetition and a lot of hand waving.

Another perhaps occurred to me. Perhaps I had spoken to two of the many tourists that must be coming over to pay their respects to this capital of capitals.

At the time it appeared to be the most plausible perhaps. The answer, ask someone who had to be a true native. The man selling the evening papers by the bend of that road yonder. I hastened there without delay or ado.

Could you please tell me how to get to Lei-ces-ter Square? please, I asked wide-eyed, eager and hopeful. The man, with a blotchy red skin and wavy brown hair generously mixed with wavy grey hair, looked up momentarily then looked down again and said, there is no such place, face and voice both utterly expressionless.

The faces and voices of the two young men, one about my age, the other hardly fourteen, one standing right behind the newspaper man the other nestling next to him, were by no means devoid of expression. I heard them no sooner I turned to walk away which I did after a brief moment's hesitation when I wrestled with the foolish notion of somehow eliciting a confession out of the florid man that he was lying and that Leicester Square did indeed exist; not realizing then that he *was* right, and that there really was no such place as Lei-ces-ter Square. The older of the young ones let out a sniggering laugh which developed into a hiccoughy laugh, the younger one hissed out, fuckin' bloody Paki; a third voice, I couldn't tell whose, said something which I did not quite understand but sounded like, and indeed was, National Front.

I felt my face go red, as red as it was physically possible for it to go red, and a surge of hate and rage and fear swept through me from nerve ending to brain cell to nerve ending. But only for one passing second. The hate and rage went almost instantly. A little bit of the redness and a lot of the fear remained.

Once the initial involuntary reactions had settled down, the overall feeling was a strange mixture of sensations, memories and impressions, not altogether unpleasant. After all, rejection was nothing new to me. I was born a reject, in the gutter; was bred in the gutter; and had learnt, very early on in life, to walk close to the gutter. And that was in my own country, the land of my birth, and the birth of my father and my mother, and their fathers and their mothers. This was a foreign land, peopled not only by my superiors, for that applied to everyone I'd ever known, from the hole in Mother woman through which I was expelled to the hole in the Mother earth by which I'd be swallowed; but by those who were superior to my early superiors; probably the most superior peoples in the entire world. At least so Great-Grandmother declared, with the exception of the Jews. Her utterly unquestioning faith in the Bible led her to believe that none could possibly be luckier or greater than those whom the love of God chooses, and if the love of God had chosen to choose the Jews, then their superiority over the rest of mankind could not possibly be doubted. Salvation is through the Jews, she often quoted Father Franklin who baptized her, for through the Jews came the Law, through the Jews came Christ, the Son of God was born a Jew, and the Holy Mother of God was a Jew and married a Jew. If all that was not the ultimate in human proximity to God, way above all ordinary mortals, she couldn't imagine what else could be.

I was neither Jew nor English nor white, or even a proper Indian or a proper Pakistani; but my travels through Europe and stay in the USA and my near acceptance there as a living entity capable of suffering pain and enjoying pleasure had temporarily given me a sort of quasi-human status, further aggravated by those willing to be my sexual partners; I had become spoilt and pampered. Obviously I would have to start re-learning my past and re-discovering my appointed place in the world. I almost felt at home, secure. The redness in my face was no longer of anger, but embarrassment, and even warmth. I was back where I belonged. However the feeling was not entirely pleasant either. The fear, though not new, was greater than I remembered, and stronger than it need have been.

The determined practical side of my nature soon took over from the lazy brooding one. I had to get to Leicester Square. I had to find where it was. I no longer cared about seeing the film, though it was to be the last with my great hero Sean Connery. I just wanted to get to Leicester Square.

The answer came from heaven. In a manner of

speaking. I looked up to the skies for no reason I can
now remember, probably a spot of rain or a ray of
sunshine. On their way down my eyes spied a policeman
on the horizon.

Now why hadn't I thought of it before!

Could you please tell me how to get to Lei-ces-ter
Square? please, I said once again, in my best voice once
again.

For a flicker of a moment as the policeman looked up
at me I thought I had struck a wall again, but then the
door opened. The policeman smiled showing large
flashy teeth. He was young and fresh with large blue
eyes and his skin shone. I would have enjoyed taking
his uniform off.

He began explaining, straight on, then first right, on
to the second set of lights ... etcetera ... etcetera ... it's
rather a long walk, sir, he concluded. He called me sir! I
was thrilled. An English policeman actually called me
sir. Great-Grandmother would have been so proud of
me. Mother would have given me a cuddle, and she
wasn't given to cuddles. Not where I was concerned.
Father's eyes would have lit up. And it takes a lot to
light up the eyes of a man dying of tuberculosis.

He could tell my mind had wandered off. I'll tell you
what, sir, he said. He said 'sir' again. I'll tell you what
sir, he said, I'll write it down for . . . here his eyes
narrowed a bit, he hesitated, you can . . . Oh yes, I
assured him, answering the unasked question, I can
read. he relaxed. Taking out a note pad from his pocket
he drew a map, writing down the names of the roads
and the turnings to take. I must have wandered off
course more than I had thought. But then the streets
had led one into another and twisted and turned and
escaped into strange territories ... There you will see the
sign, a big board ... that's where ... he smiled his big
smile again as he tore off the piece of paper and handed
it over to me.

I started getting confused halfway through, but I was

determined not to ask anyone else I didn't want another negative response to spoil the childlike happiness that the policeman's courtesy had brought to my otherwise unrewarding day.

I finally managed to get to where the directions led me. I still wasn't quite sure if I had got it quite right. Looked different from what I had imagined, but then places in real life often are different from what you imagine them to be. There was a large park spreading in front of me. Couldn't see any cinemas around.

It was only when I looked up to my right and saw the board that I realized I *had* come to the right place.

The sign read, LONDON ZOO.

The reputation of the famous British sense of humour was well deserved after all.

If a policeman could be so well endowed with it, despite the obvious difficulties and frustrations of his profession, the ordinary man or woman would surely be brimming over with a joke or two no matter what the occasion.

I could hear the young man's hiccoughy laughter all over again, this time with more telling effect. I couldn't help but join in.

The devil riding my back dug his hard pointy heels into my flesh, but I stayed my ground. I had nowhere I could go.

But to Leicester Square.

This time I decided I would try a child. For unto such belongs the Kingdom of Heaven. Leicester Square shouldn't be much of a problem.

He ran to his mother half way through my sentence. My fault. I hadn't seen her sitting on a bench not far from the spot.

I tried an Indian-looking middle-aged man with a pouchy face hidden beneath a large brimmed hat, and a paunchy stomach that seemed to run a perfect little circle round his navel hidden beneath a scruffy fair-isle sweater hidden beneath a wrinkly brown jacket hidden beneath an overcoat which brushed the homeless autumn leaves strewn despairingly across the lawns. His tie was muddy green with flowers which once must have been yellow. Sorry, no know, new . . . sorry . . . sorry . . . new, no know . . .

I decided to make one last attempt after which I would start looking for a place from where I could obtain a map of the city.

I tried a pink old lady with the future of the universe mapped on her face with linear symbols just waiting to be decoded by anyone who had the wisdom and the patience to want to do so.

It took her a while to understand what I wanted and where I wanted to go. Then she walked with me to a bus stop - I had to take one step every two minutes, and that in slow motion - waited with me, put me on the right bus and reminded the conductor where to let me out.

I was in Leicester Square. What's more. I had learnt that it was really *Lester* Square.

That was not all I learnt that day. I hadn't even begun.

Margo Glantz

'Constable? No, I'm not too keen on Constable. Or rather I am, but my favourite English painters are Stanley Spencer and Turner. And Hogarth.' I take a sip of beer, of lager. His is a pint of bitter, mine's a half. *He has bought me a drink.* How I loathe that expression. At home we say: 'Would you like a beer?' or 'do you fancy a drink?'

'Okay, I'm lying,' I admit. 'There are lots of English painters I really do like.' In any case, it's weird that whenever I say that to Keith, he looks at me with the unmistakably quizzical air of the tall thin intellectual he is, his hair on the blond side of chestnut (now heavily greying); his fair skin with his rosy cheeks reminding one of Victorian youths with perfect complexions (or so the novels of Wilkie Collins and the paintings of the Pre-Raphaelites would have us believe); his eyebrows bushy and deliberately unkempt; his classic tweed suit of the old school, worn with a shamefully Byronic air somewhere between hippy and academic; his accent public school, as befits his education, although he also speaks a passable Spanish, so we can keep switching languages whenever linguistic difficulties develop. Last but not least, Keith is an historian who has frequently visited Mexico and it doesn't faze him that I,

as a Mexican, should come to his country to write about
its artists. He's in favour of it, perhaps even likes it, and
approves of the Third World rather as some of the
English also evince my approval, Malcolm Lowry and
Graham Greene among them. And Keith is one of the
few Englishmen I know who really likes Spencer, the
rest dismiss him as representative of an imperial,
conservative, rural English idyll. 'Not so,' I insist, and
Keith agrees: 'But I like Spencer too.' He then continues:
'There are only three great English painters this
century: Stanley Spencer, Wyndham Lewis and Francis
Bacon.' I add Burra.

We've just emerged from an exhibition at the Royal
Academy, 'British Art of the Twentieth Century.' 'Yes, I
like Hogarth, but Spencer intrigues me. Did you notice
they both concerned themselves with the everyday?
Spencer has his characters busy washing sheets,
making beds, tidying cupboards, and Christ and his
apostles appear in Cookham as though attending a
summer regatta.' 'Fine,' he says, rising from his chair,
'I couldn't ask for more proof of realism, of everyday
life...' 'But,' I interrupt, 'for English snobs of the upper
classes . . .' 'Members of the aspiring middle class
hankering after nobility,' he continues, 'these paintings
offer what they most of all dislike: a celebration of the
people.' 'They'll be better off when they're part of
Europe,' I rejoin, now in the pub doorway.

Keith says goodbye, impatient to be off. I carry on
talking with the same chattiness and speed that got
Jane Austen's heroines into trouble. He is not to walk
out on me before I run out of steam. 'England is an
island without sea, or else an island that used to be
sea-bound, only so long ago that the sea's now evaporated.' He impatiently plants a swift kiss on my cheek
and ... and is already gone. I like – I'd like – to smoothe
his eyebrows with my tongue and maybe more besides.
But it's too late now, I've frittered away the time, as
usual.

Sunday and it's very cold. I'm waiting at Charing Cross station and I'm wrongly dressed in a black hat and coat, whereas I should have come in jeans and a heavy Shetland jumper. I'm off to Boulogne-sur-Mer with Rosita, Keith, Brian and Sue. Not by plane, we'll catch the train and then the ferry like before, almost nostalgically since when the tunnel is open, there'll be no more frontiers to cross: the sea, I think again, has already ceased to exist for England. Where are those boats beloved of Conrad? Nowadays it's the regular ferries that capsize

'D'you remember last year's Zeebrugge catastrophe?' We're sitting in the train, knocking back gin, and I'm continuing the same line of thought, aloud. 'England has an archaic style; that's why I like Spencer.' I take another slug, and ignore the amused smile of those around me. I talk and talk, they drink and drink. 'And what with the tunnel and the European Market, what'll be left of England? Will the pound sterling be done away with, the last relic of that ancient monetary system of shillings, pennies and guineas?'

We carry on with the gin, nobody paying any attention to my sentimental reminiscences, contradictory and literary as they are and unable to express my conflicting desire that England be an island in a timewarp and that the English behaved like Continentals. Nobody listens but instead they stare out at the countryside, the classic English landscape. Then suddenly the white cliffs, a salty tang in the air, a few sheep and a funereal sky.

We've arrived in Folkestone, to leave the train and board the ferry. We continue drinking, gazing out at a sea now almost as redundant as five o'clock tea or straw boaters, both commonplace back in the 1950s when the children in *Lord of the Flies* became violent in the midst of their paradisical island, at precisely this magical hour of five o'clock, and in the living room, that sweetly British interior, flowering the semi-darkness into a

plethora of chair covers and curtains, sprigged bone
china and mums in Liberty-print dresses . . . 'The tea
itself,' I reflect aloud, 'is transformed by bleaching it
with milk, so it no way resembles the complexions of
those *swarthy people*, least of all the inhabitants of a
tea-producing Indian subcontinent. (What of novels of
Somerset Maugham, Forster and Conrad? No, consider
first and foremost Emily Brontë's *Wuthering Heights*,
for who was Heathcliff other than a *swarthy bastard*
who spoke gibberish in preference to the Queen's
English.)

'Such people,' I continue aloud, 'who are rendered
suspect of nothing more than their *swarthiness*, are
repulsive in their manifestation of a sinister attraction.
All the more important, then, to stand protected from
the like and ensure that all things – not excluding
alcohol – conspire to bear visible witness to that ruddy
hue sported by the English living in the Tropics.' For
some time it seems I've been talking to myself. Nobody's
listening but I insist: 'This *fairness* of skin obliges them
to shield themselves so that if they do catch the sun they
avoid the obvious danger of peeling. Shedding their
skin puts them in the same position as Jane Austen's
heroes, prematurely aged by the treacherous sun of the
West Indies.'

The wind off the Channel is brisk and fierce and icy.
We're now at Boulogne, totally drunk. The others are
dozing while I chatter, attempting to cure their som-
nambulism with my words. A jolt, and a voice booming
through loudspeakers to announce our arrival in
France. I wake them up and we shamble along towards
the Customs. We reach the station at the same moment
as an elegant train loaded with ladies preening themselves in their furs and hats, the men all wearing dark
suits. The compartments have little curtains in the
windows; the lamps are lit; it's eleven a.m. but still
winter. Am I dreaming or is this the Orient Express of
the inter-war years? Irresistible memories of Agatha

Christie and Hercule Poirot.

The customs officer checks our passports, notes the absence of a visa in both the Mexicans'. Having failed to obtain one means I've forgotten my status as a foreigner in Europe, Latin American, undesirable. I need a visa and have failed to obtain one, Rosita likewise, and so they put us behind bars like prisoners.

Keith, Sue and Brian have British passports and enter Boulogne without visas. Rosita and I are to be punished, stuck there with long faces, alongside our fellow wrong-doers, representations of *swarthy people*, black as tea taken without milk. But with a sliver of lemon?

'You should see the care and tenderness Burra bestowed on his portraits of Blacks and Mexicans.' I'm advising Rosita, by the way reminding her of Malcolm Lowry, of whom we're all fans. Rosita glances at me impatiently. 'And so,' I continue, 'the suntan becomes fashionable and it's no longer as necessary as it was – taking Robinson Crusoe by way of example – to hide from it under a parasol in order to conserve that *fairness of skin* threatened by the desert island climate. So that when he returns to Mother England he's still sporting that delicate shade of complexion so beloved of English males, and above all English females.'

'Do you understand the precise meaning of *swarthiness*? It's quite difficult to translate: would "negritude" be the correct term?' Rosita looks at me indignantly, with a furious gleam in her eyes, a look of hatred that exactly transmits the colour of my question. The customs officers run their eyes over us as if we weren't there.

Keith, Sue and Brian reappear weighed down with shopping bags, flashing their teeth in wide grins which set off their milky skins. They show us an exquisite quantity of French cured meats, smoked crayfish, mayonnaise, salads, champagne, pâté, patisserie and chocolates.

We retrace our steps to the station, wait a while for the ferry to take us back to Folkestone. We settle ourselves down in a First Class cabin, lay our delicacies out on the table, open some wine and champagne, set the crayfish on to plates that don't look paper, and eat, drink and devour vast quantities of pâté, hors d'oeuvre and champagne. We talk, laugh, guffaw, sing in English and Spanish and suddenly, just before we dock I demand: 'And now, all of you, who do you prefer, Spencer or Constable?'

translated by Amanda Hopkinson

IF ENGLAND WAS WHAT ENGLAND SEEMS

Naomi Mitchison

Yes, we get some lovely views from the railway, just as you say, but - oh dear! - the industrial side and the back streets and the mess! Yes, that was Birmingham.

> If England was what England seems
> And not the England of our dreams
> But only putty, brass and paint,
> How quick we'd chuck her -

That's what Kipling wrote. He decided that after all England wasn't what she seemed. But now? It looks sadly as though only too much of England - or shall we say the English populace - is what it seems. And should be chucked by those who still have some idea of what a good society should be.

What is Englishness, then? I remember well, during the air-raids of the forties when I was in London and we waited as darkness came for the first sirens and the deep breath to get one's courage up, that we felt we were part of the will of the capital of England. Knowing that if they break our will, they win. So it must not be.

But this was different from Englishness. So what can that be? Looked at from Scotland, it is sadly tied up with Thatcherism, which, we hope, is something that will pass, since it goes against a better, more basic feeling which is still there. People of my generation were brought up to admire the sacrifice of life and happiness for others, the hope that we can live up to what this means in ordinary, dull practice. We wanted, on the whole, to be good, not just through fear of punishment, but perhaps with an element of pride. You may remember E. Nesbit, the great children's writer and inventer of the family of Wouldbegoods, who were very English, trying to do the right thing but often falling over themselves – or others – when it came to practice.

This surely is the basic English policy of helping and solidarity, which took us through the last war and into the first Labour Government and the welfare state. Much of it still remains. But the present doctrine of competition is destroying it, and with it the picture of our Englishness. Children are mostly friendly, only accidentally cruel. But soon enough they learn competition, useful at first, but dangerous when it becomes, as it easily does, the only atmosphere. Not 'His need is greater than mine.' Not Grace Darling.

You teachers realize well enough what is happening, but teachers have to play the competition game, assessing pupils, pushing them on. One of their problems, of course, is Englishing children from other cultures. Which England should they hold up as a pattern, a reasonably true pattern? Whichever it is, the more it is rubbed in, the more it will fail to click.

Yet, haven't we tried to teach and think in non-racial history? That isn't easy. There is so much of it! I would be surprised if it wasn't still possible to go through ten years of education with only the faintest idea of what has been happening in the world, even your own country. In my day and at a good school, it was easy, as you moved up from class to class, to miss out totally on some period of English history – the only history that was taught. It ended grandly with Queen Victoria's jubilee, having skipped over the Crimea and the Indian Mutiny. But at least we knew a lot of Shakespeare by heart, especially Agincourt. But you are a teacher yourself! Well now: this decision that all children must learn two languages, forgetting the thousands in many English cities who already have a home language, with a literature of its own.

Nowadays it may well be world history, deeply simplified. Does it mean anything to most children? What do they think Englishness is? I suspect that most of them identify it with being white. And because white, superior. So Englishness is corrupted from the beginning. If they think of history, it may be hard not to see it in dressing-up terms from telly watching.

Teachers may try to tip the balance about this Englishness. Radio and telly make great efforts – at least sometimes. But it is a struggle. Good Englishness doesn't dress up, indeed it tends to hide itself. There are parts of Asia and Africa where there are good memories of English people who devoted themselves, sometimes gave their lives, to the practical good of the indigenous population. They were just and merciful. Most of them, perhaps, were doctors, government servants of one degree or another; a few were farmers (I can think of one, still remembered) and some were just friends, as I myself have been for the Bakgatla and, I hope, for the whole new country of Botswana.

Up until recently the English have had certain virtues assigned: honesty, loyalty, fair dealing, kindness to animals (and women). But how much is true now?

From Scotland we are apt to look at and condemn Thatcher's England, south of Birmingham, the greenbelt-eaters, the yuppies, the Sloanes. That is no doubt wrong and covers our blindness to our own Scottish variety of unpleasantness, but easy to see how it happens. Again, most women have at some time come across specimens of English anti-feminism, though the geography of this unpleasant addiction does not follow national boundaries or even religious ones although both have their own special effects. In some ways people in London (flower of cities all, as a Scots poet put it long ago), both men and women, have more freedom to live as they want than they have in most other cities. But is that Englishness?

So, does dream England always disappear at dawn? Well, there are strange little bits of old-fashioned good Englishness about, dating perhaps from the late forties, when city streets were safe and when people of good will in England were happy and even proud to see the end of Empire. I think that Englishness, for all that we pull it to bits, had a certain important moral structure, which has been eaten away by unchecked competition, an underground civil war breaking our roots. Can it ever come to life again, not as a bait and hook for politicians to use, not as a shouting for soccer fans? The true dyed-in-the-wool, deep down Conservatives may feel uncomfortably that the sacred word has come into the hands of unsuitable people; including the Americans. We, the people of good will, feel this even more strongly. Can Englishness ever become clean again? If so, it must change.

Fleur Adcock

You can't be it at home: they won't notice;
there are too many kinds of it around.
But abroad it's what you've suddenly become;
and it's cute, if you're in the United States,
or threatening, if you're somewhere else, or just
puzzling, if you're the only English-speaker
they've ever met who's not American.
You have to tell them, shyly naming the place
you never name at home, where 'in this country'
serves to avoid a tricky semantic choice.

At least with real 'abroad', where they're all foreign,
you're braced behind passport, phrase-book and
   hopeful smile.
What's more unsettling is when you're in a country
where they all speak English, and you understand
   them,
and you ask for something simple – a return ticket,
say, or a pint of milk, or a bag of crisps –
and just for a moment *they* don't understand *you*.
(They know about Englishness, but you don't fit
into any of its three varieties:
EastEnders, Coronation Street, and posh.)

You have to repeat your question, mouthing the words
like a goldfish: 'No, not two, I said a return.'
Or: 'Milk - you know?' (You could try pronouncing it
    'moowk'.)
Or: 'What I want is paper with *narrow* lines,
not *no* lines.' (Ah, they've got it - the phrase, that is:
you'll have to go elsewhere for the actual paper.)
And suddenly you've become the thing you are:
no longer a Commonwealth citizen, one with them.
'Crisps? Aw, chippies, you mean.' The eyes narrow.
'Whaddarya, mate?' they ask. 'Some kind of Pom?'

FISHWANDA

Susan Daitch

1

Playing on the third floor of Loew's Thirty-fourth Street Multiplex, in Cineplex 3: *Fishwanda*. The abbreviation as it travelled around the dot board, sounded as if someone were reading a map accordion-folded between Africa and India. I went on to the next level to see *Midnight Run*. Robert de Niro chased a mafia account-ant from Brooklyn to Las Vegas, and afterwards as we walked down Second Avenue we repeated lines from the movie. *Do I know you? Wait a minute, I don't think I know you.* We instinctively understood that de Niro was referring to *Taxi Driver*, even in this much later movie and it's funny. We know the language. We get the joke. *Fishwanda*, seen briefly in a preview, disappeared, forgotten. On lower Second Avenue we passed the Telephone Bar and Grill whose front was constructed from a series of British telephone boxes. They could be copies, but they look real enough. One red box is actually the entrance to the bar. I continue to be surprised all those little panes of glass haven't been smashed in, but a metal door comes down at night and the neighbourhood is full of tourists anyway.

2

Money was supposed to be wired to her soon from somewhere. As she walked from the post office empty handed, she pretended to be an American tourist, one who could leave in a few days, one for whom the trip would soon be nothing more than a few travel stories and postcards. She wasn't sure she wanted to return, but seemed not to have much choice anymore, and so she stayed.

Dedham from Langham, long blues, long brown shore, brush strokes in the clouds; *Rockets and Blue Lights (Close at Hand) to Warn Steamboats of Shoal Water*, painted light rippled the sand and waves into a vortex and what were those people doing on the shore? Who were they waiting for? Smugglers, escaped convicts, drenched fishermen, or they might have been just watching the storm, voyeuristically curious to see a boat break up in choppy water. Some of the paintings almost reminded her of the Hudson Valley, but she hadn't seen the Hudson River in nearly a year. She stood before Constables and Turners and imagined Algonquin Indians on a western embankment. She imagined tiny villages far to the north of England which had no electricity or telegraphs, which believed in lake monsters and King Arthur, and were not so different from northern towns near Canada. The northern English towns might not know or care that Wall Street had crashed. What does it mean that a market has crashed? Boom, a couple of awnings tumble, a horse runs away, apples roll into the gutter. Tiny American villages might by now have read about Black October and stockbrokers jumping from windows, fortunes utterly lost, but the crash mightn't mean all that much to them either, in northern American towns with names like Chateaugay, Champlain, Swanton, and Saddleback. She hadn't quite determined what it was going to mean to her. Perhaps nothing, but as she waited for money which didn't seem to be coming, it was fairly certain the crash was going to mean something. American travellers became stranded in Europe and turned into expatriates or exiles in Henry James's novels, shadowy amalgamations of foreign manners with shreds of familiar accents that were up to the narrator to decipher, but it couldn't happen to her, not in 1928, even with a crash. The money to return home would have to come. Mercurial changes in painted light were due to fog, not smoke signals. She tried to remember the Hudson River as she had travelled down it by train, and the weather seemed constant although she knew it wasn't. In memory, when the sun shone over Reinbeck, it would be bright in Reincliff as well and all the way down to New York. In London she lost umbrella after umbrella, as if with each accidental leaving behind lay the idea that she might not need that particular umbrella again. She left the museum and walked to her rooms to save money.

When she had arrived from France she was supposed to contact friends of her family, but the bag which had contained their address had been lost or stolen. Weeks passed, but still she didn't bother to try to find them. After travelling around the continent to a constellation of cities linked by who her father knew, it was a relief to cross the Channel alone and to arrive at a place where it was not generally such a struggle to make herself understood. She liked to take walks alone, and occasionally pretended she completely belonged in St James's Park or Kensington and always had. She invented a new history for herself, one of privilege, with distant relatives living in colonies who would send her ivory totems from Nairobi, tea from Ceylon, a three-eyed, many-armed brass Devi with a moon on her head. The reality of a painted postcard of a log cabin and box of arrowheads disappeared. As long as her money held out and she didn't open her mouth, she could almost make the artificial history stick.

She rented rooms from a woman whose husband died

in Suez and had left her a small income and a house in Whitcher Place. The widow claimed to be particular about who she let to and told her a great deal about the other lodgers; a musician and a German student, both women, and one man, a writer. His room was closest to hers and she often saw him coming and going. He was simultaneously working on two projects: a glossary of regional expressions and slang terminology, so far mostly from London; and a Gothic novel. He was often broke and was gradually forced to sell off his library. On odd days he would work on the novel. On even days it was the glossary. She could hear him repeating phrases to himself through the thin wall between her room and his. The landlady told her he would drive them all round the twist, he was born to chase a bob without success, and he left queer books lying around. The landlady repeated that she was being very lenient with him but generosity on her part was not without limits, *my girl*. She pretended to agree, suspecting that her time for trying the landlady's leniency would be next.

On even days he whispered about the five different meanings of *how's your father* and the etymology of *knackered, Bob's your uncle*, and *taking the piss out of X or Y*. On odd days, a young woman who had gone to work as a governess at a remote Scottish house wrote to an employer she never saw about portraits which moved in the middle of the night and which, the governess wrote, appeared to speak monosyllabic expressions of agony. None of her letters were answered.

When he stopped his work for tea, the prying landlady being out at the shops, he would try to arrange to meet her, either in the house or at the British Museum if she were going near the West End that day. He could justifiably be at the British Museum if asked. There was always research to be done. They met in the Egyptian wing, at the same place each time, near a fragment of papyrus which was labelled, *The Opening of the Mouth*

Ceremony. This ritual restored to the mummy all his faculties so that he might enjoy the afterlife to the full. She read all the labels as she waited. He was often ten minutes late, as if the minutes had been timed exactly. She didn't know what to think of these solicitations. He rarely actually touched her, apart from taking her arm. They began to meet in pubs, sometimes in the evening, near the centre of London where it was unlikely they would be noticed.

'Tell me about the funny Dutch houses and Red Indians,' he would ask. 'Describe the historic fort, the table with a colonial's dried blood on it that's never been cleaned. Whose blood do you think it is really? Maybe it's a recent murder after all.'

It was a stupid idea but nothing she said seemed to make any difference. She wanted to say screw the colonialist blood but didn't. She kept waiting for him to do something, but he hesitated, as if he were waiting for her. She enjoyed hearing about the governess's letters which would never be received and translations of East End rhyming slang, but didn't think he actually listened to her, he often asked her the same questions. It was as if he were memorizing her life so he could sail to New York, adopt a different accent, and claim to be a long lost relative due a piece of her fortune which hadn't been considerable and might all be gone now. Sometimes she caught him looking at her, but he never really kissed her and the vagueness of his attentions made her anxious and say bitter things she didn't mean. She didn't know what he wanted from her. She thought she might have to move to a cheaper place anyway.

At breakfast he grew nervous and left in a hurry. She was disappointed that he hadn't arranged to meet her during the afternoon or even later on. She knew that his Gothic romance and glossary were being turned down by publisher after publisher and he grew despondent as he rewrote and rewrote again. She caught him in the hall as he put on his hat. *Later, my dear*, and he kissed her quickly, when the landlady's back was turned. Upstairs, alone, feeling left out of something she couldn't define, she looked through a pile of books left by his door. She picked up *London Labour and the London Poor,* Henry Mayhew, and began to read.

I continued walking the streets for three years, sometimes making a good deal of money, sometimes none, feasting one day and starving the next. The bigger girls could persuade me to do anything they liked with my money. I was never happy all the time, but I could get no character and could not get out of the life. I lodged all this time at a lodging-house in Kent Street. They were all thieves and bad girls. I have known between three and four dozen boys and girls sleep in one room. The beds were horrid filthy and full of vermin. There was very wicked carryings on. I can't go into the particulars but whatever could take place between boys and girls squeedged into one bed, did take place and in the midst of the others.

She shut the book and walked out, down Camden High Street, Hampstead Road, past knots of schoolchildren in uniforms, prams, and grocers with horse-drawn carts. She walked and walked, up Shaftesbury Avenue, Holborn Viaduct, she gave nothing to buskers, veterans of the Great War, gassed blind, missing limbs, clinking cups, Cheapside, Threadneedle, Bishopsgate to Spitalfields. She circled back, stopping at Cleopatra's Needle, leaning over, looking at the river. It was growing dark, and she thought of sleeping on a bench or under a tree in a remote part of Regent's Park, but she was afraid that, having spent the night out and returning in a dishevelled state, her landlady might assume the worst and not let her in again. She could make up a story, say she suffered temporary amnesia, or that she was knocked unconscious by thieves and all her money was gone, but she doubted she could make it sound believable. By the time she returned to Whitcher Place it was night.

On the first floor, a radio had been left on. *Trio Snotta in F,* an announcer's voice said. The room was empty.

She reached into a cabinet and turned the radio off. The
pretence fell apart. As long as she had money, she could
pretend she had always been here, but the prospect of
destitution tested her false history in a way which made
her feel it wasn't her fault. She didn't know the
language.

On the second stairwell she could see the landlady
peering from the doorway of the writer's room, pink
with anger. Look, she said, he's left, bolted, owing three
months' back rent. She looked in. The room indeed was
nearly bare. His books and clothes, all his things were
gone, he had even stolen bits of china and a lamp. He
had give his name as E. Thomas Reardon and it turned
out to be a pseudonym, so cheques left on the mantel
were useless, and he must have known that they would
be. She had gone right to the bank with them when
she'd discovered he'd gone. Why ever did he bother to
write them out? the landlady asked, gravely vexed and
insulted.

She was hungry and sorry she'd turned off the radio.
The landlady stared at her in an uncomfortable silence.
She felt tired and cold from all her walking, her shoes
badly worn, and without thinking she asked the landlady if he had left a note for her. Only afterwards did she
realize how foolish her request sounded. Foolish in that
it gave a great deal away to the other woman, and she
could tell the woman looked at her as someone who
could be aggressive and perhaps a bit vulgar, someone
who said things which ought never even to have been
thought. The landlady looked at her with suspicion as
she backed into her room and she resolved again that as
long as she stayed in London she wouldn't speak to
anyone. She would be as if mute.

3

Eleanor Marx left Liverpool for New York on 31 August
1886. She was thirty-one years old. The first Americans
she observed were on the boat and she wrote, 'they

laughed at the poor immigrants lying on the deck in their wretched clothes . . . without the least sign of sympathy.'

She was seen with a man in a loud checked suit who favoured bright ties. Edward Aveling's interests in the signs of class were not the same as Eleanor's. *Nobody is as bad as Aveling looks*. Her friends, with the exception of Engels, loathed him. He was the great love of her life. In photographs his face looks pasty and his expression petulant; it would contradict his reputation as a seducer, and of his alluring voice there is no record. Besides women he was pursued by financial scandals. All that remains of his seductiveness are the historical traces of a bad lot.

Infamy
Disrepute
Scheming

In a letter posted shortly before departure, Aveling wrote, half ironically, but perhaps also partly believing the possibility existed, that he might make millions of dollars in America. He was to see the beginnings of the great urban slums of New York and Chicago, and he must have had some sense of this if they were going to speak to American working people, but still, there was the mythology, the possibility of millions of dollars waiting to be made. Though not an out-and-out cheapskate, he was thought the kind of man who would try to squeeze a shilling into a pound by whatever means. On board ship he invariably tried to hoodwink other people, even a cabin boy, into paying for his sherry. He was to have one heroic moment in America although the mythological fortune eluded him.

He looked over the women in the ship's dining room, just checking, a few glanced his way. There were opportunities to flirt with other passengers, moments when young American women returning from a long tour left mothers and aunts below deck, and, standing a few feet away from Edward, they stared out at the Atlantic. He could do little more than watch porpoises and gulls with them. He might have listened to complaints of how stifling an aunt could be when one wanted to wander around London alone, or how one got sick in Venice or Paris, but he could only touch an elbow with mock sympathy or pat a sea-sprayed hand. Ten days on the ocean gave him a few chances to visit the cabins of single women, but until they arrived in New York, there were no places to escape once the liaison ended, however passionately, half-heartedly, or ephemerally it had begun. If he needed to give the object of his desire the slip, he would have to hide in steerage or the boiler room. (Even in the cause of evasion, Aveling was not known to have spoken to any workers during the course of his tour.) A boat was not the best place for the kind of romance Aveling preferred. As rumour circulated within its confines, Eleanor would surely discover his infidelities. He leaned over the rail and watched porpoises and gulls. Except for the burial at sea of a woman travelling to meet her husband, it was a dull voyage. Once in New York he couldn't disappear into the city either. If he could have, if he had no responsibilities, he would rent hotel rooms, write plays, and go to auditions. He would meet American women of all kinds whose faces he imagined would reflect mixed nationalities, and he would tell them he was an actor who had performed before the Queen. The American women wouldn't have seen his picture. They wouldn't know that his trip had been sponsored by the Socialist Labor Party of North America and his time, if he stuck to his commitments, was to be all booked up.

The Statue of Liberty had just arrived from Paris and was being assembled so it was not in New York harbour when they arrived. Lower Manhattan must have looked confusing to them as several different neighbourhoods met at the end of the island, at Coenties Slip. Already the new world was not easily reduced to one thing. These contradictory elements drew Eleanor's first image of New York: smokestacks, horse-drawn carts, the steeple of Trinity church, shipchandlers offices, and English spoken in unfamiliar accents. The black metallic S curve of the elevated train shadowed the squalor of the lower east side which had begun to grow under it.

They were taken deeper into that neighbourhood and Eleanor wrote to her sister Laura in Paris that she considered New York a 'very dirty, shoddy town'. She stayed in the apartment of Wilhelm Rosenberg at 261 East Tenth Street between First Avenue and Avenue A. It is a street of tenements and railroad apartments and Rosenberg's apartment was one of these. She didn't think to compare the German-speaking neighbourhood to Spitalfields or the East End. It was dirty and shoddy in a way that was very symbolic of New York: square blocks, square buildings, several storeys higher than English ones, packed full of people, no yards, no gardens, not even mingy ones with soot covered plants.

Eleanor and Aveling spoke to 25,000 people at Cooper Union, a school for artists, architects, and engineers. The building is large, brown, a series of Romanesque arches in tiers that span Astor Place and Cooper Square. There is a small triangular park behind it and the crowd may have spilled out from the Great Hall. That night there was one Buddeke present, a Pinkerton agent. Originally the Pinkertons were detectives but they became known for spying on union organizers and breaking strikes by violent means. Buddeke, probably a German immigrant, was actually hired to tail Wilhelm Liebknecht, but on their American tours Liebknecht's and Eleanor's paths intersected. (In a sense they must have worked in tandem since Liebknecht, whose English wasn't very good, addressed primarily German-speaking crowds. Eleanor and Aveling were able to reach non-German-speaking Americans.) When

Eleanor spoke at Cooper Union police entered the crowd and tried to disrupt the meeting. As she saw movement near the doors Eleanor said, 'I have been told that you in America enjoy such freedom that socialism is not needed. Well, all you seem to enjoy is being shot by Pinkertons. I speak not only of what I have seen, but of what I have read in your labour statistics. You have no more freedom than us.' Buddeke wrote bits of her speech into a notebook as he examined those around him and made note of the enthusiastic individuals who happened to be standing nearby, describing dress, attitude, or making little sketches. At the same time he tried to determine the identities of the Americans on the podium. He was kept very busy.

When he saw the blue uniforms of the New York police, did Buddeke show them some sort of identification or did he just leave? To flash a badge was to risk someone in the crowd remembering his face and in the future, on another job, he could be fingered as the stoolie he truly was. His cover would have been blown. On the other hand, by refraining from identifying himself he risked being bludgeoned or arrested. Photographs of Eleanor Marx survive but Buddeke's image has vanished. His bill for spying on the English Marxists was $712.10.

The attempt of the police to cause a riot was called 'a disgrace for New York' by one paper. Eleanor, Aveling and Liebknecht wrote to another, *We have never seen in Europe such wanton interference on the part of the police with the liberty of the subject as we saw today in a country proverbially known as 'the land of the free'.*

There was no quiet retreat, no time to rest between speeches and meetings. Tenth Street provided no refuge. Rosenberg's railroad apartment, one room following the next, offered little privacy. Tenements were noisy and smelly, and then they left for New England. If a movie were to be made of her American tour, one would see pages fly from calendars, clock hands spin and headlines slapped one on top of the next. The headlines of the *New York Herald*, for example, read 'Socialist Pleadings. Cooper Union Crowded. Spurred on by a Woman.'

'In European countries, it took the working class years and years before they fully realized the fact that they formed a distinct and, under existing conditions, a permanent class of modern society; and it took years again until this class-consciousness led them to form themselves into a distinct political party, independent of, and opposed to, all the old political parties formed by the various sections of the ruling classes. On the more favoured soil of America, where no medieval ruins bar the way, where history begins with the elements of modern bourgeois society as evolved in the seventeenth century, the working class passed through these two stages of development within ten months.'

Engels also believed in the myth of a new society which could be moulded in a sensible modern way, without 'feudal traditions or appendages.' The Buddekes, however, were to win.

Eleanor made notes on the differences between English and American workplaces and unions. Corporations, banks and trusts controlled a great deal and, although machines replaced workers more frequently in America, certain trades, Eleanor wrote, were 50 per cent more labour intensive than in England. American labour politics were complicated and deemed a 'slippery business' by Engels. Workplace observations notwithstanding, for Rosenberg, one judgement echoed: New York, shoddy and dirty. Did she fault the landlords or tenants for shoddiness and dirt? It seems obvious she must have known it was the former but he wished she had said so, after all this remained his city. Rosenberg worked hard to raise the money to have them give the American lecture tour, and he was beginning to be suspicious of Aveling, but Eleanor was devoted to him and deaf to all his antics.

In her loneliness Eleanor found no comfort in the geography of New York's lower east side. The nearby Tompkins Square Park was dangerous, and walks by herself, Rosenberg told her, were out of the question. Moments alone were limited to climbing his tenement stairs, smelling different cooking smells on each landing. When she reached the apartment she tried to write, but sounds of crying children and raised voices came through the ceiling and walls. She chain-smoked and stopped eating.

Eleanor used to say that she inherited her father's nose and she would one day sue him for damages. She must have seen many similar noses in Rosenberg's neighbourhood, but how she felt about the similarity has not been recorded.

They travelled to Chicago by train. Aveling eyeing hats and legs in the dining car, both fascinated and repelled by mid-western accents. He was collecting notes for a book of random observations, a Thackeray-like Sketch-book, called *An American Journey*. He observed that American women spoke and chewed gum simultaneously and took copious amounts of snuff. Under the pretext of research he spent hours trying to observe a woman 'hiding' snuff. He also observed that Americans wiped their noses on their sleeves, employed spittoons and had poor aim.

Coarse, money-grubbing provincials.

One of the myths Eleanor would speak against was the idea that socialists wanted to have women in common, and the men who made these accusations, she said, were the owners of the means of production anyway. Chicago was in a state of siege in the aftermath of the Haymarket trial. The Chicago Eight, anarchists unfairly tried and convicted had been sentenced to hang. The Chicago press warned of 'Dr

Aveling and his vitriolic spouse', in the language of a carnival sideshow. The anarchist paper *Freiheit*, in opposition to the Marxists, thought Eleanor should have been shot on sight upon arriving. Yet they drew huge crowds and all their meetings seemed a success.

Aveling preferred actresses, but they were more difficult to locate once he left New York, and he rather looked down on what passed as theatre in America, although he admired Buffalo Bill's *Wild West Show*. He made no secret of what he thought of as the poverty of American culture. His disdain was a source of embarrassment to his sponsors, but a greater embarrassment developed as they prepared to return to London.

He developed an aphorism, *New York is over-eager to get rich*. He repeated it constantly, goading Rosenberg.

Rosenberg's suspicions of Aveling multiplied as piles of receipts were turned in. He had demanded exorbitant fees for his speaking engagements and billed the Socialist Labor Party for theatre tickets and corsages which he claimed were for Eleanor. The irony of excessive expenses incurred for Karl Marx's daughter wasn't lost on Rosenberg, but Aveling called his accusations ridiculous, and he was defended from England by Engels who brushed off Aveling's embezzlements as the pranks of a boyish 'noodle'. Rosenberg could sense the counter-accusations ringing across the Atlantic, the worst of them perhaps unspoken: Americans had idealist and somewhat puritan expectations of how Dr Aveling should have behaved, Americans are a simple people, literal-minded and dependent on secondary sources of information.

London papers in fact ate up the scandal, writing that the New York socialists would 'nevermore import a professional agitator from the effete monarchies of Europe. The luxury is too expensive.' When questioned about the contradictions between his enormous lecture fees and his supposed interest in the disenfranchised,

Aveling replied, *Well, it's English you know, quite English.*

When Eleanor left, the Statue of Liberty had just been unveiled in New York harbour. Icon for future paper-weights, imitation foam tiaras, and torches covered with foam flames, an image to be printed on bumper stickers, T-shirts and sweatpants, some of which, through donations, will find themselves passed out by evangelical missionaries in Central America one hundred years after the unveiling. But in 1886, when Eleanor Marx sailed back to England, the statue was a symbol in its infancy, a giant thing, a gift from France, constructed in parts and shipped across the Atlantic.

4

If you walk east from the Telephone Bar and Grill, you arrive at the block where Eleanor Marx stayed when she came to New York. The buildings are the same as they were one hundred years ago; there has been no development on this block. Crack dealers operate on the west end of the street, near the Good Medicine and Co storefront theatre. The Russian-Turkish baths are directly opposite 261 East Tenth Street and were prob-ably there when Eleanor Marx spoke in New York. They reserve one day for women, and in 1886 there may have been no day reserved for women at all. 261 is between a Reggae music store which has T-shirts and records in its window, and the Osgood Fulfillment House, a half-way house for runaway children.

Cooper Union is a few blocks west. In front of the building people sell junk either stolen or scavenged from the garbage. They have bundles and shopping carts full of things, old magazines, books, used clothing, shoes. When it rains they huddle against the building, leave the objects on blankets or broken up cardboard boxes, only to return to selling when the rain stops. The park behind the school is full of homeless people who have set out their blankets and mattresses near the statue of Peter Cooper. There is a methadone clinic nearby and on Saturday morning, if it's raining, junkies, too, meet under the Romanesque arches. Lately none of these groups have been present in the park, but as it gets warmer they will return.

5

On a London bus she had heard a driver announce Stoke-Jewington when driving through Islington. She had heard rhyming slang, she knew what *four by twos* meant, and she'd once been asked if she could speak with a Jewish accent. The man had come up to her at the entrance to the library where she worked and just asked her. *Can you speak with a Jewish accent?* She thought he might have meant a New York accent, but she was from Los Angeles and wouldn't have tried anyway. She'd also been addressed near Notting Hill Gate in Arabic. When she couldn't answer, the man turned to his friend and said in English, *she's not one of ours.*

At work everyone was talking about the television dramatization of the Jack the Ripper story. Michael Caine played a highly emotional, fairly hard-drinking detective who finally uncovered the Queen's physician as the Ripper.

—Did you know he was Jewish, someone asked?

—The Queen's physician?

—No, Michael Caine.

The head librarian expressed incredulity. Judy Holliday, Piper Laurie, Laurence Harvey, Cary Grant (half), a woman in the cataloguing department who claimed to be Polish, those he knew about, but Michael Caine? He said he was going to start a Secret Jew of the Week Club. A different one every week but they had to be believable. The Prince of Wales was out, and so on. It was funny for awhile but the novelty soon wore off. It was hard to top Michael Caine, and later the woman confessed she wasn't even sure about that one.

6

In New York in 1882 I met Oscar Wilde. After lectures, theatre openings, at private parties, I would infiltrate his circle, usually posing as a reporter or a photographer, and while he tried to snub me, I pretended to ignore his ignoring me. It was difficult to see him alone, but I did manage a few times. I knew that my presence annoyed him, and if I'd stop to nurse hurt feelings, I'd travel home each night on the el, lonely and defeated, in the way one can be on a train. So I just barged on. I made my way home each night with at least some notion of hope and plans for a new assault on Wilde. With what little money I had I would try to wear unusual suits or hats, learning a combination of subtlety and the unexpected in order to gain attention. After leaving me outside a restaurant in the theatre district while he and his friends dined inside with Oliver Wendell Holmes or P.T. Barnum, I realized it was stupid to pander to his interest in aesthetics. I was neither aspiring poet nor actor and had never been further east than Brooklyn. I wanted to offer him something no one else would. One night as he waited for a young man to find him a cab, I saw my chance. He was alone for just a few minutes and I made my offer.

Oscar, I said, *let me take you to Coney Island, it's like Brighton, I think, the Brighton of the New World.* I really had no idea if this was true.

He wasn't interested.

Oscar, I tried again, *after engaging in a critique of American culture in speech after speech, will you fail to visit the spot where Walt Whitman had been known to read Homer and Shakespeare to the waves?*

He became mildly interested. I nearly told him Coney Island was also known as Sodom by the Sea, but thought better of it. Some subjects, I'd learned during the weeks I followed Oscar Wilde, were better left only as implications.

We arranged to take the train out on a Saturday. I

knew Oscar would have preferred a quieter, less raucous
venture, on a weekday perhaps, but I had to work on
certain days and those days came up during his visit.
On the train as we rode past the spines of Manhattan to
the flat rooftops of Brooklyn, he told me something of
his travels in north America, indeed, he had been much
further west than Jersey City, even beyond Chicago. He
told me how he had been deceived by a young man who
claimed to be the son of a banker, and he had lost money
in a gambling casino because he believed the con artist.
It had been a narrow escape and I was impressed. He
had next invested in Kelly's Perpetual Motion Company
and lost more money. In one city he had been imper-
sonated by a woman named Helen Potter, and in
another a boy of sixteen managed to get into his hotel
room. He'd left school and wanted his advice on becoming a writer. *I just gave him a piece of fruit*, Oscar
said, *and told him to learn French.* Yeah, I'll bet, I
thought. I was curious about Kelly's P.M.Company.
Was it to do with zoetropes or physical fitness? Afraid to
ask seemingly stupid questions, I kept my mouth shut.
At about high noon we arrived at Coney Island and
approached the boardwalk. People pushed and shoved,
stared at his madder lake suit, trousers cut off at the
knee. He looked faintly uncomfortable and began to
sweat. I pointed to the bathing lockers where we could
leave our things and go for a swim. No, he shuddered.
Wrong again, I realized, of course Oscar Wilde wouldn't
swim with the immigrant masses. I had the sinking
feeling of failure.

Look, I pointed to the site of the former Coney Island
House. Do you know who used to stay there? Melville
and Edgar Allan Poe.

Together? he asked.

The day, though hot, turned more promising. We took
a long walk down the Iron Pier. Oscar took his jacket off
and I offered to carry it for him. It would have been easy
to nick his wallet at that point. The crowd was full of

pickpockets, as I pointed out to him, and I could have easily said, well, I am sorry Oscar, but you know it is one of the risks here. I bought him a red hot, a sort of sausage on a roll with mustard. He wouldn't eat it, so I did. Later when he was hungry, he ate three of them in a row, washed down with bottles of beer which he said he didn't much care for. American beer, pooh. The Atlantic Ocean splashed against the pier, and he stared out to sea and began quoting Homer. A few people stared. Coney Island is about staring and he seemed to enjoy being a spectacle even for dirty children with candy-smeared mouths. He was invisible here, just a man in a strange suit and a funny accent. Some mimed dances and twirled around him, humming popular songs. Little did they know this was the fellow for whom *The Flippity Flop Young Man* was written, and I wasn't about to tell them. Would it have made any difference if I had? Did he enjoy being a temporarily anonymous spectacle, or did he believe these seamstresses and pipe fitters knew who he was? I couldn't quite tell, and as a sort of curator of the afternoon, it made me nervous. One woman pointed to his madder lake trousers, said she wouldn't mind a pair like those. Oscar didn't pay any attention to her.

By late afternoon we'd stopped in at a number of bars along the pier. I managed to keep boys away from him, but in one alley he disappeared. It was the worst of all Coney Island's dark corners, and I ventured down it, calling his name and looking in dirty windows. It occurred to me that he might well have heard me and decided not to answer. I still had his jacket, but he had taken his wallet out at one of the bars and had that with him.

It was growing dark as I walked down the pier alone, his jacket draped over my shoulders, and I wondered if I should really look for Wilde at all. He could find his way back to New York somehow. He could speak English. He could ask directions. I sat on the shore and stared at all the junk left on the beach: beer bottles, paper wrappers, bits of clothing, shreds of cigarettes. I thought I saw something purple floating in the tide, a pair of trousers, or a skirt, an upsidedown umbrella even. In the twilight and without my glasses, I couldn't really tell. Would I one day show people this jacket and say that it had been a lovely afternoon in Central Park when he gave it to me and, in closing, would I say that as he disappeared into the trees, I never saw Oscar Wilde again? The purplish thing drifted on to the beach, but I felt too lazy to walk over and examine it. The stars were clouded over, the gas lights were dim then grew a bit brighter, and I could hear a tinkly organ out of tune, the sound came from the direction of the Iron Pier. Perhaps he thought I was the impersonator, dressed as a man, hoping to win his confidence and thus learn the kind of mannerisms and opinions he might reveal only in private. Perhaps he thought that, and he'd given me the slip. I brushed sand from my suit and strolled towards the pier, stepping on a rotten orange. I nearly slipped on the convex peel as it made a squishing sound underfoot, doing small damage to my shoe. The Bowery looked ominous but I wasn't afraid. It was time to make some attempt to look for him.

7

Finally we give in and rent the movie we ignored a few months ago when we went to see *Midnight Run*. As we listen to Kevin Kline run through every possible cliché about the English, the people who live upstairs begin to fight. The noise gets louder and louder and we wonder if they are beating their children. *You think you have balls? Well my balls are bigger than your balls.* Father to eleven-year-old son. Sound of slaps. John Cleese tells Jamie Lee Curtis he doesn't like being English all that much. It's a pain being so repressed, he more or less says. I call the police and describe the sounds of the fighting going on above my head. It's Saturday night and they may not come. Sometimes they do, sometimes not. We could turn up the movie but it doesn't help. Before the end of it, we rewind and just wait. A brain-damaged man who lives with his mother near the top of the tenement comes in at eleven o'clock, after sweeping out Seventh Street Pizza. He always repeats certain phrases over and over. Sometimes it's *No news is good news. No news is good news. I always say, no news is good news.* Tonight it's the story of his uncle and as he stands around in the hall, he talks about his Uncle Rocco who was stationed in Ipswich. His uncle was fond of French fries and he tells the empty corridor for the hundredth time that they are called chips over there and they are eaten with vinegar. *Normandy Beach,* he repeats as he climbs the stairs. *Normandy Beach. Normandy Beach.*

Fleur Adcock's most recent collections of poetry are *Selected Poems* (1983) and *The Incident Book* (1986). Her book of translations from medieval Latin poetry, *The Virgin and the Nightingale* was published in 1988. She lives in London.

John Agard came to England from Guyana in 1977 and now lives in Lewes. His collection *Man to Pan* won the Casa de las Americas Prize. His adult poetry collections include *Mangoes and Bullets* and *Lovelines for a Goat-Born Lady*, both published by Serpent's Tail.

Hanan Al-Shaykh was born and brought up in Beirut. She studied in Cairo, returned home to pursue a career in journalism, moved to the Arabian Gulf in 1975 and then to London, where she now lives. She has published four novels in Arabic, *The Suicide of a Dead Man, Praying Mantis, The Story of Zahra* and *Women of Sand and Myrrh* – the last two also published in English.

Jean Binta Breeze was born in Hanover, Jamaica, and at the moment lives in Brixton, London. She has published a collection of poetry, *Riddym Ravings*, and two albums of poems and music, *Riddym Ravings* and *Tracks*.

Kevin Coyne was born in Derby, 1944, lived in London, 1968–1984, moved to Germany in 1985 and is now resident in Nuremberg. He is a professional musician/songwriter, occasional actor, and artist/illustrator, and is motivated by the humour, loneliness and general strangeness of existence; an optimist. His collection of stories, *The Party Dress*, is published by Serpent's Tail.

Susan Daitch has taught at many writers' workshops, including Sarah Lawrence College, Columbia University and the Iowa Writers' Workshop. She is the author of two novels, *L.C.* (1986) and *The Colorist* (1989). Her short fiction has appeared in *The Village Voice, Bomb, Between C & D* and *Top*

Stories. She lives in New York City.

David Deans lives in Scotland and is writing a novel called *The Peatman* part of which, 'The Problem of Gathering Winter Fuel', has been published in the *Edinburgh Review*.

Leena Dhingra was born in undivided India, but came to Europe as a small child following the partition. She was educated and worked in India, England, France and Belgium. Her novel *Amritvela* was published in 1988. She lives in London with her daughter.

Shirley Geok-Lin Lim was born in Malacca, Malaysia. She received the Commonwealth Poetry Prize (1980) for *Crossing the Peninsula*. She has published two other books of poetry, *No Man's Grove* and *Modern Secrets*, and a collection of short stories, *Another Country*.

Margo Glantz lives in Mexico City. Her books, including *The Family Tree* (published by Serpent's Tail), have won numerous awards in Mexico. She is one of many Jewish writers whose voice is an essential part of Latin American writing.

Andrew Graham-Yooll was born in Argentina in 1944. He lives in London. Editor, *Index on Censorship* since 1989. Books: *The Forgotten Colony* (1981), *Small Wars You May Have Missed* (1983), *A State of Fear* (1986).

Bonnie Greer was born in Chicago in 1948. Her plays have been produced in Chicago, New York and London and she has lived in London since 1986 where she teaches in inner-city schools. Her first novel, *Hanging by Her Teeth*, will be published by Serpent's Tail.

Judith Grossman is the author of *Her Own Terms*, a novel. She has lived in the United States, near Boston, since 1961, after failing to find a way to live in the UK.

Roy Heath was born and educated in Guyana. He has written eight novels, one of which, *The Murderer*, won the

Guardian Fiction Prize. *Orealla* was short-listed for the Whitbread Prize. His book of Caribbean memoirs, *Shadows Round the Moon*, came out in 1990.

Gabriel Josipovici was born in Nice of Russo-Italian, Romano-Levantine parents. He lived in Egypt from 1945 to 1956 when he came to Britain. He has published eight novels, the latest of which is *Contre-Jour*. He is also the author of two volumes of stories, including *The World and the Book* (1971) and *The Book of God* (1988).

Judith Kazantzis has published four poetry collections: *Minefield, The Wicked Queen, Let's Pretend, Flame Tree* and the political poem cycle, *A Poem for Guatemala*, and she has shared a collection, *Touch Papers*. She is a watercolourist and lives four months of the year in Key West, Florida, otherwise in London with her two adult children.

Gohar Kordi was born into a peasant family of a Kurdish mother and Turkish father in Western Iran. When she was four the family moved to Teheran. She was the first female blind student at Teheran University, where she studied psychology. She came to England in 1971 and now lives in London.

Kathy Lette, born in Australia, has written three plays, been half of an act called the Salami Sisters, and published three books, *Puberty Blues, Hit & Ms*, and *Girls' Night Out*. After working in Los Angeles on a sitcom (and being nicknamed Crocodile Dundette), she moved to London, where she now lives.

Deborah Levy was born in 1959. She now lives in London. Her plays include *Pax* and *Heresies*, and her collection of stories is called *Ophelia and the Great Idea*. Her first novel, *Beautiful Mutants*, was published in 1989.

Mario Vargas Llosa was born in Peru, where he now lives. He has spent long periods of his life abroad, including several visits to London. His novels include *Conversations in the Cathedral, The City and the Dogs, The Green House* and

Aunt Julia and the Scriptwriter. He writes literary criticism and plays and was a presidential candidate in the 1990 elections in Peru.

Duncan McLean was born and brought up in Aberdeenshire. He now lives in West Lothian, Scotland.

Naomi Mitchison was born in Edinburgh in 1897, educated in Oxford and returned to Scotland in 1937 to Argyll, where she has lived ever since. Since her first novel, *The Conquered*, was published in 1923 she has published over seventy books, including *The Corn King and the Spring Queen, The Blood of Martyrs, When We Become Men* and *Cleopatra's People*. She was made an Officier de l'Académie Française in 1924. She has been tribal Advisor and Mother to the Bakgatla of Botswana since 1963.

Jill Neville is the author of *Fall Girl, The Girl Who Played Gooseberry, The Love Germ, The Living Daylights* and *Last Ferry to Manly*. Her sixth novel, *Songs for a Blue Piano*, was published in 1990. She is also a literary critic, poet and broadcaster and has lived in London since the age of eighteen.

Grace Nichols was born in Georgetown, Guyana and came to Britain in 1977. Her children's books include *Come On In To My Tropical Garden*. Her books for adults include her novel, *Whole of a Morning Sky* (1986), and the poetry collection *i is a long memoried woman* (which won the 1983 Commonwealth Poetry Prize). She enjoys slipping in and out of English. Difference, Diversity and Unpredictability make her tick.

Ben Okri is a Nigerian writer resident in London. His novels include *Flowers and Shadows, The Landscapes Within* and *Incidents at the Shrine*. His short stories have appeared in the *New Statesman, Firebird* and *PEN New Fiction*. He has published a collection of poetry.

Kate Pullinger was born in Canada in 1961 and moved to London in 1982 where she has lived ever since. She published her first book, a collection of short stories called *Tiny Lies*, in

1988, and a novel, *When the Monster Dies*, in 1989. She was writer-in-resident at the Battersea Arts Centre, London, during 1989–90.

Moya Roddy was born in Ireland. She now lives and works in London.

Emma Tennant grew up in the Borders of Scotland and now lives in West London. Her novels include *The Bad Sister, Woman Beware Woman, Wild Nights* and, most recently, *Two Women of London* (1989).

Lynne Tillman was born in New York City, where she now lives. She has written two novels, *Haunted Houses* and *Motion Sickness*. A volume of her collected writings, *Absence Makes the Heart*, has been published by Serpent's Tail, including the film script of *Committed*, which she also co-directed.

Colm Tóibín was born in Ireland in 1955. He is the author of two travel books, *Walking Along the Border* and *Homage to Barcelona*, and a novel, *The South* (published by Serpent's Tail). He lives in Dublin.

Nicole Ward Jouve writes fiction in French (novels and short stories) and some in English (*Shades of Grey*). She has written a study of the Yorkshire Ripper case, *The Street-cleaner*. She is currently working on a fiction and a family history – 'in French or in English, that is the question.'

Fay Weldon, novelist and dramatist, was born in England, reared in New Zealand and educated in Scotland. Her novels include *Praxis, Puffball, The Schrapnel Academy* and *The Life and Loves of a She-Devil* which, after being screened on BBC Television, was turned into the feature film *She-Devil*.

Adam Zameenzad spent his childhood in Africa and his youth in Pakistan. He has travelled in Europe and North America and now lives in Kent, but says he is looking for another country which will have him. His novels are *The Thirteenth House, My Friend Matt and Hena the Whore* and *Love Bones and Water*.

Also published by Serpent's Tail

The Seven Deadly Sins
Alison Fell (ed.)

'Seven fine writers, seven vices probed to the quick.
Splendid.' ANGELA CARTER

'These seven writers represent . . . a newer and more
knowing feminist strategy . . . Mischievous and
exhilarating.' LORNA SAGE, *The Observer*

'Rich in experiment and imagination, a sign of just
how far contemporary women's writing might go.'
HELEN BIRCH, *City Limits*

'All of these stories cut deeply and with a sharp edge
into the main business of life — death, God and the
devil.' RICHARD NORTH, *New Musical Express*

'A rich but random survey of recent women's
writing.' JONATHAN COE, *The Guardian*

'An exciting, imaginative mix of stories.'
ELIZABETH BURNS, *The List*

'Witty, modern, female.'
KATHLEEN JAMIE, *Scotland on Sunday*

'Extremely entertaining.'
EMMA DALLY, *Cosmopolitan*

Is Beauty Good
Rosalind Belben

'A startling record of life preserved in the face of increasing desolation . . . Rosalind Belben's gift or burden is to press on to the painful edge of what is possible. It is an achievement to celebrate.'
MAGGIE GEE, *The Observer*

'In her work Belben gives us glimpses of such beauty that one can only choose, like her, to celebrate life.'
LINDA BRANDON, *The Independent*

'Spare, lucid prose, reminiscent of Woolf's *The Waves.*'
The Guardian

'Belben has an ability to tap deeply into the process of thought itself with all its fragmentation, puns, jokes, obscenities and moments of transfiguration . . . In this case beauty is certainly good.'
ELIZABETH J. YOUNG, *City Limits*

The Crypto-Amnesia Club
Michael Bracewell

'Slips a razor-sharp knife into the ribs of London's Groucho gauchos and is as quick witted yet poetic a first novel as you are likely to read this year ... in five years time when the Booker Prize winner is announced you'll be able to say, "Ah, but did you read Michael Bracewell's first book." '   *Over 21*

'More than leavened by a spiky and self-deflating humour . . . One of the most impressive British debuts in recent years.'   *Time Out*

'This flashy debut has a voice of its own.'   *TLS*

'A compelling read, especially for the cynical.'
Look Now

Leslie Dick
WITHOUT FALLING

'A debut of great conviction and profound originality.'
NEW MUSICAL EXPRESS

'A boldly overambitious novel . . . promising stuff.'
BLITZ

'Thankfully a million miles from the rosily worthy world of seventies feminist fiction.'
WOMEN'S REVIEW

'It is rare these days to find a novel which is so fresh, harsh, exciting and funny.'   NEW STATESMAN

'In a literary culture dominated by gentility and middlebrowism, *Without Falling* is itself something of a bomb.'
LONDON REVIEW OF BOOKS